TALES
OF
SOUTHERNERE

VOLUME 2

TALES

OF

SOUTHERNERE

VOLUME 2

INDRA ZUFAYRI HAMDAN

LitPrime Solutions
21250 Hawthorne Blvd
Suite 500, Torrance, CA 90503
www.litprime.com
Phone: 1-800-981-9893

Published by LitPrime Solutions   10/22/2021

ISBN: 978-1-955944-35-9(sc)
ISBN: 978-1-955944-36-6(e)

CONTENTS

PART 9
The Battle of Southernere

All praises to Allah for giving me the inspiration to write this story. An inspiration received through playing soft toys with my two sisters. A story I am elated to share since I was ten. And of course there were changes along the way, all with intention to make the story more interesting and logical.

(THIS STORY COMES IN SERIES)

PART 7

RISE OF THE OUTLANDS

THE WEDDING OF
TWO WINTERAINS

King Edward of Combination was getting married to Queen Flyangel of White Woods. It's been a year since the war. Just before the annual Inland National Day, the wedding was to be held at The Royal Court. Just a few minutes ride by horse carriage from the castle. It's a surprise indeed. Even for Edward and Flyangel themselves. They had fallen for each other since their adventures started. Everyone was excited. Nobody cares that both of them are somewhat related. Edward's father, King Henry, was the half brother of Flyangel's mother, Lady Matilda. Technically, they're not fully cousins. And there's nothing wrong at all for cousins to get married, unlike siblings. Besides, Edward and Flyangel grew up not knowing each other. Why a year later? Some people asked. Edward and Flyangel wanted the time to get to know each other better. And they wanted to experience ruling solo first. Now they're ready to join their lives together. Before this, White Woods was a part of Combination. After the war last year, it became an independent city.

After the wedding, both cities will merge together as one. In some ways, it's the same as being a part of Combination as before.

It has been a little more than two months through winter. Snow was just starting to fall in the northern parts of Southernere. Edward took the opportunity to compliment his bride-to-be.

'Look, even the snow is happy for you' he said. They were already in the carriage, waiting for the coachman.

'Are you teasing me right now? At this very special moment?' Flyangel laughed.

'That was a compliment! And besides, this isn't the special moment yet' Edward grinned.

'Oh shut up. Oh I can't wait to see you in your king robes!'

'Same here angel. Same here' Edward smiled romantically. They had given each other sweet names. Edward calls Flyangel "Angel". Flyangel calls him "Eddie", which actually isn't the first time for someone to call Edward that.

'Good morning your majesties' the coachman said walking past the carriage doors to the front.

'Morning Ackley, good breakfast?' Edward replied in a very friendly tone.

'Yes your majesty, best eggs in the land' Ackley said, getting on the boot. The horses were all ready to move.

'That's good to hear' Edward said.

'Ackley, why don't you share with me next time? I

actually haven't had breakfast' Flyangel said, keeping a straight face.

'Oh goodness your majesty!' Ackley said, alarmed and concerned.

'No Ackley, she's just kidding' Edward said. They all started laughing.

'Don't scare me, your majesty, I'm an old man' Ackley laughed.

'I'm sorry Ackley! I thought of joking with you for a while. Didn't think it would be bad'

'No worries your majesty! No problem for me! I appreciate the humor' Ackley laughed. He actually liked Flyangel tricking him. She was only joking. Who wouldn't love a royal who knows how to acknowledge your existence, especially with humor? People generally love Edward being their king. The idea of Flyangel joining the throne thrilled them as well. Those two combined together are a powerful mixture of goodness.

The carriage pulled away, out of the royal grounds and onto King's Road. King's Road is one of the oldest roads in Combination. It stretches all the way from SHAW Academy, turning at the small path to the royal gates, and goes south, ending at South Districts Market. Estimation, that's probably about less than five kilometres. One of the changes Edward had done for city developments were, adding more signboards on the streets, making Combination more systematic. He gave names to every street on the map. Even those small lanes in between buildings.

A few minutes later they stopped at the side of the road. The Royal Court is a magnificent one storey building. It's high ceiling is the reason why the building is taller than any two storey house around the area. The Royal Court is a building with few massive empty halls for multi-purposes. It's a happy place, so it's usually for festivities. It was built in the time of King Harry, Edward's grandfather. Edward took one good look at the building as he stepped out of the carriage. Another one building to be added into his renovation project.

Citizens had gathered around the entrance of the multi-purpose building. Some fanatic ones came up to the carriage.

'Oh your majesty! I'm so happy for you!' an old lady exclaimed happily, bowing repeatedly.

'Thank you ma'am' Edward replied, placing a hand on his chest as a sign of respect. Flyangel stepped out of the carriage. She gave the lady a warm smile.

'Thank you for being here!' Flyangel said sweetly. The lady was now in heaven. She was extremely elated that the king and queen acknowledged her presence.

There were more people who got past the king's guards guarding the area. They waved excitedly at the royals, shouting happily. The double doors into the building were wide open. Barriers had been placed by the side of both doors to prevent the citizens from overcrowding the building. More king's guards were tasked around the area. Inside the building, there were more people waiting for their arrival. Bobby, dressed very smartly in his tuxedo, rushed out of the building towards them.

'Your majesties, five minutes before the official time!' Bobby said in a hurry.

'Oh right' Edward said and he and Flyangel rushed inside with Bobby leading the way. The sound of the excited citizens, screaming and calling their names, became muffled as the doors were closed.

'You look amazing, your majesty' Laura said, helping Flyangel place the finishing touch, the crown on her headscarf. Flyangel was mostly dressed in red. Her queen robes, headscarf, and the gems on the crown.

'Thank you Laura' Flyangel said.

Laura had moved to White Woods to serve Flyangel permanently. She became the head of the maid and servants in White Woods Castle.

There was a knock on the door. Master Mousy entered the dressing room.

'Look how beautiful you are!' Mousy complimented.

'Thank you Master Mousy. Where's Master Lillain?'

'Oh she's already in the hall. Preparing for her moment. You know, she practiced a lot!' Mousy said. Lillain was now the royal master of Combination. It's one of her responsibilities to marry off people, especially royals.

Annie and Dewi entered the room both with a vase in hands, each full of flowers.

'Oh you look very beautiful your majesty!' Annie

exclaimed excitedly. They placed the vases on any empty tables in the dressing room.

'I'm so happy for you!' Dewi said, her fingers intertwined with Flyangel's.

'Thank you, both of you!'

There was a knock on the door. And King Nathan and Prince Jake entered.

'Boys are not allowed!' Mousy said sternly, but she wasn't entirely being serious. Both of them laughed.

'We are her brothers' Jake said, giving an expression like "duh!".

'It's alright Mousy' Flyangel laughed. 'Thank you guys for coming, although we can see each other later'

'We came to congratulate you. Come on, you're our sister. We're technically VIPs to this room' Jake laughed.

'And we're so happy for you Flyra... I mean Flyangel' Nathan said.

'Still not used to the name aren't you' Flyangel smiled.

'I called you Flyra for twenty years!' Nathan laughed.

'It's no big deal. Thank you Nathan. Thank you Jake' Flyangel said. She gave a very heartwarming smile.

'Alright, see you later. Dazzle the crowd Flyangel' Jake said. And they left.

'Is it going to start soon?' Flyangel asked, starting to feel butterflies in her stomach.

'We'll have to wait for Bobby' Annie said.

Edward was in the room opposite Flyangel's. A male dressing room. A squire was helping him, adjusting and perfecting everything that could be done to his appearance. Bobby was also there to supervise. Queen Darleen of Barenge entered the room.

'There's my royal nephew, soon to be a husband!' Darleen said excitedly. She gave him a hug.

'Aunt Darleen. It's good to see you again' Edward replied. 'How is Barenge?'

'It's a small travellers town but it's growing. The city of musketeers will be one of the prides of Inland once again, just wait' Darleen said with full of hope.

'I know you'll do your best, your majesty' Edward said.

'Now don't waste time and hurry up and get married!' Darleen laughed. She left the room.

'Are you ready sire?' Bobby asked. Edward took one glance at the squire who nodded as a reply that he's all set to go.

'Yes I'm ready' Edward said.

'Happy wedding day, your majesty' Bobby said happily. 'You can come out five seconds after I leave'

He left the room.

'Five seconds?' Edward laughed, thinking how funny it was to have been given a time limit to leave a room. 'Thank you Oscar, for everything'

'It's an honour my king' the squire bowed. 'Five seconds have passed, your majesty'

'Oh right! Wish me the best' Edward winked and left the room. The door of the female dressing room was opened and Laura exited with Flyangel right behind. Both Edward and Flyangel were astonished by each other's appearance. Edward's red king robes and Flyangel's queen dress were a combination of richness, grand, and royalty.

Down the hallway where they will walk later on, down the aisle between round tables filled with guests, awaiting their arrival, and awaiting their time to venture the food served on the buffet tables, an announcement was heard. It was Bobby's voice. He was obviously very excited that he got out of the male dressing room, informed Annie and Laura that they were ready, and walked to the hall to make the announcement, all very quickly.

'Kings, queens, royals, masters, ladies and gentlemen, please rise for the arrival of the groom and bride, King Edward and Queen Flyangel' Bobby spoke from all the way at the front, where Edward and Flyangel will be walking towards. The Royal Court was built in a way that allows voice to be projected very easily. Edward and Flyangel could hear Bobby's voice very clearly.

'This is it!' Flyangel said softly, full of excitement.

Edward smiled and opened up a space between his right arm and his body. Flyangel placed her left arm through the space. They locked their arms together.

'Walk with me' Edward said. Flyangel gave him a sweet smile. They started walking down the hallway through an opening into the main hall, the biggest room in The Royal Court. Every guest watched in awe at the two beautiful people with their magnificent clothings as they made their way towards the end of the hall. Lillain was standing in a gorgeous white dress and a green headscarf, waiting at the end. Bobby was standing close by. Edward and Flyangel looked around at the different faces that were very excited to see them. All the SHAW masters were there. Every royal from all the cities were there, Queen Lady Lith, King David, and King Harold. Captain, Bale, and Oliver were standing in one corner, beaming. Every other person that has always been by their side was present to witness their special moment. Not far from where Lillain was, a group of five children dressed very smartly were standing close together. They all seemed very bright and happy to see them. But Edward and Flyangel have no idea who they are.

Edward stopped in front of Lillain on her right. Flyangel stood beside him, on Lillain's left.

'Please be seated' Bobby said. 'You can proceed' he whispered to Lillain. Lillain nervously flipped through a booklet, a wedding script for the person marrying someone off.

'You can do this Lillain' Edward said softly. Lillain felt a sudden rush of confidence.

'Combi Nation, we're gathered here today to witness two beautiful Winterains tying the knot. Marriage is one of the milestones of someone's life. This is when your hearts beat as one. When one of you gets something bad, the other will feel it. When one gets something good, the other will feel it. Flyangel, daughter of Adam, do you accept Edward, son of Henry, to be your husband?' Lillain said with confidence. She referred to the booklet only a few times.

'I do' Flyangel said confidently, very genuine with her decision.

'Edward, son of Henry, I marry you off with Flyangel, daughter of Adam, with a gold ring as a dowry for the bride' Lillain said, making eye contact with Edward. Bobby came close to her carrying a gold tray covered in red cloth with a gold ring on it.

'I accept the marriage of Edward, son of Henry, to Flyangel, daughter of Adam, with a gold ring as a dowry for the bride' Edward said.

'Then I pronounce you husband and wife' Lillain said happily. She took the ring from the tray and placed it on Edward's palm. Edward and Flyangel turned to face each other. Both smiling very widely. Edward slipped the ring on her right ring finger and kissed her forehead. Everyone clapped.

'Royals, masters, ladies and gentlemen, you are invited to dine now. The buffet tables serve many kinds of food. Enjoy!' Bobby announced. Those very close to the newlyweds cheered even from far. Those who were nearer went to meet them. There were many who congratulated the newlyweds. Queen Lady Lith and her daughter, Princess Nathaliya, talked to them for quite some time. King David was being overly friendly. King Harold seemed to be kind of envious, but he was mostly happy for them. Lillain was the last in the queue. There were a lot more people who wanted to meet them, but Bobby set a limit so that Edward and Flyangel could enjoy the food as well. Lillain came up to them with the group of five children they noticed earlier. Their expressions were speechless. Everyone could tell that they are huge fans of the king and queen.

'Your majesties, I want to introduce you to representatives from each class of rank five' Lillain said, referring to the children.

'Oh, they're your students?' Edward asked in amusement.

'It's nice to meet all of you' Flyangel said, always maintaining her heartwarming smile.

'It's an honour your majesty' a handsome blonde boy spoke for the rest.

'That's Cardinal, head of Class A' Lillain said. 'Introduce yourselves'

'Yes, I'm Cardinal sir' Cardinal bowed.

'Nice to meet you Cardinal' Edward said, nodding his head once in response to the bow.

'I'm Baron your majesty, it's an honour' a black haired boy spoke next. He was handsome in a mysterious way. He was wearing mostly dark colours.

'I'm Eva'

'I'm Evius'

A copper red haired girl and boy spoke at the same time.

'Sorry about that. I'm Eva' the girl said.

'I'm Evius' the boy said. He wore a pair of circular glasses. So he looks like someone who is very smart.

'We're twins!' Eva said.

'And I'm Izalora' the fifth student, a girl with a headscarf said shyly. Edward could tell just from Izalora's face that she's a brunette.

'Nice to meet all of you' Edward said.

'They've been looking forward to this all week. I would like to discuss some arrangements with you later for a study session at the castle, if that's alright with you Edward?' Lillain said.

'Sure! Lillain, no problem, I'll inform you soon when I'm free' Edward replied.

'Thank you very much Edward' Lillain said gratefully. The students exchanged excited looks among themselves. It made Flyangel laugh a little at how cute they are. She and Edward made their way to the buffet tables.

'Rank five, how old are they?' Flyangel asked.

'Twelve years old' Edward replied.

'Your majesty! Congratulations on your marriage!' a random citizen exclaimed, probably a businessman, seeing how wealthy his outfit was.

'Thank you mister...'

'Donald!'

'Mister Donald' Edward finished.

More people meet the king and queen while they're taking food, eating, and even conversing with friends and family members.

The rest of the ceremony ended very smoothly

with people going about the buffet tables, eating more than three servings, communicating among each other, and then leaving with a full happy stomach.

That night, Flyangel was back to living in Combination Castle. White Woods and Combination joined as two forever united cities. Edward and Flyangel spent the remaining time they had that night romantically. Both of them went to sleep feeling very happy. Tomorrow's a new day. There will be more work to do since two cities are under them. But none of them are leading alone anymore. They have each other to work as a team. As king and queen, as husband and wife.

THE RAIN

It was the first of April, marking one year after the battle of Alhora and the first massive independence parade. The annual Inland National Day was today. Snow was already falling at a much faster rate. But everyone was not intending to miss the parade or the festival. The city square, and the entire Business and Merchant's District were bustling with activities. Here and there, people are hanging colourful decorations, singing songs, playing with their kids, and even walking alone and admiring everything that was going on around.

Academy Road, the road by the side of SHAW Academy was packed with many carriages and coachmen waiting for the parade to start. The parade will start with the carriages being driven onto the starting point of King's Road and will end at its ending point at the South Districts Market. As the parade passes the royal grounds, the king's carriage will join by cutting in into the centre. There will be many different music and magic shows on the different carriages. But walking by the sides of all the carriages will be a musical band that will play a uniform tune. The parade should be commencing at around noon. It was eleven in the morning, people were already crowding along the road. A lot of them had started to crowd around the area since nine.

At the castle, King Edward and Queen Flyangel were getting ready to leave. Bobby seemed to be the busiest, giving instructions here and there. Annie, Laura, and a few other squires and handmaidens were catching up behind the royals as they got onto the roofless carriage. All carriages that were to be part of the parade were roofless. They were specifically made solely for this purpose. After the parade, they'll not be in use until the next parade next year, unless there are certain reasons or requirements to use them.

'Your majesty, there's no need to hurry, the parade isn't starting until fifty minutes later' Annie said, stopping outside the carriage, catching her breath.

'We're going somewhere first. It'll be a rush' Edward said.

'To where sir?'

'SHAW Academy Annie, please finish your own task first' Bobby scolded. Annie rolled her eyes.

'Don't forget to bring the prisoners for their weekly community works' he said again.

'Could you find someone fiercer than Jerry?

Pertum and Lydia aren't cooperating everytime'
Annie said.

'We'll look into that Annie, thank you for the
feedback' Edward interrupted. 'Let's go Bobby'

Bobby boarded the carriage and sat opposite to
Edward and Flyangel. Annie curtsied and headed off
with Laura and the other servants following behind.
The sound of the horses neighing with delight, happy
to be moving at last, drifted away.

Annie and Laura headed to the entrance of the
dungeons.

'How much longer for Jerry to arrive?' Annie asked
impatiently.

'You don't want to miss the parade right?' Laura
said, grinning.

'Laura, it's the best show I've seen in my entire
life!'

'I'm sure Jerry will be here soon. He's always been
late' Laura reassured.

'I'm just disappointed that the first of April must
fall on a Saturday. The day when we'll be taking
those prisoners and unremorseful avengers out' Annie
expressed her annoyed feelings.

'It's only for an hour, after that we'll be watching
the parade!' Laura said, staying positive.

'But now is already ten minutes past eleven, by
the time we're done, the parade would have already
started!'

'Annie! Calm down!'

'Ma'am' a male voice said. It was Jerry. Jerry is

a combat trainer for new recruits. He was given the task to watch over the prisoners as they do their weekly community works. But being a junior trainer himself, he has not much experience, and not really that tough. So strong and mean avengers like Pertum and Lydia most of the time simply rebel against him. And Bobby had to step in when the situation turned ugly. Avengers like Pertum and Lydia are a different classification of prisoners. They are the only ones with the dungeon locks around their wrists specially made for this weekly routine. The locks are enchanted with anti-magic, so Pertum and Lydia couldn't harm anyone with their powers.

'Why are you late?!' Annie asked angrily. Laura immediately tried to calm her down.

'Ma'am, how could you speak to me like that?' Jerry said dramatically. His actions most of the time are girlish and very irritating to whoever is talking to him.

'Shut up Jerry' Laura scolded. 'Are you alone today?'

'Yes, I've given my men the day off to enjoy the parade with their fam...'

'You what?!' Annie shouted. 'You think this is a funny job?!'

'Ma'am! I didn't say that!'

'Get lost! Now! Forget it, today we cancel the community works' Annie ranted. Jerry stormed off like a drama queen.

'How such a person became a combat trainer' Annie said, rolling her eyes in disgust.

'You should see him fight, he's actually very good with his sword' Laura said.

'Not helping Laura'

'How are you going to tell Bobby? Or his majesty?' Laura asked.

'I'll tell the king alright'

'Bobby's going to be very cross'

'That's why I'm skipping him and tell sir straight'

'You think he won't find out?'

'He will, if you tell him' Annie said, annoyed.

'I'm not a telltale!' Laura laughed, hitting her playfully.

'Let's go prepare for the parade' Annie rushed off.

The royal carriage pulled up at the end of King's Road. There was no space for them to enter Academy Road. Coachmen and performers were crowding around their carriages waiting for instructions. SHAW Academy stood by the side. A very clean building. The cleaner is always free, and clearly doesn't have much to do. Magic sparks that always surround the school due to the massive occurrence of exerting powers, helped clear away most of the dust.

Edward, Flyangel, and Bobby made their way to the academy's conference room. Royal master and headmaster of SHAW Academy, Lillain, the royal welfare advisor, Dewi, Master Mousy, Master Kitty, Master Asher, and Sir Everos were already seated around the conference table. They stood immediately in respect to the king and queen's arrival.

'Your majesty, we have a lot to discuss' Lillain said.

'Yes we do, we have to hurry, the parade's in forty minutes' Edward replied.

'There have been suspicious sightings of people hidden behind cloaks, wielding dark magic, near the rural areas of Arstar' Asher reported. 'We believe they're Outlanders'

'What did King David deduce?' Edward asked.

'He sent soldiers looking out for those people. No further news yet'

Edward nodded. The nod also meant that they can proceed with the next matter.

'Trisnarim wants to hold a second ice competition to get back at us for winning that time' Mousy reported. Edward laughed a bit.

'They're already so good! We won that time because Flyangel was on our team, she brought us up' Edward said.

'They love to win it seems' Mousy said.

'I'm sorry but I have to reject that. Tell Queen Lady Lith she does not need to worry. I'll make the ice competition an annual event. Right now we can't have another, we have other events and matters to discuss' Edward decided.

'Yes your majesty'

'Your majesty, there have been quite a few feedbacks we collected from our students. It will be a dream come true for them if like once a month, their class, especially for subject History of Combination, to be held at the castle' Lillain said.

Edward looked at his wife. He was letting her decide for this one.

'Yes, sure! The castle is open anytime for a tour. Except, the dungeons are out of bounds' Flyangel said.

'Noted your majesty, thank you'

Edward glanced at the clock by the window. The parade will commence in thirty-five minutes.

'Anything else?' Edward asked.

'Yes, regarding the five representatives you met yesterday. They've shown their best and I would like to grant them the best learning opportunities with your permission, your majesty' Lillain said.

'What are the learning opportunities?'

'We don't have sword fighting lessons. That's an example of the learning opportunity. They'll be taught subjects that are not in the syllabus of SHAW Academy. Like sword fighting by Bobby, royal living by the head servant or handmaiden in the castle, and others. They could even get a special lesson from the king or queen!' Lillain said enthusiastically.

Edward thought for a moment. Then he looked at his wife.

'We'd be happy to be tutors ourselves for them' Flyangel said kindly. Lillain was very elated. She was so proud of the five students and wants to provide them with more knowledge since they're too talented for their age level already.

'So when can I schedule for any of the sessions at the castle?' Lillain asked.

'We can start next weekend' Edward replied.

'Yes sir'

'Anything else?'

'Yes, your majesty' Dewi said. 'It's about the missing pieces of jewelry again. Another case reported yesterday while the wedding was happening, a hooded figure was seen running from a jewelry shop. Later it was reported, the shop was missing a piece of jewelry. It always happens when people least expect them. But they're unpredictable and not really a massive concern'

'This has been happening since last year' Kitty added.

'That many cases should be a concern by now. Put the matter under urgent case. We finally have at least one description, a hooded figure' Edward said.

'That's not helpful at all!' Mousy said.

'At least we got something. Anything else?'

'Sire, our undercovers from Silverside reported that Silverside has been receiving threats from an unknown source, and the threats are quite frightening as they're now too afraid to tell anyone else' Everos reported.

'Put that among our urgent cases as well' Edward said, glancing at the clock. They have twenty-five minutes left.

'We have to end the meeting for now. Thank you everyone for attending. We'll get back on every matter soon. If I can't reach you, I'll send a raven. I want everyone to stay vigilant. Our fight with the avengers is not over. They might even be rebuilding their army as we speak. Anything happens, take note, report during the next meeting. Anything urgent, report immediately' Edward said, he stood up as he ended his speech. Everyone stood up as well.

'Yes, your majesty' they replied.

Edward, Flyangel, and Bobby left. They returned to the castle. Edward and Flyangel quickly changed into a more formal attire.

By eleven, they were already seated back in the carriage. This time it was only the king and queen with a coachman. Bobby will be marching into the parade by foot leading a squad of king's guards. The castle has been left with Bobby's assistant, Kelly, in charge.

The sound of the band playing Sofya's song signified the commencing of the parade. Many colourful carriages made their way onto King's Road. At the same time, Bobby gave a command for his squad to stand at attention. Two commentators' voices sounded distant. It came from the centre of King's Road where the big cross junction is. The four-lane Harmony Lane stretches from the Encampment District, cuts through King's Road and stops at Merchant's Road in a "T" junction.

'Ladies and gentlemen, it's the second year we're celebrating Inland National Day. Many appreciations to our beloved king, King Edward, for this special occasion' said a female commentator.

'It's still fresh in our memories, one of the worst times in Southernere history. Our enemies tried to take over Inland. But our heroes remain strong and we regain our independence' a male commentator said.

'That's right, happy national day everyone! And now the parade commences!' the female commentator said.

The band started playing louder and a more exciting tune. The band started marching forward together with the carriages in between. In each carriage there are different things happening. Some are just displays of food, art, or jewels. Others have performances like singing, magic, or even just people waving happily. As the centre point of the parade reached the castle gates, the front half continued moving. The back half stopped. The carriages halted. The performances were still carried on. The band marched on the spot, stomping both their feet consecutively and rhythmically while playing their music. The gap between the first and second half grew bigger. Bobby gave a command for the squad to turn to their right, facing the open gates. Everyone turned at the same time, even their feet shifted together. Bobby then gave a command to march. The squad marched forward, out of the royal grounds and onto King's Road. The royal carriage followed closely behind the marching squad. They filled in the gap formed. When the royal carriage was a few metres to the front, the parade's second half started moving forward again. The parade progressed towards the

Business District. The roadsides were swarming with citizens and some tourists from other cities, waving, and the girls fangirling at the performers. The snow seemed to be following the beat of the band. They're playing a fast tune. More snow falls. As the parade passed the cross junction, the royal carriage exactly in the middle of the cross junction, the band started to march on the spot again. The king's guards squad were doing the same thing as well. Then the band members that were on the right side of the parade's second half, started marching forward, turned to their right onto Harmony Lane. Bobby gave a command for his squad to turn to their right. Everyone turned at the same time while still stomping and finished with a single loud bang on the ground. And they immediately marched forward, following behind the band. The royal carriage followed behind afterwards. The parade continued forward on King's Road. The second half of the parade followed the royal carriage onto Harmony Lane. They've reached the Merchant's District. The snow was falling even more rapidly. The sky was so much darker now. But everyone was having so much fun to notice. However, there are still few who noticed. Edward was one of them. He has a strange feeling, like something bad was going to happen.

'Angel, I don't feel alright' Edward said, sitting back and stopped waving. Flyangel turned her attention immediately from the crowd.

'Eddie what's wrong?' she asked with full of concern.

'Something's happening' Edward said, looking up at the sky. Flyangel followed his gaze. The sky was very dark. Snow was falling very fast. The band was still playing. And the commentators' voices were competing with the band. But upon looking up, the world seems dead and scary.

Suddenly, a droplet of water fell on Edward's cheek. Edward sat up straight immediately, wiping his cheek with his hand and observed it.

'Water' Edward murmured. Suddenly more water droplets fell. Flyangel felt it, almost everyone else felt it.

'Rain?' Flyangel said, shocked and confused. Without warning, it started to rain heavily. Everyone exclaimed shock expressions as they started to rush indoors. The streets became chaotic. Everyone was running or walking fast in every direction. As a result, some fell down and got stepped on repeatedly. Lightning struck kilometres away, out of the city. It was followed by a thunder. Everyone started to move faster. Many were screaming in fear. The rain washed the snow away. Edward and Flyangel stayed in the carriage, but the coachman had fled. Bobby was already rushing towards them.

'Rain in winter. That's impossible!' Flyangel exclaimed.

'Come your majesties, the carriage can't move through this crowd' Bobby shouted. Everyone had to raise their voices over the rain, bellowing thunder, and screaming people. The situation was out of control for Edward or Flyangel to say anything. They got off the carriage. Edward quickly untied the horses.

'Thank you, your majesty' the horses said before galloping away.

'This way!' Bobby shouted, leading them back onto King's Road. There were still so many people running around.

'We won't be able to make it back to the castle, we'll have to go to The Royal Court!' Bobby said, leading them south. The Royal Court was less than a hundred metres away. Edward did not lose his grip on Flyangel's hand a single second.

There was another thunder. The loudest, like an explosion. People screamed. The rainwater had nowhere left to flow to, the water level started rising.

'Hurry! It's flooding!' Bobby shouted. The water level had rose just above his ankle. They passed by closed market stores. There were people inside for sure. They could hear arguments. The water level rose to the shin. The Royal Court was just a few metres away.

'Your majesty, in here!' a helpful citizen came out of the building they're heading to, covering himself with a cloak. Edward, Flyangel, and Bobby rushed towards him. The man attempted to cover them with the cloak.

'No, it's alright, that's yours' Edward said. They entered the building. A few people were waiting at the entrance, they closed the doors. The sound of the rain became softer. But the sound of thunder still could not be blocked.

'Thank you, kind man' Edward said.

'William, your majesty' the man said.

'Thank you William. Thank you everyone'

The citizens were kind of smiling, somehow the royals' presence made their day.

'Now we have to help, there are many others still out there' Flyangel said, very worried.

'Forgive me, your majesty, but can't magic stop the rain?' William asked.

'Magic can't stop natural events' Edward replied. 'But we can try to direct it elsewhere. But us alone won't help the entire city' Flyangel said.

'It's something, I'll channel the rain' Edward suggested.

'I'll channel the water!' Flyangel said quickly, liking the idea of teaming with her husband very much.

'I'll help too! With the people' Bobby said.

They opened the door, cool wind blew the rain inwards.

'Get inside!' Edward told the citizens. They did as he said. Edward focused on the rain. Flyangel focused on the flood. Edward managed to stop the rain completely, just for the area around The Royal Court. Flyangel controlled the water to sink into the ground. The water sank very easily. But only the area around the building. There was still water and rain from everywhere around. The water took interest in this sudden dry area and flowed towards it. The wind was still blowing wildly, rainwater splattered into the area as well. Bobby noticed some people still rushing around and called for them. They slowly made their way close together towards the building.

'Angel, I could stop the rain! Someone's doing this' Edward said, still amazed that he could stop the rain.

'Then we have to stop it! Together' Flyangel said, her mind was still on the flood, sinking every flow of water that entered the area.

'Flyangel, you'll gonna get yourself tired. We can't stop this alone. We need all SHAWs we can possibly get' Edward said. Edward gestured for her to step outside with him. They went closer to the road.

'Perhaps a signal and a little bit of motivation is what everyone needs' Edward said. He held up his palm facing the sky. Blue light appeared on Edward's palm and shone brighter every second. Edward tossed the light into the sky. The light moved briskly high up above the buildings and stayed there. Everyone could feel the energy radiating from it.

'Now, we begin!' Edward said, turning his attention towards the flood. He made the ground absorb all the water near him deep into its body. Flyangel joined in immediately.

'Are you sure this is gonna work?' Flyangel asked.

'If no one sees the light, they can feel the energy radiating from it. We'll get this' Edward replied.

The doors of The Royal Court burst open and a few citizens came out with Bobby.

'Your majesty, we can help' one lady said. She wore a hat above her headscarf.

'Yes, I'm a Winterain myself' a man said.

'Yes please, we need all the help we can get. Thank you' Edward replied. The citizens got to work. They did the same as what Edward and Flyangel were doing. Those who have no skills in ground and water, they did other things possible. Some controlled the wind to blow the rain in other directions, and others stopped the rain bit by bit. It was quite difficult at first, trying to stop the rain in the entire Combination. But with all the help, it got easier. And soon, many others came out from the shelters they hid in to help. The rain stopped and the flood disappeared deep into the ground. The sky turned bright and clear once again. But there were lots of mess on the streets. Injured people and random objects lay here and there. The royals and the council got to work immediately, aiding the survivors, restoring the city. They were fortunate that the disaster did not last long. If it were to happen that way, there's sure to be more casualties or even deaths.

Edward called off the celebration immediately. Everyone should head home and rest. Those who were injured have to get themselves checked immediately. Dewi was the busiest after the king at the moment. Being the royal welfare advisor, she has to listen to every complaint and report the citizens made.

Towards the end of the next day, everything was back to normal. There are minor damages on buildings, but that is an exception. Edward planned to get them fixed as soon as possible. As for now, Edward reallowed people to leave their house freely again. And exactly that night, markets, stalls, and businesses started. People did not care that it was already late. Usually, shops start to close just before the sun sets. But that night was different. Being stuck indoors for a whole day was enough to get them restless. Some of the managers and stall owners like the idea of their business booming until night. They planned to try starting night business from then on and see how it goes.

LADY FERAMEIN'S WARNING

The Business and Merchant's districts were very lively that night. And so were the royals. They came down to join and mingle around with the citizens, while of course staying close together at all times. No one can separate newlyweds from each other. By now, news of the flood has reached all across Southernere. King Edward and Queen Flyangel received letters of concern from White Shore, Arstar, and a few other new settlements. More came when Bobby caught up with Edward and delivered the messages.

'Your majesty, there are two new letters of concern from Silverside and Trisnarim. Queen Darleen of Barenge sent a letter, notifying that she'll be coming here latest by midnight' Bobby tried to tell everything as loudly as he could but still remained cautious as to not reveal anything to the citizens walking nearby. The crowd's noise was a challenge for him.

'Is there anything else?' Edward asked, trying to focus on Bobby but the environment easily distracted him.

'Yes, your majesty. There's an urgent matter to be discussed immediately. Someone wants to meet you. He's waiting back at the castle' Bobby said. There was a pause as Edward was distracted by a group of performers dancing by the side of the road.

'Who is it?' Flyangel took over, shaking her head and smiling at the same time at her husband.

'Master Nvago' Bobby replied. Flyangel perked up upon hearing the name. She grabbed Edward's hand immediately which released him from the distraction of the dancers.

'I've never seen you attracted to something that way before' Flyangel teased. 'Come on, we have to leave. There's an urgent matter to discuss' she said. Flyangel pulled him away back to their carriage on King's Road. Edward glanced back at Bobby who was following them like a loyal servant.

'What's going on with her?' Edward mouthed the words to him. Bobby only managed a short laugh. He has no idea what to mouth back in reply.

They all got on the carriage and it pulled away back to the castle. Annie and other servants were waiting for them at the main doors. Everyone seemed to be rushing here and there.

'Your majesty, the master just entered the castle

and went wherever he intended to go' Annie said very quickly. 'He even went past the guards to the dungeons. They're now still under his sleeping spell'

'What master?' Edward asked, clueless.

'Where is he now?' Flyangel cut in.

'He's in the library' Annie said. Flyangel hurried to the library.

'Angel, what's going on? What master?' Edward caught up with her, still very clueless of what's going on.

'This is why you should listen to Bobby and not be distracted by some random dancers' Flyangel snapped.

'I'm sorry Angel. Come on, it was a good performance' Edward said.

'Oh, was it the performance, or the ladies, you're watching?' Flyangel replied. Edward was taken aback by that.

'Angel, how could you say that?'

'Your distraction is nothing I've seen before' Flyangel said, stopping in front of the library doors. Bobby, Annie, and Laura had just caught up with them. Embarrassed, Edward did not press the matter further. They entered the library to find Master Nvago sitting on one of the couches by the fireplace, sipping on a cup of tea.

'Oh I prepared for him tea if you don't mind, your majesties' Laura said.

'Thanks Laura' Flyangel replied.

Flyangel sat on the couch opposite to the master. Edward awkwardly sat beside her.

'Don't blame him for that, Flyra. I was the one who distracted him' the old master said suddenly, placing his cup of tea on the tea table in front of him. 'The three of you, if you would please, I would like to have my meeting alone with your king and queen'

Bobby, Annie, and Laura left.

'Why did you do that?' Flyangel asked calmly, starting to feel guilty for scolding Edward earlier.

The library doors suddenly went open and another Master Nvago walked in.

'I did not!' the second Nvago said. Flyangel looked back and forth at the two persons having the exact same face. Out in the hallway, Bobby, Annie, Laura, and a few other servants were crowding around, looking inside, equally confused as well. The first Nvago laughed and changed form. His skin moved around like liquid. Now in its place was a younger man, who no one recognised. No one except Nvago. And he smiled, a very wide smile.

'You caught me Nvago. You know as soon as I heard that you are delivering Feramein's message to them, I see there's an opportunity for me to have some fun, you know, just to show Feramein that she's not as fun as me, not as fun as she used to be' the man said, crossing his legs.

'You're far from home Grindel' Nvago said. 'Go back north'

Flyangel thought about the name Grindel. She remembered seeing or hearing that name somewhere, but she couldn't recall anything.

'I'm exactly where I want to be at this point in time' Grindel replied.

'You are no match for Feramein. Might as well head home and stop with your tricks. You are just wasting everyone's time, including yours. Alden's not going to like hearing that you meddled in Feramein's affairs' Nvago said.

'Yes, I'm no match for Feramein's magnificent elemental magic. But, when it comes to curses and spells, you know exactly who's the best in the council' Grindel said.

'Alden is'

Grindel scowled at that.

'I am where I want to be' Grindel said stubbornly, folding his arms. Nvago took a deep breath, calming himself down. He glanced back, the servants were still curiously looking inside.

'Don't you have your duties?' Nvago said. Most of the servants immediately rushed away. Nvago shook his head as he swiped his hand, closing the doors magically.

The fire in the fireplace suddenly crackled and spat sparks. It grew in size until it was the height of a human. A little bit shorter than an average height. Then it died down to its normal size, and standing on it was a lady in a magnificent emerald gown. She has straight long brown hair that shimmers under a crown of white flowers.

'Feramein? Oh Lady Feramein, what an honour!' Grindel exclaimed. He was shocked at first, but he quickly made it sound like he's more excited than surprised.

Feramein stepped out of the fireplace.

'Go home Grindel' Feramein said. Her voice sounds like calm water flowing down a river.

'Okay okay, wow, you guys are no fun. But I really came here to meet her' Grindel said, pointing at Flyangel.

'That's why I messed with his mind, I don't need him' Grindel said, referring to Edward, who is now sitting like he is waiting for orders from Grindel. Flyangel had forgotten about him. She realised now Edward had been acting like a hypnotised man since they were at the market areas.

'You can keep your tricks and threats to yourself, now leave' Feramein said.

'Lady Feramein, if you don't mind, I would like to know what he has to say' Flyangel said. Feramein seemed disappointed by that. Grindel on the other hand was smirking like an immature adult. Feramein nodded her head, granting him permission to speak.

'You should know me by now...' Grindel started.

'Cut to the point' Nvago interrupted.

'I was given the permission to speak, you keep your mouth shut!' Grindel snapped. He moved too fast. At the start of his sentence, he already sent a wave of forcefield at the old master. But Feramein was faster, she froze the forcefield a few centimetres before it could touch Nvago and absorbed the force into herself.

'Just focus on your message. Nvago leave him be' Feramein said. Grindel rolled his eyes.

'Alright Flyra, you should know me, I am Lord Grindel, high master in the council, twelfth member of The Fifteen, protector of Forges of Beasts and the Northern Kingdom, keeper of beasts and curses. I am not in my true form. You'll be frightened if you see me in my true form, cause I ain't human' Grindel said. Now it all came back to her. Flyangel had heard about Grindel from Nvago about more than a year ago.

'And I see that you know who I am' Grindel said, happy that he could make an impression. 'The cursed bracelet is one of my creations. Your husband has it. Speaking of which, when I go, he'll be conscious once again, so you not need to worry'

'So are you here just to introduce yourself to me? Me alone?' Flyangel asked.

'You got some fire miss. And I don't like it. Now I'll tell you why I'm here. Marcala, remember her? Oh the person you destroyed during the war last year. She was one of my best students...'

'She was mine too, Grindel, before she became evil!' Nvago snapped.

'That isn't my point! Once my student will always be my student. And my students are a part of me. Destroying her means you're destroying a part of me. And I'm pissed. And do you know what I do to people that pisses me off?'

'That's enough' Feramein interrupted.

'I cursed them forever' Grindel just carried on speaking stubbornly.

Feramein held her hand up by her side. A little of the fire in the fireplace shot upwards, forming a solid long hot crimson spear in her hand. She used both hands and turned its tip to point at Grindel's neck.

'I said enough!' she exclaimed. Grindel laughed evilly.

'One tip, I don't come into someone else's property without the proper protection for myself' Grindel said. He tossed a coin in the air and it fell back down on the couch, where he used to sit a second ago. There was no one there on the couch. Grindel had vanished into thin air. And immediately afterwards, Edward was back.

'How did I get here?' Edward asked, rubbing his forehead. Flyangel was speechless for a while.

'Lady Feramein's here Eddie' Flyangel said simply.
'Who?'

Edward opened his eyes wide. He looked around, Nvago was there and a lady he had never seen before, holding a scary looking spear in her hand. Feramein broke apart the particles of the spear, it changed back into fire and she sent them back into the fireplace. Feramein took the coin from the couch and sat down.

'I'm sorry, your majesties, Grindel coming here wasn't part of the plan. My appearance either. It was simply only Nvago had to deliver the message. But matters got difficult, so I had to come down myself' Feramein said.

'It's an honour… um… Lady Feramein. We heard a lot about you from Lady Lith. How can we address you?' Flyangel said.

'Lady Feramein is enough' Feramein replied.

'Yes, great. Um, what message do you have for us?'

'A threat is coming your way. I'm not talking about the avengers, not the recent magic weather, not even from the Outlands. I'm talking about something bigger than all those threats. Among the laws of The Fifteen, I can't be involved in affairs of my people. I can only watch and guide from behind the scenes. But when it gets out of hands or in this case, it's something foreign and doesn't belong in this land, I have to step in. A foreign threat is coming. I've seen it. People in Southernere are very kind people, easily trust and help one another. But I have to warn you, the threat I mentioned. The people involved, you must be extra careful. They are not like us. I'm not saying they'll definitely be your enemies. I'm saying don't easily trust these new people you'll encounter soon. You will know who I'm talking about when you see them'

'Dewi's kind of people?' Edward said suddenly. Feramein smiled, impressed.

'Did Nvago mention Edward has one of the brightest minds Southernere has ever had?' she said.

'He did' Flyangel replied, also impressed and wondering what Edward meant by that.

'Dewi is of foreign blood. She doesn't belong here. But she's one of a kind exception. Her kindness is beauty in their lands. As the world gets older, that beauty fades. That's why she's a gem. She is someone you can trust. When the time is right, tell her. She could help you against the threat. If you make a wrong move, she could help the threat destroy you. Yes, her people are coming'

'What about the recent flood? Can't you help us?' Edward asked.

'You'll manage that. Like I said, I can't be involved in the affairs of my people' Feramein said. 'Please remember my warning. You are strong, you don't need me to settle your problems. If you needed me, the war couldn't have been won. Alden summons me, I'll be off'

Her form changed as her particles loosened. She turned into wind and flew out of the castle through the fireplace.

'She's amazing!' Flyangel said.

'I'll be off too, but I'll have to walk. I'm not that skilful' Nvago laughed. He turned to leave but stopped again.

'Oh yes, before I forgot, Fly… angel, you should know that your mother wasn't purely a human. That explains why you're so good with water. In fact, try putting your face in a basin of water, you'll be able to breathe. She wasn't from here too, that's how she obtained the seed of Gratultyn. That's just a tip I'm sharing, just in case when you need to use a lot of power, just believe in yourself, you have it in you' Nvago pushed the doors open and stepped out before the doors closed back a second later.

'Master Nvago' Flyangel called, curious as to what he meant. She was confused. Edward however was amazed.

'You're a mermaid?' Edward asked excitedly. 'I mean part mermaid?'

'Nvago did not say that' Flyangel replied.

'Well, he said you could breathe in water. What other creature could do that and walk on land?' Edward said.

'Water fairies or sprites I guess' Flyangel said. She got up to catch up with Nvago to ask him. But when she opened the doors, along the hallway from one end to the other, there was no one except a few servants walking about.

'He's gone' Flyangel said sadly to herself.

THE INDONESIAN VESSEL

*Before you start reading the next
chapter, finish what you're supposed
to do first. Done? Carry on!*

The fire in the fireplace crackled like as if someone else was about to make an entrance. Queen Flyangel and King Edward were discussing the information that has been shared to them earlier.

'Why would he come all of a sudden to talk about something that happened a year ago?' Queen Flyangel said, full of worry.

'He didn't come all of a sudden. He had planned since the day he found out. But he just came now because he saw the opportunity. Master Nvago wanted to meet us. He thought that if he disguised himself as Nvago, and told you whatever he wanted to say, you would listen. But his plan didn't come to work, so he improvised and threatened you instead. Threatened us. Threatening you means he threatened me too'

Edward explained. Flyangel felt very touched by that. She held Edward's hands in hers.

'You really amaze me everyday with your intellect' Flyangel said, moving her hand up to caress his cheek. 'No one else I know can figure that out in a few minutes'

They both looked deeply into each other's eyes.

'About the threat Lady Feramein mentioned. What are we going to do about it?' Flyangel asked.

'We wait first. Lady Feramein only warned us to be careful. She did not say they are a confirmed threat. But I do believe we have to talk about this with Dewi soon' Edward said.

'I agree. But for now, let's have a good night's sleep' Flyangel replied, smiling sweetly. She got up and led Edward out of the library and into their chamber.

The following day, they had a very busy morning. There were quite a number of citizens who came to complain about last night's events. Some were complaining that their family was already ready to sleep but the noise outside prevented them from falling asleep. Others complained that the streets were so dirty and were filled with rubbish here and there. King Edward and Queen Flyangel addressed them one by one with patience and reason. After that was settled, Bobby came and delivered exciting news. Information that will help them with investigations on the recent disaster. It was reported that citizens living near the edges of the city found pieces of jewelry in random locations. Those that were stolen from the shops. They were all in random locations all around the perimeter of the city. But Edward believes that they were not randomly placed. The good thing was that all the pieces of jewelry were returned to their respective owners.

It almost seemed like all the royal duties for the day were over but then it just got more exciting. News came from White Shore informing that a large ship has crashed into the docks. The ship, a standard far from the Guardians, because unlike the Guardians, this ship was made out of wood. And along with it were people with looks clearly not from this land. Strange and foreign, just like Dewi when she just came around twenty years ago. So Edward, Flyangel, Bobby, Laura, and a few squires and king's guards proceeded to White Shore immediately. Edward asked Dewi and Lillain to tag along as well. A larger road was built the past year to allow easy travelling in between the two cities. With three carriages and two spare ones to hold the newcomers, they reached White Shore Bay in less than thirty minutes. The docks stretched from one end of the bay to the centre. The remaining half was a beautiful sandy beach. Indeed White Shore got its name from the clear white sand of its beaches. It will always be magical and breathtaking to view. But everyone's attention was towards the huge ship that had crashed into one part of the docks. A crowd of passersby had formed up around the entrance. Looking through the carriage window,

Edward and Flyangel could make out King Nathan and Prince Jake along with the royal staff of White Shore acknowledging a group of people exiting the ship. As soon as the curious passersby noticed them approaching, they quickly gave way. They whispered curiously and some admired the newlyweds. Flyangel smiled gracefully, humbly following her husband who was so focused on entertaining his curiosity. And clearly, everything that was reported to them was true. The newcomers are not from around here. Edward looked back to see his wife who also turned to look at him. They exchanged looks of worry. Lady Feramein's warning was just hours ago. And it is happening now. Flyangel went closer to stand beside Edward.

'This is too fast. What are we going to do?' she asked softly so that only Edward could hear.

'They posed no threat yet. We can't do anything. We'll just have to wait'

'What about Dewi?' Flyangel said.

Just then Dewi's voice exclaimed in happiness.

'*Ayah?!*' she exclaimed in an unknown language.

'*Ayah!*' she exclaimed, sounding more sure than before, and ran to an old man that had just exited the ship.

'This will be difficult, she knows someone among them' Edward said.

Dewi hugged the old man. The man was so shocked and elated to see Dewi.

'Dewi, you know him?' Nathan asked, he was standing close by.

'He's my father!' Dewi replied excitedly. She turned her attention back to the man, ignoring the surprised looks of everyone who heard her.

'Ayah tidak tahu ayah akan menemukan kamu di sini' the man said, not letting go of his daughter's hands. Suddenly more excited voices filled the air.

'Dewi?' a handsome middle-aged man said. He stepped to the side, letting others behind him pass. Dewi does not seem excited to see him.

'Rajah membantu ayah. Ayah mencarimu, dia setuju untuk membantu' Dewi's dad said.

'Apa yang ayah janji padanya? Dia tidak akan menolong kecuali ada perkara yang dia inginkan!' Dewi exclaimed, sounding very mad.

Edward and Flyangel finally went to greet Nathan and Jake.

'What's going on?' Flyangel asked.

'We're not sure. They're speaking something we don't understand. Only thing we know is that he is Dewi's father' Jake replied, pointing to the old man. Edward and Flyangel watched shockingly.

'Dewi! Dewi! Jangan begitu. Kita kawan bukan?' the handsome man laughed awkwardly, extending his arms, gesturing that he wanted a hug. Dewi aggressively pushed the man away and stormed off back towards the carriage.

'What's going on?' Edward said out loud, couldn't take it anymore.

'That's my daughter' the old man said.

'Yes, we already know that. But I sensed tension going on'

'When she left twenty-two years ago, we're not exactly on good terms, well for everyone else. She's still close to me' the man said. His accent was so obvious and clear that he doesn't speak English very often.

'I'm Rajah, Dewi's fiancé' the handsome man said suddenly. As he spoke, Edward noticed Dewi's father rolling his eyes. Clearly, even after twenty years, there's still so much tension going on.

'You must be… a king?' Rajah said, observing the crown on Nathan's head. He suddenly bowed in a weird manner.

'Uh, we don't do that here' Nathan replied. 'Yes, I'm King Nathan of White Shore. Welcome to Southernere. You aren't the first people we met from another world. King Edward here will be hosting your hospitality' Nathan said in a very formal way.

'You a king too?' Rajah asked, pointing at Edward with his whole arm. Edward was not wearing his crown. He was dressed simply in a shirt and a vest. Rajah couldn't possibly know that he is a king.

'Yes he is, and we don't point fingers visibly at others, it's rude' Bobby snapped.

'I'm sorry king, queen, I am curious. What you mean by we are from another world?' Dewi's dad asked politely.

'We don't exist in the same world. You are very far from wherever you came from' Edward replied.

'That's impossible!' Rajah interrupted in a very

annoying tone. 'We only sailed the Indian and Southern Ocean, very close to Indonesia'

Bobby wanted to give him a piece of his mind but Edward held him back. Then an old lady came out of the ship. Unlike the rest, her white hair was so visible because she wore her scarf very loosely. She seemed different compared to the rest as well. Her whole aura gave a weird impression. Like any normal SHAW in Southernere, they have a magical aura, anyone can tell they are magic-abled the longer he or she looks at them. But this lady has something different. Edward and Flyangel felt a dark presence just for a short moment when she appeared. One thing for sure, it wasn't dark magic. And it's impossible to say if she is magic-abled, since she is from the other world where Dewi came from. There is no such thing as magic in their world. She looked at the surrounding atmosphere, the beautiful town of White Shore, and took a deep breath while closing both eyes. Rajah has been very quiet ever since she came out. He only respects this lady, Edward thought. The lady opened her eyes again. That was when Edward noticed her eyes, they were beautiful grey. She acknowledged their presence.

'You have a very clean land' she said. She made eye contact which made her look very intimidating.

'Thank you' Nathan said, bowing his head. A gust of cold wind blew past them. The lady made her way towards the others.

'That's Lizyati, everyone calls her Yati' Dewi's dad said.

'Yes and she's my…' Rajah was saying confidently when he paused thinking of the right word to say. 'My assistant' he said.

'So am I right to say you're the captain or leader of this ship?' Edward guessed.

'Yes, isn't it obvious?' Rajah replied.

'Yes, and it is very obvious that you are a very conceited person' Bobby snapped.

'Excuse me?' Rajah said, offended.

'Oh you know that word? I thought you're too full of yourself to know uncommon words' Bobby said.

'Bobby, that's enough' Edward said. Edward nodded once to Nathan which he understood immediately. Nathan turned to one of his men.

'Charlie, can you gather them in the town hall? Thank you very much' he said. As the newcomers were escorted away, Edward and Flyangel met up quickly with the two brothers.

'Nice seeing you again' Jake grinned.

'It's only been a few days guys' Flyangel said.

'Nathan, why do you tell him I'm hosting them? They landed in your town' Edward said, smiling.

'What? Combination is five times bigger than White Shore! There's no place for them here. And besides, you are the king of Southernere. The king of Combination is also the king of Southernere'

'Who said that?' Edward said, raising one eyebrow.

'Me' Nathan replied.

'Me too' Jake said.

'I do believe it too. I mean, it doesn't state in books but everyone sees it that way. Combination is where it all began' Flyangel said. Edward was not going to win this debate, so he gave in.

The four of them proceeded to the town hall. Every chair was already occupied. Charlie had to order movements of chairs from storage for the royals to sit. But none of them sat.

'Greetings, people from the other world, I'm King Edward of Combination' Edward began his speech. The crowd went whispering, they were confused by what Edward meant by the other world. But everyone was behaving nicely like obedient students. Everyone except Lizyati. She was standing in one corner observing the new people she just met. In a way, it was creepy.

'You are now far away from your homes. You're in a land called Southernere. I know you will have lots of questions but I can't afford to answer them one by one right now because your welfare is more important. But I'll open only three questions to the floor'

A few hands raised. Flyangel stepped up to the front to assist Edward in choosing a random person. She pointed at a timid young lady with very black hair.

'In which part of the world is Southernere? Is it Australia?' the lady asked. Edward paused for a while, obviously not knowing what is Australia.

'I don't think so. Like I said before, you're from

another world. You are very far from home' Edward replied.

More people raised their hands. Flyangel was about to point to someone when Charlie approached. He whispered something in her ears. Flyangel tried not to react, with eyes widened a little, she stepped onto the small stage to inform her husband.

'There's a spotting of a familiar figure in the streets of Merchant's District. Widow' Flyangel whispered into Edward's ear. Edward too was shocked but he controlled his expression well.

'I'll head back Combination first. I'll bring Bobby with me' Flyangel continued.

'Be safe' Edward said. He pushed the thought away calmly and turned his attention back to the crowd. Charlie helped him point a random person. A young man stood up.

'By any chance are you the fallen empire of Othmaniyyah? Or wait, English is Ottoman' the man asked.

'I'm sorry what?' Edward just blurted out his confusion.

'The Ottoman Empire fell five to six years ago, right after world war one. So we see you, the king and queen dress modestly, I thought you are the Ottoman Empire'

'Oh, I have never heard of Ottoman and we are certainly not. We're the descendants of Combi'

That just made them more lost.

'Alright, one more question'

A lot of hands were raised. Charlie pointed to another man.

'How many cities are there in this land?' the man asked.

'Only counting major cities, we have about six of them' Edward replied. That got most of them imagining how big this land might be.

'Now, since you are a very big group. And it'll take at least a week for our builders to build guesthouses for you. A quarter of you will remain in White Shore, King Nathan's man will assist you in repairing damages on your ship. The rest shall return with me to Combination. Majority of you will be staying in houses that are still vacant or guesthouses, and a few of you will stay in the castle. This is only until the builders finished building the guesthouses. Or your ship is repaired and you're ready to set sail again. I'll need your group in charge to assign who's going where' Edward said. Immediately Rajah got up and turned to the crowd.

'Alright simple, our fisherman crew and tinkers will stay here. The rest of us shall follow the king' Rajah decided. Edward felt unbelievable how simple Rajah made that sound. If Edward was in his place, he would have to consider as well whether the people will like what they're assigned to. Nevertheless, everyone seems to agree with the arrangements. The tinkers and fishermen were assigned to guesthouses and small cottages at the edge of the forest by the shore. And all the others boarded the carriages and King Edward led them back to Combination. It was early evening when they arrived and the sun making its way down in the west made the city seem more magical. Rajah and Omar was on the same carriage as Edward, and Dewi was there too. The whole time they talked about their home back in Indonesia. When Rajah opened his mouth, it became awkward.

'Here we are' Edward said, alighting the carriage first. The Indonesians glanced up at the tallest tower of the castle, amazed by its beauty. A few servants came down the stairs to greet the king. Edward asked them to bring the guests to their temporary assigned houses. Rajah, Omar, Lizyati, and a few others, probably Rajah's other assistants or his men working close to him, altogether a total of seven of them will be staying in the castle. Annie and Laura were the ones who will guide the seven through the castle.

'Annie' Edward called before she could go away.

'Yes your majesty?'

'Has Angel returned?'

'I have not seen her majesty since this morning, I apologise sir' Annie said, getting worried. That means, Flyangel was still at Merchant's District.

'That's alright Annie, I know where she is. You may proceed' Edward said. Annie curtsied and left.

'William, Merchant's District please' Edward told the coachman before getting back into the carriage.

JEWEL TRICKS

*Before you start reading the next
chapter, finish what you're supposed
to do first. Done? Carry on!*

Although there were people walking about the streets, it was very quiet. Queen Flyangel met up with the informant in front of a jewelry store. He reported to her everything that he saw. A hooded person exiting the store, met up with another hooded person. There were a few others as well, without a hood, circling the area, but no familiar faces. He claimed to have seen Marcala as one of the hooded persons.

'How long ago was that?' Bobby asked the man.

'I'm sorry, your majesty, I thought you would come sooner, I've been waiting for an hour. They're gone now' he replied.

'Which way they went?' Bobby asked.

'North'

'That's towards the castle' Flyangel said, alarm in her voice. She and Bobby rushed back to the carriage. Before she could open the carriage door, a hooded person came from around the back, attempting to stab Flyangel with a knife in his hand. Bobby drew his sword, knocked the knife upwards in time. The knife landed on the road, tip pointing down. Bobby rested the sword on the person's neck.

'Reveal yourself' Bobby said. The person was motionless. Flyangel used her magic to pull the person's hood back. There was no one. Automatically the entire cloak fell to the ground like as if a ghost had attempted to murder her. Flyangel looked around fearfully while Bobby bent down immediately to inspect the cloak. He picked it up to find a small ruby on the ground.

'Your majesty, I need to get you back to the castle immediately' Bobby said, feeling uneasy. He had no idea what was going on, but something definitely doesn't feel right. But everything that comes next happened so fast. A big black bird swooped down towards Bobby, transformed into a man and kicked him on the chest. Bobby fell back a few metres away. The man closed on him. Nearby, a hooded person was summoning a fireball on his palm, his whole body facing Flyangel. Innocent passersby screamed in shock and ran away. The sky was growing darker. It was just the same as when the city got flooded. The hooded person threw the fireball at Flyangel who rolled to her right. The fireball crashed into the carriage, burning it completely. The man who was facing Bobby took out a knife. Bobby had his sword in his hand. He got up quickly. The man eyed his sword carefully. Bobby watched his knife. There was no way this guy's knife could defeat his sword. But he wasn't planning on letting his guard down. Bobby stabbed him in the stomach. His whole outfit fell to the ground and the man disappeared. Underneath the clothes was a sapphire.

Flyangel observed the hooded person. But she couldn't see the face properly. He summoned another fireball, whereas Flyangel played with water. From between her fingers, water flowed out and followed her directions. She moved her hands in circular motion in front of her and the water followed. The man threw the fireball and summoned another. Flyangel directed the water to wipe the fire out and continued the motion again. This happened the same way for a few more rounds before Flyangel directed the water towards him. The water soaked the cloak and the cloak fell down into the huge puddle of water. There was no one standing there. Flyangel rushed to pick up the cloak and found a diamond bracelet. It was then that a few groups of soldiers arrived. They came from the southern districts, stationed there to patrol. Word got out fast and they rushed to assist.

'Your majesty, we received reports' a soldier asked.

'Yes, I'm confused about what's happening. But something is definitely happening. Random attackers and then they disappeared. Or turned into this' Flyangel lifted the bracelet in her right hand.

Suddenly, there was an explosion from a nearby shop. Fire erupted from inside. Flyangel caught sight of an eagle flying away from the scene. She knew, that must be one of the avengers. She noticed one of the soldiers carrying a bow. She politely gestured for him to give her the bow and the arrow in the quiver behind his back. The eagle was circling back. She nocked, aimed, and released. The arrow flew straight into the eagle's body. Black fog appeared around it as it fell. The eagle changed back into a man. The arrow had pierced his chest. He fell hard a few blocks away. There were distant screams. Flyangel handed the bow back to the soldier and rushed to get to the body. She ordered some of the soldiers to aid whoever needed help in the burning store. Bobby and the rest followed.

People were running away, some were curiously inspecting. When they reached, some of the soldiers cordoned the area while Flyangel and Bobby took a good look at the body.

'I recognise him. One of Widow's strong followers' Flyangel said.

'Your majesty, I believe there is more coming, I need to get you back safely' Bobby said.

'No Bobby, it's my responsibility, I can't be a coward and hide myself. And I won't' Flyangel replied.

Another carriage arrived. King Edward stepped out.

'Angel, what happened?' he asked, remaining calm. Even though he has seen the body and the smoke rising a few blocks ahead.

'Widow is behind this I'm sure of it' Flyangel said, but she wasn't sure of it herself.

'Yes she is' Edward said. 'I had felt her dark power months before we wed. I just kept it as my suspicion. I shouldn't have. The power is getting stronger'

Flyangel was sceptical.

'But she's dead' she said.

'We thought she was. So what is this and that smoke?' Edward said, quickly changing the topic.

'Believe me, we've been facing different attackers but they all were… fake. Only this was real. Like the rest disappeared and we only found jewels in their places' Flyangel explained, showing him the bracelet. A look of realisation on Edward's face. He touched the bracelet with his fingertips.

'We have to get back to the castle now!' he exclaimed. 'This was just a distraction. We'll gather the council once this is over'

Edward rushed back to his carriage with Flyangel and Bobby. The soldiers knew what they should do without being told. Some proceeded to clear the body, the remaining went to assist the others at the burning store.

OLD FRIENDS

*Before you start reading the next
chapter, finish what you're supposed
to do first. Done? Carry on!*

Annie led the guests through the castle main
doors. The awed looks on their faces put a smile
on her. But one was expressionless. The lady named
Lizyati. She expressionlessly said "nice". Her head was
always tilted upwards, like how an arrogant person
walks, except that she doesn't give the arrogant vibes,
she was intimidating.

Suddenly, the sound of magic could be heard from
the castle gates. Annie's eyes went wide in horror. She
knew something wasn't right. They have guests who
are not accustomed to the lifestyle here. To introduce
magic, obviously the king would have to hold an
event. So this impromptu magic couldn't have been
the castle men. 22 years ago, Dewi was introduced
to magic, she was alone. Now this is a huge group of
strangers. Annie could imagine the chaos that would
come. She turned to face the guests but they were all
already looking curiously outside. Apparently, only

she was thinking that way. Laura and the others were stupidly going out to check even though they are not magic-abled.

'Everyone, let's proceed!' Annie was panicking.

'That's impossible!' someone Annie expected the last to ever speak with expression said in surprise. Lizyati was shocked. They saw fireballs thrown from people's hands and burnt the plants and staff around. Those with magic were defending the front. If they don't deploy SHAWs and troops now, the line of defence will be broken and the avengers will enter the castle. Annie could make out some familiar faces and amongst them were Alphaga and Marcala. The guests were staring in shock. Annie went in front of them and called for their attention.

'Everyone, it's dangerous!' Annie shouted fearfully.

Behind her, one guard was charging at Alphaga who easily sent a forcefield at him. The guard was thrown very far backwards. He was about to land on Annie. They all followed the movements except Annie who was clueless. Seeing that they were staring at something, she turned around and was almost scared to death. However, the guard did not land on her. He stopped midair, there was no forcefield or anything. No one at all standing in their place were magic-abled. Something slowly brought the guard back down on his feet. The guard looked back in surprise. Annie looked around as well. Still no one near was magic-abled. The fight continued. Annie tried again to get the guests' attention.

'Everyone, it's safer inside. Listen to me!' she eventually shouted angrily. Rajah, Omar and the others followed. Lizyati stayed for a while more before entering.

'Whatever happens to Rajah, you all will pay for it' Lizyati said fiercely. Annie couldn't stand any longer. First, she saw a dead person standing strong and was about to kill them, probably, second, she almost got crushed, and third, Lizyati is now threatening her. Who does she think she is? Annie thought.

'Alright if you think you're so great, fight them!' Annie snapped. A few seconds later she regretted saying it without thinking. How could she say those words to the newcomers, she thought.

Lizyati breathed in and out.

'I can't' she said.

'I'm sorry, I shouldn't have said that' Annie apologised. Somehow, a certain someone was not being himself the entire time, a chatterbox. Annie glanced at the person, Rajah.

'That's alright' Lizyati said, and gave a smile. The kind of smile that will give you chills. But Annie was happy enough to receive a smile.

'Let's go somewhere safer' she said, quickly leading them into the castle.

Outside, the battle was intense, more of the guards were dying. Fortunately, Masters Mousy, Kitty, Lillain, and Asher arrived.

'And of course all of you have to step in and spoil

the fun' Marcala said, grinning at them. Somehow she seems more powerful than before. She stopped all magic in the air with a single hand. There was like an invisible barrier between her side and the castle men, preventing fights from continuing.

'What's the matter? Don't want to greet an old friend?' she laughed.

'How are you still alive?' Lillain asked. She still couldn't get over the moment when she found out her grandmother was The Avenger.

'Oh Lillain, that's no way to talk to your grandmother' Marcala said teasingly.

'You're not my grandmother'

'Ouch' Marcala was still teasing. That was followed by her evil laugh.

Lillain brought the ground that was separating both sides up high above the castle towers.

'This child' Marcala muttered. The powers that were stopped resumed, crashing into the thick dirt wall. Marcala tried to bring the wall down but her efforts were to no avail.

'Everyone help me, what are you doing just watching?! You're much stronger than me now. You know I'm still depending on the conductors' Marcala scolded. They all used their force to bring the wall down. It started sinking slowly but the resistance was very strong.

'Just destroy it!' Marcala exclaimed. She punched the air with her palm. A strong forcefield slammed the wall, creating a big hole bigger than enough for

Marcala to walk through. Marcala grinned again at Lillain who was staring in front of her. She stepped forward, Lillain brought the wall back down. The wall crumbled down. Marcala managed to step back in time before she got devoured.

'How dare you!' Marcala glared. She force-choked Lillain. But nothing happened. Mousy and Kitty had both shielded Lillain from the force.

'Strike them down! We have been preparing for this, no retreat!' Marcala shouted. The avengers all at once sent their magic towards the four masters and the other remaining guards and staff. But it was too many, some of the powers collided, causing a forcefield that threw both sides away. Some were deflected and attacked other random people instead.

'Split up! Just find a weak spot around the castle and charge in! Do what we came to do!' Marcala shouted. She transformed into a black bird and flew high around the castle, observing for weak spots. Aside from the guards stationed randomly around the castle, the castle has a magical layer of resistance that resists every unwanted magic from entering. But it does not mean it's totally impossible to go through. Alphaga remained at the gates, keeping Kitty and Asher busy. Lillain and Mousy went to stop those who have gone to break into the castle. Lillain glanced above as she neared the main entrance steps, her black bird grandmother swooped down and crashed through one window on the second floor. The avenger has made it through.

THE WITCH

*Before you start reading the next
chapter, finish what you're supposed
to do first. Done? Carry on!*

While the chaos was happening outside, inside the castle was noisy as well. Servants rushed here and there to follow the emergency procedures. The king's guards that were assigned inside were moving about to look out for the avengers that had made it through, based on Master Lillain's report.

No one has any clue that Marcala was creeping around the second floor, finding her way down to the dungeons. As she walked along the main hallway, she heard a group of servants from around a corner and was about to bump into them. She quickly entered one of the chambers without thinking. She turned around to find Lizyati staring at her with no expression on her face. Marcala smiled.

'You must be new here. I'm Marcala…' Marcala said. She was planning her next move already, kill this lady and carry on.

'You almost killed my leader just now' Lizyati said,

Marcala could feel the room starting to get colder. Enough being nice, Marcala thought. She swiped her hand at Lizyati, intending to throw her to the side. But nothing happened.

'I'm so glad you chose to use a power that my friends can easily handle' Lizyati said, smiling mysteriously. Marcala had no idea what she meant by friends until she felt something, no it was a few things, beings, grabbing her all around. She could even feel them inside her. Soon, her feet were off the floor. She felt like vomiting. Her whole body felt weak. From the head to her toes, she felt like there were beings moving around, in her blood, in her soul. Her face tilted upwards and she gasped for air. From the bottom corner of her eyes she could make out Lizyati forming a smile. She tried resisting, using all the abilities that she has. But she was too weak to exert any force.

'*Letakkan di katil*' Lizyati said in a foreign language, asking to place Marcala on the bed. Marcala was brought to the bed by something and as she lay on the bed unable to resist the power, Lizyati took out ropes from a bag she had been bringing along with her since she exited the ship. She tied all of Marcala's limbs tightly to the corners of the bed. Marcala had given up on resisting, she used her strength to speak instead.

'What are you doing? Who are you?' she asked weakly.

'Don't worry lady, I'll be gentle, I know you are

very old, that's why I asked my friends to be more gentle with you' Lizyati replied. If this is gentle, what's not? Marcala thought.

'What friends? Who are you?'

Lizyati ignored. After tying all the ropes, she proceeded to take out a sharp dagger from her bag.

'What are you doing?'

Lizyati placed her face in front of Marcala for her to have a good look.

'I'm sacrificing you. Something you wouldn't understand. Your land is clean, your people know nothing about my magic. I'm here now, my friends will spread and we will rid of this land of your people. Any last words?'

'High Master Lord Grindel of the Northern Kingdom, save me' Marcala said, closing her eyes, tears rolled down the sides. Lizyati held the dagger in both hands, lifted it above Marcala's stomach with the tip pointing down, said a few words in the foreign language, and brought it down deep into the body. Marcala let out a short gasp before lying back down dead. Her eyes wide open in shock. Lizyati breathed in and out deeply. With her bloody hands, she gently touched Marcala, smearing blood on her face.

'Thank you for coming into this room. I've needed that sacrifice for days' Lizyati said, staring into Marcala's dead eyes. She turned around, grabbed a towel out of her bag, wiped her hands dry. But it was still red.

'*Kamu tahu apa harus dibuat. Jangan sesiapa tahu itu bukan dia*' Lizyati said. (You know what you have to do. Make sure no one suspects it's not her). She was telling something.

CURIOUSER AND CURIOUSER

*Before you start reading the next
chapter, finish what you're supposed
to do first. Done? Carry on!*

Master Lillain walked up the stairs to the second floor. She went to search the hallways. Marcala was nowhere to be found.

Down in the entrance hall, magical explosions were starting to take place. The avengers had gathered up there to combine powers. Lillain rushed back to the balcony overlooking the first floor entrance. Avengers were killing helpless servants, injuring the king's guards, and pressuring Master Mousy who was the only master there. The others were still outside, facing Alphaga and other avengers. Lillain sent a wave of the air. Wind blew some of the avengers outside. And Mousy finished off the rest. Lillain joined them back on the first floor, starting back the defence and drove the enemy back.

'Enough!' a sudden piercing voice sent shivers to

all its listeners. Surprisingly everyone stopped. Even Alphaga and the avengers. They turned to see Marcala walking out of the main doors and down the steps. The good guys giving way to her automatically. Even Lillain has nothing to say.

'I couldn't find what we're looking for' Marcala told her men. 'Everyone is badly wounded. We'll be back on another day'

For some reason, she did not transform into the bird she always transformed into when she's making her leave. Instead, she walked all the way out the gates. Some of the avengers like Alphaga felt something was weird, but they all followed her obediently. The masters, servants and king's guards who suffered minimal injuries helped those who are wounded. There were quite a few bodies that were needed to be cleared. One thing for sure was, everyone was relieved that it was over, for now.

King Edward, Queen Flyangel, and Bobby returned just in time to see the avengers walking out the gates. It was kind of funny. But seeing Marcala's face was enough to bring back anger.

'Don't let her get away' Edward said, stepping closer and releasing a blue current from his hand. Alphaga stepped in front of Marcala and released black currents from his eyes. Edward caught the second in his other hand.

'Enough Alphaga, I said we come back next time' Marcala said.

'Then we should have left since just now. It was your ridiculous idea to walk' Alphaga replied while trying to maintain the currents. Edward did grow stronger than when they last fought in the war.

'I warn you, that's enough!' Marcala scolded. Alphaga ignored her. One second later, Marcala swiped her hand and a great amount of black silk swirled around them. Shadows and darkness devoured the currents and Marcala grabbed Alphaga's stubborn hands and flew high into the sky in the form of a big black bird.

'What magic is this?' Edward asked. When the shadows disappeared, the avengers were no longer there.

'Your majesty, it was a relief they didn't take anything' Annie cried as they walked onto the royal grounds.

'How were they allowed to leave peacefully? They entered the castle, the same very castle of our great mother Sofya. And look, look at all those damages. And you let them go?!' Edward was infuriated.

Silence. No one has anything to reply. No one dares to talk back as well. Edward rarely gets mad, and when he does, it is very scary. Fortunately, he calms down very fast as well.

'Excuse me, I need a moment alone in my chamber' Edward walked away.

Later on, Bobby supervised the cleaning of the

mess and the few dead bodies. The SHAW masters worked on repairing the damages. And Flyangel went to check on Edward. He was looking out the window at the royal grounds entrance below where the servants were busy cleaning up. He glanced at the King's Road that leads into the city.

'She should have been dead' Edward said without turning. Flyangel thought of the best words to speak as she went to sit at an armchair by the tea table.

'All of them should be dead' Edward continued voicing his unhappiness.

'That's not my Eddie speaking' Flyangel said, trying to sound like she was joking.

Edward took a deep breath.

'I'm sorry' he said, finally turning around to face his wife.

'That's alright' Flyangel said. She went closer to him. His beautiful brown eyes made contact with hers. Flyangel can't help but feel weak in his gaze. The good kind of weak. She loves him dearly. She found herself caressing his cheek. Edward took her hand in his and kissed it.

'Even after marriage we rarely got time to be together, just the two of us' Flyangel said, longing for more of Edward's affection.

'There are so many things happening' Edward replied, not breaking eye contact even for a second.

'Can you make it up to me?'

Edward smiled. He leaned in closer and kissed her gently.

Meanwhile, down at the castle entrance, Master Lillain was leading a group of five SHAW students through the castle gates. The mess was not a pleasant sight.

'Oh dear, I think our lesson will have to wait. You go along, Cardinal, lead them into the castle, stay safe, I'll see you again later' Lillain said. Cardinal led his friends into the castle as Lillain went to help the masters.

Cardinal and his friends were very excited to finally step foot into the castle. It was their first time. During the dark years when King Henry was heartbroken over the death of his wife and children's disappearance, there weren't any celebrations at the castle. Even after he recovered from the incident, he had never opened the castle doors to the city. It stayed that way until Edward took back the throne from Marcala and his sister, Erieka, a year ago. Seeing the magnificent interior of the historic home of Combi, the children stared in awe.

'I'm telling mom everything' the girl with the copper red hair, Eva, said.

'Not if I tell her first' her brother, Evius, said.

'Guys, let's appreciate their majesties, the king and queen, and our masters for letting us on this amazing opportunity. So let's put in our best to learn all we can' Cardinal said.

'Absolutely!' Izalora, the one with the headscarf, said dreamily.

'I wonder where might the king and queen be'

Baron, the last of them who has been quiet the whole time, said.

Annie passed by them, and Cardinal stopped her.

'Excuse me kind miss, may we know where we might find King Edward and Queen Flyangel?' he asked.

Annie was mainly surprised he stopped her just for that. It was obvious that the servants were too busy to be stopped by some children wanting to ask a silly question.

'I'm sorry, I'll get back to you later okay?' Annie said quickly and rushed off.

'Cardinal we should just wait. It's clear they do not want to be disturbed' Izalora said.

'You're right'

They spent almost a half hour more waiting for Master Lillain to get back to them, and an additional ten minutes for the king and queen to meet them.

'I apologise for keeping you waiting' Edward smiled at them and clapped his hands together.

'That's alright your majesty' Cardinal said.

'No no, it's not alright, as a courtesy of the royal family, I invite you to stay the night. We shall start on your lessons tomorrow. How does that sound?' Edward told them excitedly. The children looked at each other in amazement and disbelief. From Eva's face, Edward could tell she was screaming inside with joy.

'That is the most... I'm extremely honoured your majesty' Cardinal said, taking a bow.

'That is absolutely wonderful' Lillain said, smiling proudly at Edward. 'I'll tell your parents you won't be coming home tonight, and that you will be needing your stuff for tonight' she said to the students.

'Your majesty, can we explore the castle?' Izalora asked.

'Sure! Why not?' Edward said. 'Penny will lead you to your chambers. Later on in the evening at six, we'll have a performance by the masters at the ballroom. Don't be late'

He and Flyangel went off to do their royal duties.

A handmaiden introduced herself as Penny, and she assigned servants who will show the children to their chambers. Their parents came minutes later delivering their bags filled with clothes and toiletries.

'You won't be needing toiletries, the castle has plenty of them' Lillain told every one of them.

They hugged and kissed their parents goodbye and headed back in. All of them had their chambers beside one another on the second floor. Cardinal being the first, and Izalora had the one closest to the end. After settling their bags down, they went venturing around the castle. They were left alone. Lillain placed Cardinal in charge of the group as she had to attend the royal council meeting soon.

'Where should we go first?' Cardinal asked them.

'We should split and explore wherever we like!' Baron suggested.

'I don't think that's a good idea' Cardinal said.

'Say whatever you guys want, Izalora and I will

be sticking together' Eva said, holding Izalora's hand excitedly.

They were standing in the middle of the hallway. They were not blocking anyone as not many servants use this way much. The servants prefer to use the servants' walkways, their tunnels cover a huge part of the castle's body system. They can get anywhere at a faster rate through them. And we haven't even touched on the hidden chambers. Mostly the royals and the senior staff know about it.

'Okay then. Evius, you want to come with me or Baron, or alone?' Cardinal asked. Evius looked at the both of them, thinking.

'We don't have all day!' Baron said.

'Alright, I'll go alone' Evius said. He would feel very guilty if he had chosen one of his friends. So he decided to go alone.

'Meet back here at five-thirty, we'll go to the ballroom together' Cardinal reminded. They parted ways, eager to explore the castle. They have about an hour to explore. Cardinal went to find the royal library. Baron went down, looking for the dungeons. Evius went to find the entrance to the towers, looking forward to the view of the city from up there. Eva and Izalora strolled around the hallways. They don't have a specific place they wanted to see. So they just followed wherever their curiosity brought them. They passed by some servants along the way. They met some painters, handmaidens, maids, and even cooks. There were some who were not in uniforms they do not recognise.

Rajah, Omar, and even Edward's friends, Captain, Bale, and Oliver. But no one was as suspicious as Lizyati. They noticed her walking slowly, which isn't that suspicious. It was an aura she emitted. It may fool adults, but kids see past the fog with their wild imaginations. Izalora felt it more. Eva was sceptical. But Izalora convinced her to follow Lizyati secretly wherever she goes. There was something mysterious about Lizyati that Izalora wanted to find out. They followed her all the way to her chamber which was back on the second floor, not that far from theirs. She entered leaving the girls standing a few metres behind like they're stranded somewhere.

'She feels scary, dangerous' Izalora said.

'You said the same thing for the hundredth time now. It's clear, she was just strolling around and now back to her room. At first, yes, I agree there was something weird, but enough, just let it go' Eva expressed her annoyance. She had wanted Izalora to drop the subject minutes ago. Now they have wasted their time. Ten more minutes and their sightseeing time will be over.

'I'm sorry' Izalora said.

'That's alright. We shall wait for the boys to return'

They boys were a little late by 2 to 3 minutes. But only Cardinal and Evius came. Baron was nowhere to be seen.

'What took you boys so long to come?' Eva asked.

'I got carried away reading in the library' Cardinal told guiltily.

'And you?' Eva looked at her brother's face, annoyed.

'Relax Eva, what did you see that made you mad?' Evius said.

'It's my fault' Izalora said. She wanted to explain but Eva asked her to drop it, saying that it was nothing. They finally realised Baron was not there.

'And where in Southernere is Baron?' Eva asked.

A moment of silence as they all looked at one another for answers.

'Where do you think he went?' Izalora asked the boys. They could only shrug their shoulders.

'Let's split up and find him' Evius suggested which made Eva glared at him again.

'We shouldn't split' Izalora replied.

'Yes, another one of us might go missing again' Cardinal said.

'Where to first?'

'I say we go to the towers, he likes thrills, the towers have great scenery I guess' Cardinal said, looking at Izalora. He depends a lot on her. Izalora is a very smart girl. Aside from that, she's a good friend.

'No, I just came from the towers, he isn't there' Evius replied.

'You came from all of them?'

'No, but...'

'Then we'll go to the towers'

'No' Izalora said quickly. They all looked at her in surprise.

'He's in the dungeons. I think' Izalora said again. They were still staring at her, speechless. What a random suggestion from the towers to the dungeons. But they know she isn't lying or tricking when she says something. Izalora never lies. And it's kind of her gift to be able to sense beings around her. It's perhaps also because she is a sprite, they're stronger in nature. And the castle was built from nature, rocks and all.

'I just feel it' Izalora said.

'Then we'll go to the dungeons' Cardinal concluded. They proceeded down immediately.

'How are you always doing that?' Eva walked beside her and asked.

'I don't know. It's just my feeling'

'Well, that's a very powerful gift you got there! But sometimes it's just a waste of time. Like the lady just now' Eva said. That actually hurt Izalora's feelings but she just let it go. Eva might be right. Maybe it was nothing. But the feeling is too strong for Izalora to push it away.

As they turned a corner of a hallway on level one, they bumped into Baron.

'Where have you been?' they asked. Baron was almost speechless. His face was very pale.

'Guys, I've got many things to say, and that the castle is not safe is one of them' Baron spoke in a rush, like he badly wants to get out immediately. Eva and Evius were about to say that he has gone mad.

But Izalora stopped them by asking the most basic question.

'What happened?'

'Not here…' Baron said quietly, looking around for anyone watching. He brought them to his chamber and shut the doors.

BLACK MAGIC

*Before you start reading the next
chapter, finish what you're supposed
to do first. Done? Carry on!*

Baron was very excited to explore alone. He was always the type to look for thrills. And by doing so alone, without any help or what he calls "disturbance". He went straight looking for the entrance to the dungeons. He found it in less than five minutes, it was obvious as the only way underground is the only way to the dungeons. Surprisingly no one was guarding it. He was about to confidently run down the stairs when he heard some mysterious conversations going on. He decided to creep downstairs slowly, making sure his ear was nearer down than his legs. His foot was on the second step and he stopped. He hid behind the wall, the only cover he has. Straight ahead is a corridor with rooms in which all are empty except one, the treasure chamber. A sharp turn on the right leads to the dungeons. The voices were obviously coming from the right. It could be the prisoners talking. But there was something darker. Colder. Baron tried his best to peek but he couldn't get a clear view. Like there was an invisible barrier blocking, but truthfully there wasn't. However the voices were clear.

'All you need to do is join her. She will be the reason you are safe from what's to come' a hoarse male voice said.

'We told you before, we won't agree to anything, not without the consent of Marcala' the voice belongs to a woman.

'So I suggest you get out of here creep. I don't know who you are, coming in to offer some ridiculous deal. For all we know, you might be working for Edward' that was the voice of a man. Not hoarse, a different man. It was Pertum and Lydia but Baron has not the slightest idea who they are.

'If you reject her now, you'll regret it' the hoarse voice said.

'We won't' Lydia replied.

Then there was silence. Baron knew the conversation was over. Any second the owner of the hoarse voice will make his way to the stairs. Baron ran up to find his friends.

'Who do you think the voice belongs to?' Izalora asked. They were all gathered at Baron's chamber's lounge corner, hearing the story.

'I have no idea'

'We should tell Master Lillain. She's the only person I trust' Cardinal suggested.

Suddenly, there was a knock on the door. Then Master Lillain spoke.

'Children, are you ready for the show?'

Eva was about to reply very loudly just like she always does. But Izalora cupped her hands around her mouth. Only a soft murmur came out.

'What are you doing?' Eva asked in annoyance, pushing Izalora's hands away. The rest were also unsure of her actions.

'Master Lillain never calls us children. And how does she know all five of us are in here?' Izalora explained her suspicion.

There was another knock.

'Children, you don't wanna keep the king waiting' Lillain called impatiently. Izalora raised one finger, pointing.

'Whatever you do, don't open that door' she warned. Her friends were all still clueless. Eva couldn't take the tension so she voiced out.

'Okay, so what Izalora? Are we supposed to just wait in here while our master is calling for us?' she was louder than she expected to be. Loud enough for anyone outside the chamber to hear.

'Eva quiet down' Izalora hissed. Eva shook her head stubbornly.

'Eva' Cardinal finally let out a stern voice. Which made Eva silent for a while. Izalora glanced at him. He too may not understand her opinion but he cooperated with her. She respects him for that. And since he's their group leader, he's leading by good example.

'Children, you know I could hear you from here!' Lillain exclaimed. Her voice sounded almost wild, like she had gone mad. She started banging the door.

'I agree with you. That's not Master Lillain' Evius said fearfully.

'Okay guys, we need to get out of here now' Izalora said.

'Through the window' Cardinal said.

'We're on the second floor!' Baron said disapprovingly.

'Then what's your idea Baron? Face whoever's behind that door?' Eva argued.

'Eva you're being annoying' Evius said.

'Guys! You're not helping' Cardinal projected his stern voice again. 'Bad timing for a stupid argument'

He rolled his eyes and got to work on bringing down the curtains and tying them together to help them get down.

'We're wasting time' Izalora said and stepped to the open window.

'Izalora?' Eva said, extremely worried now.

Izalora held her palm out the window facing the ground. A leaf from one of the bushes grew in size and length as it rose to the window's level. Izalora stepped to the side and signalled her friends to climb. She has a little smile on her face, proud that she did the magic without any help. Her friends climbed. The leaf was miraculously large and strong to hold all of them. Just after Cardinal gestured for Izalora to go first, a smoky presence entered through the door without it being open. Smoke rushed into Cardinal's nostrils, entering his system. Izalora watched in horror as her friend's eyes went up so that she could see only white. And he began to float as his whole body started shaking and his head tilted upwards. He was being possessed.

'Cardinal!' the rest were exclaiming in fear as they watched from outside. Eva was screaming. By now the whole castle would have heard them. But no one came.

'Please! Whoever you are, please release my friend!' Izalora begged. Cardinal stopped shaking. But he was still in midair, his eyes white, and his skin very pale.

'I've asked you to open the door. But you ignored me' the voice was very hoarse and frightening. It sounded like it could kill anytime. What is more frightening was that the voice came from Cardinal. He was mouthing the exact words but with a different voice.

'What have you done to him?' Izalora cried.

'Oh I've done nothing! He's perfectly fine. This is a form of punishment. Wait until master comes. She'll gladly take over' Cardinal said again. There was a knock on the door. Cardinal looked like he just remembered something. His shoes touched back on the floor and he went to unlock the door. Lizyati came in. Seeing her, Izalora stepped back a single step and she couldn't go any further.

Bagus semuanya tapi kamu lupa buka pintu Lizyati scolded Cardinal. (Excellent job but you forgot to open the door).

Maaf ratuku Cardinal replied. (Apologies, my

queen). The hoarseness seems to be getting worse. Lizyati turned her attention to Izalora.

'You see what my friends can do. Do you want to resist and be a stubborn girl?' she said.

'What have you done to Cardinal? What do you want? Who are you?' Izalora asked.

'Feisty this one. You think you can possess her instead?' Lizyati talked to Cardinal.

'Certainly master'

'You can't' Izalora said, getting into her fighting stance.

'We should help her' Baron said, climbing back in to join Izalora. Eva and Evius nervously followed.

'So sweet all of you, you know' Lizyati sarcastically adored. 'Uri' she kind of gave a command to something. Suddenly, Izalora was pulled up by the neck. She was choking hard.

'Stop!' Eva was screaming and crying. Baron formed fire on both hands and was about to throw them at Lizyati when smoke rushed out of Cardinal's nostrils and into Baron. Cardinal fell down unconscious. Baron was now possessed, he wasn't aiming at Lizyati anymore. Instead, he was aiming at his friends.

'What do you want from us?!' Evius exclaimed. The chaos died down. Izalora fell and Baron wiped out his fire. But the thing was definitely still inside him.

'What do I want? I found out from my friend, let's show him respect, he has a name, Uri. Uri told me one of you has been spying on him, on me. And of course, my secret will be out sooner than I planned. So now, I know you troublemaking children can't keep secrets, especially my type of secret. I'll just have to sacrifice all of you' Lizyati said, smiling the whole time.

A moment of silence.

'What amazing power you have?' Eva asked, she intended it to be a praise. Evius was not sure what she was doing so he was trying to get her attention and ask her. Except he couldn't, so he was looking like a silly person jerking his head forward while looking sideways. Lizyati was surprised that she got praised for her dirty work.

'I'm just saying, I would be honoured if you could teach me. We don't have that magic here. Evius knows that I'm the type of person who likes to learn new things!' Eva was a completely different person. She was so hysterical before but now she was very confident. Lizyati was actually speechless. And she was having doubts about killing her now.

'You know, you're making me reluctant to kill you' Lizyati said. Eva smiled. 'But you know, my work is my work. And as much as I love your compliments, that can't stop me from doing what I'm supposed to do'

'Well, we are no use to you dead' Eva said.

'You are more dangerous to me alive!' Lizyati laughed.

'How about this…'

Eva was about to propose something but was cut off by Baron.

'Master, they're coming'

Lizyati groaned.

'Usik minda mereka. Jangan sekali mereka ingat apa yang terjadi' Lizyati ordered. (Wipe their minds. Make sure they don't remember what happened).

Smoke came out of Baron's nostrils and for a short moment, Eva and Evius could see smoke coming towards them but then everything went dark.

GRINDEL'S GAME

*Before you start reading the next
chapter, finish what you're supposed
to do first. Done? Carry on!*

King Edward, Queen Flyangel, and Master Lillain entered the conference room. Everyone was already there. Bobby, Dewi, Masters Mousy, Kitty, Asher, and Sir Everos.

'Before we get to whatever it is you have to say. Flyangel and I have very urgent news to deliver' Edward began. Those who have things to say sit back, knowing their messages will have to wait.

'Lady Feramein paid us a visit yesterday' Flyangel said. Both Edward and her were cautiously trying not to offend Dewi which made them stray away from the main point.

'And not that matters are bad or anything but well, that's just it. There's nothing wrong...'

They carry on not telling until Mousy has had enough.

'Your majesties, with all due respect, if Lady Feramein came to meet you herself that's bad' she said.

Awkward silence.

'What's the problem? She definitely told you something' Kitty asked.

'Okay, directly speaking. I need to ask Dewi, are you willing to stand with us if anything happens?' Flyangel asked.

Another awkward silence. Soft murmurs around the room as some of them felt that that was not an appropriate question. Dewi let out a short laugh.

'I mean, I don't understand your question. I've always stood with you for the past twenty years' Dewi replied.

'Feramein warned us about the Indonesians coming here. Just yesterday' Edward said. He proceeded to tell them everything that Feramein said, including her terms of not interfering with her people's affairs. The news was very intriguing. But their meeting was interrupted by an unexpected guest. The room has no windows, so if anyone wants to make a surprise entry has to do it on the walls. The walls seem to be moving in wavy patterns. The very old light brown paint seems like an ocean moving in a complete cycle around the room. It even ignored the door, the paint went over it. A man slowly emerged from the walls on one side. Flyangel immediately recognised who he is.

'Lord Grindel' Flyangel mumbled. Edward heard her. He looked at her cluelessly, wondering how she knew him and he didn't. No one else does. Flyangel also didn't tell him about Grindel controlling him the other day.

'We meet again your majesties' Grindel bowed. He had a smile that was genuinely nice. But he certainly has a motive coming here. Edward was busy trying to remember when they met.

'I'm sorry, who are you?' Lillain asked.

Grindel stared at her for a few seconds which felt like minutes.

'I am Lord Grindel, high master in the council, twelfth member of The Fifteen, protector of Forges of Beasts and the Northern Kingdom, keeper of beasts and curses. I am not in my true form. You'll be frightened if you see me in my true form, cause I ain't human' Grindel repeated the same thing he said to Flyangel. She almost rolled her eyes for it but thought better not to. Besides, she was more amused by the shocking looks the members of the council gave.

'Back to business. I am both happy and angry. Probably an hour ago, I sensed the presence of Marcala who we all thought was dead'

'We already know that' Mousy interrupted.

'Yes, but then, she was gone'

There was no reaction from the council as everyone remained silent.

'But she called out to me before she disappeared. She said this "High Master Lord Grindel of the Northern Kingdom, save me". And poof, she disappeared. I can't sense her anymore'

'You mean, Marcala was calling for your help?' Lillain asked.

'Is that a way to call your grandmother?'

'She's not my grandmother'

'Want me to check?'

'She killed my father!' Lillain snapped.

'Lillain' the other SHAW masters said. They knew she was losing control. Grindel kept staring at her, expressionless. He suddenly snapped his fingers.

'Anyway, my point is, someone killed dear Marcala' Grindel said in a very low voice.

'If that's true, then her own people killed her' Mousy said.

'Yes because we saw them leave' Dewi agreed.

'You guys are not thinking straight. No offense but all of you sound like children discussing war. And that must be your doing Grindel' Edward said. He was partly right, ever since Grindel appeared, the council doesn't seem serious. Emotional, and immature not like an adult.

'Clever boy Edward! Nvago never stop talking about your mind, your intellectual mind. I see it now. But even such an intellectual mind…'

'Can fall under the hypnosis of a high master? Yes' Edward finished his sentence.

'Impressive' Grindel said. He was indeed very impressed. 'How did you know? Flyangel told you?'

Flyangel shook her head. She was impressed as well.

'I didn't remember what happened since before the festivities, then when I woke up, Lady Feramein and Master Nvago were there. I just connected the dots'

'Well I need your help, all of you' Grindel finally got to the point.

'Stop messing around with your tricks first' Edward said.

'Alright' Grindel held both his hands up like in a surrender. Nothing happened, but they could feel some magic leaving their sides.

'What do you need our help with?'

'To stop the threat that Feramein told you about' Grindel paused.

'When Marcala and I connected, I could feel the pain she was going through. Someone killed her. Someone killed her in this very castle'

'Then how do you explain the Marcala that we saw leaving the castle?' Bobby asked.

'She's not Marcala. I don't even know if it's a she'

'Does Lady Feramein know?' Flyangel asked.

'Hasn't she told you, she can't be involved in the affairs of her people?'

'Then what about you?' Mousy asked.

'Are you my people? I'm lord of the Northern Kingdom, not lord of Southernere. Besides, breaking a few rules isn't so bad'

'Wait, so you're saying Marcala was killed in the castle?' Lillain asked, remembering something. Grindel simply nodded. Lillain got up immediately from her chair and ran out. Edward, Flyangel, and a few others went after her.

'Lillain what's wrong?' Edward asked. Lillain did

not need to reply, the extremely worried look on her face answered him.

'The students' Lillain said.

Edward ran faster to the hallway where the five children's chambers are. He opened every door until Baron's, where he found them, lying still.

The five was safely cared for in the lounge. Master Lillain and Dewi kept watch. The king's guards have been alerted to gather all the Indonesians in the ballroom.

'Is there a problem King Edward?' Rajah had been pestering Edward with the same question, following him wherever he went.

'For the tenth time Rajah, kindly get back to your seat first' Edward replied, almost losing his cool. To Edward's surprise, Rajah walked away. He observed him for a while. Nothing out of the ordinary. Rajah was just being his silly self, bothering other staff. Edward continued his duties, helping the staff do a headcount and assigning seats. Amongst a crowd of people who have not yet gotten their seat, Rajah approached an expressionless Lizyati.

'*Aku rasa mereka sudah tahu*' Rajah said. (I guess they already know).

'*Tapi mereka belom ketahui siapa*' Lizyati replied. (But they don't know yet who is).

'*Yati, mereka bukan bodoh. Nanti mereka akan tahu*'. (Yati, they aren't stupid. Later they'll find out).

'*Tuan, tenang*'. (Sir, calm down).

'*Ku tak bisa, mereka berkuasa*'. (I can't, they have powers. They are powerful).

'*Semua Jinku lebih berkuasa*'. (All my Jinn are more powerful). '*Tunggu, masanya akan datang. Tanah ni akan jadi milikmu*'. (Just wait, the time will come. This land will be yours).

A servant came up to them and showed them their seats just as Edward went up a small temporary stage the castle staff had placed just for this meeting.

'Thank you everyone for cooperating' Edward addressed. 'I apologise for all the inconveniences. We have received word that we were being attacked by your people'

People started whispering.

'Of course we needed proof. Fifteen minutes ago, we found five children lying unconscious in one of the chambers. And they have not woken up yet'

The whisper turned into full conversations. All of them were talking in their native language. Edward glanced at Flyangel. He mouthed the word "Dewi". Flyangel got that fast and went to get Dewi. Meanwhile, with the help of the Bobby and the king's guards, they managed to calm the people down.

'We are more than happy to kindly host your stay, but we would appreciate your understanding. This is a very serious situation' Edward said.

One man stood up with one hand raised.

'Yes, question?'

'No your majesty, some of us don't understand English' he said.

'Ohh, yes okay, someone's coming to explain it in your language'

Just on time, Dewi went onto the stage and Edward stepped to the side.

'What do you need me to address your majesty?' Dewi asked.

'Just explain what's going on' Edward replied.

Dewi went on explaining in Indonesian. Her gaze fell on her father and other people she knows. Her father was not good at hiding his emotions, he was clearly hiding something. She reported back to Edward after she was done.

'They have no idea your majesty. Though I need to speak with my father first' Dewi said rather quickly. She was about to go, Edward gently grabbed her hand.

'Dewi, please, I don't want you to be uncomfortable with us all of a sudden. We've known each other for years. One question can't change your view on us so quickly. You are the only person we have that can understand them very well'

'Edward, I'm fine. I still love you as the small boy I met years ago' Dewi said and walked away to see her father.

'What was that about?' Flyangel asked as she got closer to Edward. She saw the whole thing and can't help but feel a bit of jealousy.

'I just feel like Dewi is getting more distant lately' Edward said.

Lizyati had left the ballroom the moment the meeting ended. She entered her chamber and Grindel was sitting comfortably on an armchair facing the bloody corpse of Marcala. Lizyati was startled for a while.

'Who are you?' she asked.

'Funny thing you asked me. You are the foreign blood here, more like I should be the one asking "who are you?"'

'You don't want to mess with me' Lizyati was getting nervous by how confident Grindel was. And the dead body is not a good sign. She stepped back as Grindel got up, stretched his arms and walked closer to the side of the bed.

'She was my favourite student' he said. 'And you killed her'

'Sacrifice'

'Still murder to me'

Grindel shot his hand out in a choking gesture. Nothing happened. Lizyati laughed.

'I guess you don't know me that well. You can't hurt me'

'I know, as long as you're protected I can't. That's why I got your protection' Grindel smirked. Lizyati's grin vanished as she realised what he meant.

'Let Uri go'

'Ooo, Uri, so that's what you call him. 'Come out Uri, show yourself. I can feel you, your whole dark presence, but I can't see you'

'Uri, don't listen to him. Don't reveal yourself'

'What are you so afraid of him showing me his true form?'

'Something about you tells me you will get control over him'

Grindel laughed evilly.

'So how many others like him you got?'

'Release him'

'No. Why would I?'

Grindel continued laughing.

'What do you want? I can't give you back your student. It's impossible to bring back the dead'

'Yes I know that witch, but I'm more interested in what is your work here. What are you trying to do in this beautiful land?'

'I am only following orders'

'Your leader? Rajah?'

Lizyati shook her head. Grindel released his choke and went to sit on the armchair again. Smoke suddenly charged at him. But it only circled around him.

'Next time, think twice before sending Uri to me. You think I have no protection of my own?' Grindel grinned.

'So who's your leader?'

Lizyati was reluctant to say.

'You're gonna tell everyone' she said.

'Why would I? Because I want you to carry on what you're doing'

Lizyati was certainly surprised to hear that.

'You're okay with me attacking your home?'

'Oh no! You're mistaken. This isn't my home. My

business is my secret. Whatever I'm doing, the reason behind it goes deeper than anyone like you foreigners can understand. Now answer me, who's your leader?'

Lizyati thought about what he said carefully and told him.

'Omar'

A HORRIBLE
TALENTS DAY

*Before you start reading the next
chapter, finish what you're supposed
to do first. Done? Carry on!*

Cardinal ducked just in time as Izalora's sword came swinging at his face.

'Izalora, I told you just now, no aiming at the head' Bobby warned.

'I'm sorry! I'm sorry Cardinal!' Izalora said sheepishly.

'Nah that's alright' Cardinal said.

'It may be alright when no injury occurs. Imagine if it does occur' Bobby said. 'You have a natural talent for sword fight Izalora, but right now I need you to play by the rules'

Cardinal gave her a smile of motivation. She smiled back and they continued training.

At the other side of the field, Baron and Evius were training their SHAW skill.

'You know your own element very well. But now

I need you to focus on other elements' Master Lillain said. She was tutoring them herself.

Further away, near the pond, Eva was training her shooting skill with none other than the master of archery, the queen.

'When you draw, you breathe in. You breathe out when you release the arrow. This helps with stability' Queen Flyangel said.

Yesterday's show was cancelled, everything was back to normal. King Edward and Queen Flyangel had not heard from Grindel since the council meeting. So they have no lead. And it's wrong to accuse. So life goes on as per normal, for now. Coincidentally it's the third of April and an annual event has been marked on Combination's calendar, Talents Day. It was a beautiful Tuesday. The sun shone very brightly over the city as everywhere people and animals work and play. Talents Day was introduced as a holiday, so the majority were having their day off. More importantly, the highlight of today, the Talents Day competition. People are making their way to the heart of the business district. The city square. A big stage has been set up for the show near the fountain. Limited number of chairs have been arranged at the front of the stage for the royals and judges. Citizens are piling into the square from every direction possible. Not all of them are interested to stay so there are still people roaming about the streets, shopping and spending time with their family. The rest of the crowd are the contestants. King Edward introduced this event a year ago to strengthen the bond between the citizens of Combination. And also as a form of art, to encourage people to showcase their talents.

At around ten, the judges, there were three, made their way to the seats by the side. Two of them are SHAW masters while the other is a teacher at a non-magic school. As soon as they settled down the royals also arrived, taking the seats in the middle. The rest of the audience were behind, either sitting on a chair they brought themselves or standing up. Some of the Indonesian guests were also there, accompanied by castle staff. A man in a fine coat walked up the stage with a long rolled up parchment. He unrolled and read.

'Your majesties, citizens and friends, ladies and gentlemen, on this day last year, King Edward declared Talents Day an annual holiday in our city and a competition for anyone to show their skills or talents. And before we call our first contestant, let us watch a performance from our very own SHAW masters of SHAW Academy, Master Mousy, Master Asher, and Master Miro'

The three masters got onto the stage. They faced the crowd, took a bow, and then faced each other. Miro started first. He rubbed his hands together, sparks of electricity jumped out between them. Fire started burning on his hands as he slowly took them apart. Mousy stomped her foot, lowering her body, and moved her hands in an upward-pulling gesture. A large tree broke the stage, creating a very big hole. First it was a small stem, then it grew into an enormous tree. By now the audience were staring in awe. Miro send the fire like a flow of water. From the top of the tree it burned very quickly. The fire spread like as if there's a trail of kerosene down to its roots. Mousy waved her hands upward again and the smoke and every air particle surrounding rose in a swirling motion. It was Asher's cue. He controlled with his eyes, the smoke trail transformed into a billow of small clouds, swirling up and combining into one massive cloud. As the tree totally vanished, Asher turned the cloud into water and made it swirl downwards. Mousy caused mist to appear around it, spreading around the square. The water swirled into the stage and Mousy gathered all the scattered wood and fixed the broken stage. Everything was back to the way it was before. They took a bow as everyone applauded. The audience loves it. They clapped for a good thirty seconds as Bobby made his way to King Edward.

'Your majesty, we still can't find Dewi' he whispered. Edward maintained a calm face as he thought of what to do next. After the meeting yesterday, Dewi had told him that she was going to speak to her father. But until now, both of them are nowhere to be found.

'I have no choice but to hold a court meeting' Edward whispered back.

'Understood your majesty'

'Bring me Rajah first'

Bobby nodded and proceeded to find the said man.

The host went up the stage again and held another parchment, a much shorter one.

'We have our first contestant, Mister Dibs'

An old man and a white cat went onto the stage. They took a bow. Their performance was a lively dance. The next few contestants gave unique performances, from melodious singing to stand-up comedy. Things started to get bad when SHAW contestants started performing magic. A boy who was supposed to perform simple water tricks, the water splashed at almost everyone. But people still enjoyed that although many of them did not notice the boy's worried look. Edward as usual noticed. He got up and proceeded to where all the contestants stand to wait for their turn or the results. The boy had just rejoined the rest as Edward approached him.

'Your majesty!' the boy exclaimed excitedly. He was so excited that he forgot about the performance. The other contestants heard him and were equally happy to see the king. Edward lowered his eye level to the boy.

'Hey, I need to ask you something is that alright?'

'Of course!' the boy replied excitedly.

'I saw that you were very worried on stage. Did something go wrong?'

'No, the people enjoyed it, that's enough for me' the boy replied, smiling broadly.

'But that wasn't your plan right?'

A look of realisation on the boy's face.

'Oh, yes I planned it differently. I guess I'm not that great yet, my magic did not work according to my plan'

Edward smiled at him.

'Thank you for being honest with me' Edward said. He made his way back to his seat.

'Where did you go?' Queen Flyangel asked.

'I believe our threat is messing with the show' Edward replied.

'We can't just cancel it now. What will we tell the people?'

'Well we can't wait until someone dies to do something'

The host was going up the stage again to call out the next contestant. Edward raised his hand.

'Edward, I don't think this is a good idea' Flyangel hissed, trying to not create a scene.

'Yes your majesty' the host said.

Edward stood.

'We need to stop the show' he said. There were a few murmurs among the audience and contestants. While that happened, Flyangel sank in her chair, embarrassed.

'For everyone's safety, please head back home immediately' Edward continued. People were very confused, they were still sitting or standing not moving. Awkward silence. Flyangel came to the rescue.

'We received an urgent message, we need to stop the show now'

Edward looked at her as they made eye contact. They gave each other assuring looks. People started heading out of the square slowly.

Suddenly, out of nowhere, a large fireball crashed into the fountain. The massive fire reached to a height taller than the tallest building in the district. The heat was unbearable for those near it that they started scalding. Fortunately Edward and Flyangel were a few steps out of the fatal zone. But it was not the case for the judges, the masters, the host, and some of the contestants. Masters Mousy and Asher barely made it out alive. They both ran away as the last spot of their fur burned. Edward and Flyangel quickly worked together. They conjured water out from in between their fingers and fought the fire. The fire was behaving like it has a mind of its own. Seeing Edward and Flyangel as a threat, the fire focused on attacking only them both.

Everywhere people were screaming, running away, falling, and trampling over one another. Mousy and Asher took refuge in a building at one end of the square that was furthest from the fire. It was a tailor's workshop. Mousy was hurt so badly that even walking was a torture. But she was in a much better shape than Asher. She grabbed a cloth from a table and rinsed it with water and went to help Asher. But Asher refused.

'You need it more than me' Mousy tried her best to speak. Moving her burnt mouth was very sufferable.

Asher shook his head slowly. He looked at Mousy in the eye. Mist filled with blue sparks left his body and pasted itself on Mousy. A few seconds later, Asher was dead. And Mousy was as good as new. The pain had left her body. She cried looking at her dead friend. Then the noise from outside got her attention again. She went out to face the fire. Up close, Edward and Flyangel were fighting tirelessly. The fire sent fire-hands to burn them but they managed to deflect with water so far. Mousy ran towards them and force-pushed the ground. The ground trembles a little and a wall of rock shot up surrounding the fire.

'That should buy everyone some time' Mousy shouted.

People were still in the streets fleeing. Just about when the fire was nearly breaking the wall, soldiers carrying buckets of water entered the square. There were some masters among them.

'SHAWs at the ready!' Flyangel exclaimed. Everyone who was magic abled got ready. The fire broke the wall. Mousy got hold of the falling rocks and threw it at a nearby building. Every SHAW controlled the water from all the buckets, letting it flow towards the fire. Empty buckets were replaced immediately as more soldiers entered the square with new ones. It was a beautiful team effort. But the fire was still huge. Seeing that many people trying to wipe it out, the fire started throwing small fireballs everywhere. Buildings and people got burned.

'Keep it going!' Edward commanded. 'Helaze, bring the fire down! Winterain, keep splashing it!'

All the Helazes work together to kill the fire. The Winterains continued using the water from the buckets to wipe the fire out. It was working. But as they gazed upon the sky, another large fireball was coming straight at them. That was when some of them spotted a pink rabbit hopping very quickly into the square and created a magnificent fiery forcefield that deflected the fireball. That helped the Helazes as they managed to carry the fire that had settled in the fountain and linked it with the one in the sky. All the other SHAWs used every last droplet of water in the buckets to send it towards the two fires and the Winterains conjured water themselves. Ardnis controlled the air and made it extra colder with the help of the water. And after a few moments, they managed to wipe out the fires completely. They cheered. Edward and Flyangel however were more bothered by the pink rabbit that came to help them.

'Alphaga?' Edward said.

'This does not mean we're friends or anything' Alphaga said. Everyone by now had noticed the rabbit and the soldiers were getting ready to attack on the king's command.

'Lower your weapons' Flyangel ordered. The soldiers stood at ease.

'I don't understand' Edward said.

'Me neither. I came here looking for answers' Alphaga replied.

'Answer to what?'

'Marcala isn't the same as the Marcala I know. She's behaving very differently'

'We also need answers, because the fireball came from out of nowhere'

Just then Bobby entered the square with a few other king's guards, escorting Rajah.

'Rajah, I need an explanation now, everything went wrong after you came into town. I don't buy your innocence anymore. I want to know where's Dewi and her father'

Rajah ignored him.

'Allow me your majesty' Alphaga said cunningly. Fire appeared on his bunny ears.

'Alphaga, don't'

Rajah was clearly very frightened now.

'Answer the king'

'You know for once I agree with you' Flyangel said, looking at Alphaga. Edward was very surprised. He never expects his wife to say such a thing.

'Answer the king now' Flyangel said strictly. Alphaga continued intimidating him with the fire. Finally, Rajah succumbed to fear.

'It wasn't me! I was merely just a tool, a puppet! Please! It was Omar, Omar and Lizyati! Please don't hurt me!' Rajah wailed.

Suddenly, Bobby lost grip of Rajah as a violent force pulled him upwards into the sky. They could hear him screaming in fear as his body was dropped. He landed so fast on the ground that nobody had the time to stop it. A trail of thin smoke appeared around the body and it went up. They followed the trail and then saw, at the top of a building, Lizyati stood there like a psychotic killer hunting her next victim. The smoke lingered around her and then in its place a hideous scary looking creature appeared. Lizyati grinned.

'Hello everyone, meet Uri'

THE JINN

*Before you start reading the next
chapter, finish what you're supposed
to do first. Done? Carry on!*

The Combination Border Woods was in flames.
Evil forces from the north were forcing their
way in. The animals living in the forest fled into
the city. Captain, Bale, Oliver, a few king's guards,
and a few knights of White Woods, were stationed
there for defence. But their defence is not enough to
contain the army of avengers and other creatures led
by Marcala. A large horn has been blown to warn the
city of the incoming attack. Everyone in the districts
nearby have already been briefed of the emergency
procedures. They made their way to the districts in
the south.

The army began to push the defence back into
the city. The battle was brought to SHAW Academy.
SHAW Masters joined in to assist and head students
escorted every student away.

Further into the city, Lizyati had started a chaotic

battle in the city square. Uri made her disappear and appear in other places. So when a king's guard aimed their arrow at her, the arrow hit somebody else.

'Stop firing! Ignore her for now' Edward shouted. 'The horn was blown, help is needed. Barracks-One troops proceed north now'

Barracks-One soldiers obeyed the order and proceeded north. Left in the square were barracks-two soldiers, king's guards, and SHAW masters.

'Lizyati, would you come down and we can talk?' Edward said. She was on a roof again.

'There's no need to talk. War is here already' Lizyati replied.

'Your people are not that many to make an army, what do you mean?'

'You see, Marcala is dead. I killed her'

Shock murmurs among the crowd. Grindel was right, Edward thought.

'And my friend that helped me was Hati. Hati is the other jinn, Uri's mate. And Hati has been disguising as Marcala since they came attacking that day'

'I knew it!' Alphaga exclaimed, extremely mad.

'And the best part, your enemies don't even know the one leading them is not even their leader!'

'*Lizyati, tolong hentikan ini semua!*' a familiar old voice said. (Lizyati, please stop all this!). It was Omar. He, Dewi, and Master Lillain entered the square.

'Omar, you initiate this?' Edward asked.

'No your majesty! They lied. They always lie. I

never expected when I asked for their help, they would go to this extent of doing what they do' Omar said. Lizyati cackled. Edward looked at Lizyati, to Rajah's dead body. It was her plan all along. She's the only one, alone, no helpers or minions except for the jinn.

'It's over, your land will be filled with my beautiful friends. Hati and Uri will make sure of it'

'Not if God forbids it!' Omar said very loudly, raising a book he has been holding on. The book was very beautiful and has very unique designs.

'Oh he doesn't alright' Lizyati replied selfishly. Omar muttered something inaudibly.

'Archers, arrows' Flyangel ordered. Soldiers with bows drew and aimed. Lizyati smiled.

'So the game begins' she said. Uri went into smoke mode and rushed into Flyangel's nostrils. Edward stared at his wife, aghast, as she got possessed.

'Focus your aim on your king' Flyangel said coldly. The soldiers were shocked and confused.

'Your majesty, step back' Omar said hurriedly. Dewi helped him, gently guiding Edward back. Edward was still in shock. Omar stepped forward with the book in hand. Flyangel hissed at him. She went all zombie-like behaviour. Omar began reciting unknown language.

'You will lose Omar' Lizyati said.

Flyangel charged at Omar. Omar held up one hand and said the foreign words. Flyangel was stopped by something. She started screaming. Omar continued reciting and Flyangel's scream got louder. Smoke came out of her nostrils immediately and rushed back to Lizyati's side and then disappeared. Flyangel fell to the ground unconscious.

'She will be okay' Omar told Edward.

'This isn't over Omar!' Lizyati said furiously. 'My army is marching into the city now. They'll destroy all of you soon'

'All of you, focus on the defence!' Alphaga shouted. No one listened to him. Lillain and Dewi were confused as to what he was doing here.

'Listen to him, your queen is unwell, the city is under attack. Threat here is manageable, threat in the north is not without everyone's help. Proceed there now' Mousy said. The soldiers headed north. Bobby led the king's guards behind them. Some of the masters followed. Above, Lizyati was laughing by herself.

'What was that you did?' Lillain asked Omar.

'It wasn't me. I just merely recited words from the Quran' Omar replied, referring to the book. 'It's God's help'

Flyangel was waking up. She touched her forehead in pain.

'You'll get a headache after that experience. She needs water' Omar said. Dewi rushed into a nearby building. She rushed back out a minute later with a cup.

'I couldn't find water, the tap is broken' she said. Edward conjured water and filled the cup. Dewi gave Flyangel the cup.

The sound of battle could be heard clearly now. It was getting closer.

'Everyone, I want you to focus your powers on Lizyati and her friends. Remember, Marcala is one of hers' Edward ordered. Alphaga and the remaining masters went north. Only Edward, Flyangel, Lillain, Mousy, Dewi, and Omar were left here to deal with Lizyati.

'*Bawa aku turun. Kamu lawan semua, biar aku bunuh Omar dahulu, dia bahaya bagi kamu*' Lizyati told Uri. (Bring me down. You fight with everyone else, let me kill Omar first, he's dangerous to you). Uri disappeared with Lizyati and appeared on ground level. Mousy and Lillain stepped forward to face them. Uri disappeared and Lizyati grabbed a dagger she'd been hiding up her sleeve. At first Lillain was about to attack Lizyati but Uri stopped her. Black fog surrounded Lillain as Lizyati went invisible.

'She's powerless without the jinn, you have to take out the jinn' Lillain told Mousy.

'Do you even know how to?'

'Just get a hold of him should do'

Mousy tried her best to force-choke or grab Uri but Uri kept himself hidden very well.

'Omar, I believe Lizyati is after you' Edward said.

'I'll protect him' Dewi said.

'I'll stay with her' Flyangel said.

Edward sucked in the black fog into his hand. But that affected him badly. He fell and started coughing.

Lillain was not in a good shape too having been breathing in the same fog.

'Edward!' Flyangel cried alarmingly, as she went to his aid.

Lizyati suddenly appeared and was about to stab Omar, but hit the Quran instead. Her hand suddenly got on fire and she lost grip of the dagger. They all looked at her as she screamed in pain.

'Apa ini?!' she screamed. (What is this?!).

'Balasan Tuhan, tukang sihir' Omar replied in a "in your face" way. (God's punishment, you witch).

Uri appeared beside her trying to help her but he couldn't. There's no water nearby. Edward and Flyangel weren't going to help her as well. The fire died down as soon as Lizyati's whole hand was beyond saving. Her whole hand was worse than scalded. Even her bones are visible in some areas of it.

Seeing the opportunity, Mousy force-grabbed Uri by the throat. Lillain grabbed Lizyati's.

'Lizyati, for your crimes against the safety of our land, I sentence you to a lifetime of imprisonment' Edward said. 'You'll be locked in a magic-resistance cell where there won't be any chance for you to communicate with your jinn'

'I'm sorry your majesty, but I guess you'll need more to prevent the jinn from entering. They are not magical creatures like yours' Omar said. Edward didn't know what to reply. He didn't even understand what he said.

'Don't worry, I'll try my best to prevent them' Omar continued.

'Take her away' Edward said. Lillain force-pulled Lizyati to follow her up to the castle.

'And as for you' Edward turned his attention to Uri. Now that they were close, he could see clearly his terrifying features. The blood red eyes, blood dripping down the eyes. Holes in the face. It's the perfect example of what people would say, a ghost or a demon.

'I need a vase with a cover' Omar said. They looked at him, confused. 'I know how to trap them. Sadly, I used to be a shaman myself'

None of the words, although it's English, but none of it makes sense to the people of Southernere.

'I'll get it' Dewi said. She went into a building. Couldn't find one in there and went to the next building. A minute later she exited a building with a small porcelain vase with a cover on top.

'Yes, okay, clear the area' Omar said. Edward and Flyangel stepped aside. Uri saw what was going on and he attempted to fight back. Fortunately Mousy was holding on tight to him.

'Ready' Omar said and began muttering unknown words. Uri started shrieking causing Mousy to struggle.

'I need help!' Mousy exclaimed. Flyangel and Edward helped. Omar muttered a few more words in exclamation and opened the vase. Uri turned into smoke form and was sucked into the vase. Omar quickly closed the lid. Silence.

'This has to be kept securely. It cannot be broken or even opened. If it does, the jinn will escape' Omar said.

'And we still got one more of them on the loose' Mousy reminded them.

'And he or she is tricking everyone into thinking that she is Marcala' Flyangel said.

'I just need another vase' Omar said.

'Right' Dewi went to get another.

'Let's finish this and make sure everyone is safe' Edward said.

They proceeded to the location of the ongoing battle.

THE NEW WORLD

*Before you start reading the next
chapter, finish what you're supposed
to do first. Done? Carry on!*

The avengers were so confused as to which side they were on when they saw Alphaga helping the good side. There was lots of jinn magic going on. Black fog, smoke, appearing and disappearing, and others.

Captain, Bale, and Oliver were together dealing with one avenger. He used electric currents to zap the areas around him as the three dodged and taunted him further. They laughed every time he missed and the avenger got very mad.

'Okay, that's enough' Oliver said and sent a strong forcefield that flung him very far back. They cheered and more avengers came to fight them.

Bobby and a few king's guards were fighting a ferocious beast, slightly larger than a griffin. The griffin attacked with its beak. Bobby dodged just in time, but it lunged at a guard nearby. Its claws pierced through his armour and he died. Three men left.

Bobby and the other two king's guards repositioned. Bobby stood a little to the side of the griffin's head. The other two on equal opposite sides of its back.

'Come here' Bobby said. The griffin turned to attack. Bobby rolled and slashed its side. At the same time, the other two king's guards stabbed its back on both sides. The griffin let out a high-pitched cry and lashed its tail. Another guard was thrown backwards into another fight between a master and an avenger. Two men left. The griffin has suffered major damages but is still standing strong. It turned to face its attackers. Bobby and the guard moved to its side quickly. But the griffin followed their movements. Bobby decided to just attack. So he lunged at its neck barely missing its claws lunging at him. The guard slashed its back legs. It cried in pain as it did a back kick. Fortunately the guard wasn't standing in the way. The back kick gave him an advantage. The guard slashed at its stomach. And Bobby, now underneath it, he stabbed its chest. As blood dripped onto Bobby's face, the griffin fell on its side, dead. The guard helped Bobby up and they did a brother handshake.

'There's still more of them' the guard said.

'And so we fight' Bobby said reassuringly.

Alphaga was in an intense battle with the other jinn, Hati, who was disguising as Marcala. Only a few know that she's an imposter. He needs to make her reveal herself. So Marcala was making black holes appear out of nowhere and disappear, trying to trap Alphaga inside. But luckily his legs was faster.

'Not using your fire powers is it Marcala?!' he said it out loud, so that others can hear. But everyone was too busy.

Marcala conjured black fog around the area. Everyone who breathed it in started coughing. Alphaga knew what was coming and managed to hold in his breath. But by doing so it took a lot of his energy and concentration. Marcala charged towards him. Arms out and attempting to grab him. Alphaga with the energy he has left, used it all to dodge and back away. After that he had to breathe in and started coughing as well. Marcala went invisible and the next thing that happened was Alphaga was being choked. His rabbit legs left the ground as the force tightened on his neck. Marcala reappeared and grinned in a very impossible way.

'Who's not using their powers now?' Marcala said in a way that sounded more like a hiss.

'Hati!' Omar's voice called out from somewhere behind. Marcala's eyes went hundred-eighty. All Alphaga could see was white. Her eyes had made a complete turn inside her eye socket. Then she went invisible. Alphaga was let go and he fell to the ground with a sore neck.

Omar was standing with Dewi, Edward, Flyangel, and Mousy. He started reciting words when he saw Marcala went invisible. A few moments later, Marcala appeared and she was unable to move. Simply stuck in front of Omar. Omar got ready the vase.

'Wait, we have to show everyone that she's not Marcala first. The avengers will surely stop if they know their leader is gone' Edward said.

'Yes, understood' Omar said. He began reciting more words even louder. At first it doesn't seem to have any effect. She was still struggling to get out of the trap and nothing else.

'Baca ayat ni dengan ayah Dewi' Omar said to his daughter. (Repeat this verse with father, Dewi). Dewi began following whatever Omar was reciting. Marcala's skin suddenly started to burn. She was still trying so hard to withstand but her face couldn't lie. Slowly, everyone could see the scary face that was underneath the mask. Red eyes, holes. She turned into Hati. Hati was even scarier. An extra feature she has that Uri doesn't is her very long straight black hair. Nearby, soldiers were already gasping.

'I need help to get everyone's attention' Edward said. They thought of shouting but Omar just recited some more and Hati shrieked in pain and annoyance. It was deafening, people and beasts were already looking. Though some beasts just don't have a smart brain, so the soldiers and masters had to kill them first. Edward just carried on anyway.

'What you see here isn't a human. It isn't Marcala' Edward said. The avengers were horrified.

'Marcala has been dead for at least a day now, killed by the master of this creature, a jinn. You are just wasting time. We can end this war right now. We have a common enemy that is far more dangerous than any of us. Let us make peace and discuss our future relations' Edward said. Everyone was actually eager to stop already. Everything went surprisingly fast. The avengers aggressively shooed the beasts away back to Alhora. Combination soldiers and masters worked together to gather the unfortunate dead bodies and clean the city. Omar trapped Hati inside the other vase and together with Edward, Flyangel, Dewi, and Mousy, they returned to the castle.

Master Kitty was so delighted to see them all again. He had been babysitting the five students in the castle and had assisted Master Lillain in locking Lizyati behind an anti-magic cell. They paid her a visit in the dungeons for Omar to set up whatever he needed to set up to prevent the jinn from entering the cell if they ever break out of their vase. He simply recited some words. Lydia, Pertum and the other avenger-prisoners laughed at how pathetic it looked. They just ignored them, and released them anyway. Edward mentioned that for Alphaga's short service to do the right thing, they are lifted off from their sentence. But there is a condition. All avengers have to return to their respective homes in the Outlands by the end of the day. Anytime, the only person who can return is Alphaga, to discuss possible ties and peaceful relations. Everyone agreed because Alphaga agreed. A lot of them were reluctant but they had to listen to their new leader. Alphaga was second in command to

Marcala which automatically makes him the leader once she dies. And Alphaga was in a very good mood that he just agreed to everything Edward said.

There was a massive farewell held for Master Asher and all of those who have fallen today. Edward addressed everyone about what has been happening, what has been solved, and what further actions will be taken to ensure everyone's safety.

By the end of the day, every single soldier that fought in the battle was relieved of their duty for the night to rest. Edward and Flyangel hung out with Edward's old buddies, Captain, Bale, and Oliver, in the castle lounge before going to bed.

In the dungeons, Lizyati sat alone in the dark. The location of the vases that hold the jinn were unknown. But someone visited her that night. He sat inside the cell with her.

'How did you get in? It's anti-magic' Lizyati said.

'Being me has its own benefits, you should know that by now' Lord Grindel replied.

'What are you doing here anyway? Your little show didn't even help me with anything'

'The more important issue here is you lied to me'

Lizyati was expressionless.

'You said that Omar was the leader'

'So what?'

'I planned a lot of scenarios. Because of you, now I am at risk of being caught!'

'You are afraid of getting caught for setting the fountain square on fire?'

'That was for your whole amazing plan of setting chaos to Southernere. You can't do fire magic, your jinn can't. Who else can? It's only a matter of time before they realise!' Grindel was very mad. 'You know I could kill you right now!'

'And make yourself more suspicious?' Lizyati laughed cunningly. 'You need me Grindel'

'You're good'

Lizyati smirked.

'What are you going to do now? I can't do anything without getting caught with you now locked away'

'Why are you so eager to do this?'

'Didn't we discuss this before? My business is my own and yours is yours. But now that we come to it. There's one question that I want you to answer me. Because if not I won't do anything to help you. Face it, we need each other. I need you so that I won't be suspected. And you need me since you're already locked away and can't fulfill your mission'

Lizyati was as usual with her expressionless face.

'How did you come to know about Southernere?' Grindel asked.

'People used to disappear occasionally. Dewi wasn't the first. We also had strange visitors from unknown places in our small town sometimes. When Dewi disappeared and Omar got sick, I took the opportunity to find out. My jinn are very useful helpers. Slowly I learn. Although it took twenty-two years, but I still progressed. Now I just need help to continue with my third step'

'I know what's your mission already. You're here to seek revenge on the people that disappeared. Because you feel like this place had took a lot of your people'

'How stupid. The mighty Lord Grindel came up with a pathetic reason? You'll never know the reason unless I tell you so'

Grindel was annoyed, but he kept his cool.

'So what do you need my help for?' Grindel asked.

'I need you to expose this land. I know there's a magical barrier that separates this land from the rest of the world. And I know that's the reason why this land is very clean. Not a single jinn, bad or good, to be found. Open the barrier. Let the whole world know of this place's existence. I want you to influence every single military personnel. You know how wild humans can be when they are competing for something. Make Southernere, Earth's eighth continent'

The sky lit up very brightly that night. From the furthest ocean line visible to the human eye up to the sky, lights and translucent silk-like substance lit up rhythmically. Whoever was near the source of power could hear loud blasting magic. As the last sequence of the rhythm stopped, cool breeze mixed with the smell of the ocean blew throughout the cities. The air was different. The world is different.

PART 8

THE 8TH CONTINENT

THE ANCIENT MAGIC

*Before you start reading the next
chapter, finish what you're supposed
to do first. Done? Carry on!*

It was nearing the end of winter in Southernere. It has been almost thirteen days since the horrible Talents Day. Dusk had just arrived and many were already relaxing at home. The snow had melted and signs of spring had started to appear. People were getting cozy with their family by the fireplace, waiting for the cold season to end.

King Edward, Queen Flyangel, and the rest of the gang were hanging out in the ballroom playing charades. It was so much fun that even the king's guards, knights, and servants who were standing and watching also enjoyed their time. Flyangel, Queen Darleen, Captain, Bale, Bobby, Annie, and Laura were on Edward's team. Oliver, Dewi, Omar, Masters Mousy and Kitty, and Sir Everos were on Master Lillain's team. It was Flyangel's turn to act out. She stepped out to the front where a box filled with papers folded in half was placed on a chair. She took one and read its content, "Trisnarim Palace". She dropped the paper on the floor and faced her team. Everyone was sitting on a chair, both teams opposite to each other, diagonally facing the centre.

'You can do this angel' Edward said. They exchanged warm smiles.

Flyangel started by rubbing her fingers together like the sign language of money. Snowflakes floated out from between them and scattered everywhere. Flyangel shot ice out of her hands and a magnificent sculpture was formed. The ice piled up together and ended in the shape of a castle. A building familiar to Master Kitty. But Master Kitty wasn't in Edward's team. But it was too obvious already, there's no such thing as an ice castle in the world.

'Ice castle!' Captain exclaimed excitedly.

Flyangel shook her head.

'There's no such thing as an ice castle' Annie said.

'Trisnarim Palace' Edward guessed.

'Yes!' Flyangel cried excitedly.

'Trisnarim isn't made out of ice?' Captain asked.

'Trisnarim Palace is mostly made out of diamonds and trisnal. The remaining portion is ice' Kitty explained.

Just then, the doors opened and in came King Nathan and Prince Jake.

'Sorry we're late' they both said. Flyangel went to hug them. There were hugs and the usual kisses by the ladies (begin with one cheek, then the next, and back to the first).

'You look beautiful sister' Jake said looking at Flyangel's elegant dress. A long dress trimmed with white lace and a white headscarf on top.

'Thank you!'

'How are you? How's the baby?' Nathan asked.

'I feel amazing! It's wonderful' Flyangel replied, grinning from ear to ear. It has been one week since the announcement of the happy news. Flyangel was expecting.

'Hope we're not too late for the game' Nathan said.

'Not at all'

Nathan joined Edward's team and Jake joined Lillain's. The game continued up till midnight with a few breaks in between. Nathan was the last to go, taking the last piece of folded paper from the box. "Ship". Nathan let out dirt continuously from between his fingers and formed a ship out of it. Nathan's powers are unique. People always know him as an Ardni, specialised in air. But Nathan has never settled on either. He could conjure air or earth from nothing anytime he wants. That is another mystery no one will ever know since both of his parents died while he and his brother were still young. Their actual birthdays no one knows. No one could ever determine whether Nathan is an Ardni or a Sprite.

'That's too obvious' Mousy commented. Nathan shrugged.

'It's a ship' Dewi said.

'Yay, so who wins?' Oliver asked.

'There isn't a winner. We just played for fun! To enjoy the time together' Flyangel said.

Suddenly, the ballroom doors opened and a very familiar master walked in with urgency.

'Master Nvago?' some of them said softly.

Master Nvago stopped a few steps away from them.

'I'm sorry to intrude on your gathering your majesties but urgent matters are much of a priority at the moment' Nvago said, his expression filled with worry.

'No worries master' Edward said. 'I fear everytime you come. Because you only come when matters are urgent'

'I'm afraid they are' Nvago said. 'Decades of secrets, big and small, finally now one of the biggest secrets is out in the world. The real world'

Nvago noticed their confused looks.

'When your ancestor Sofya stopped the problem of overflowing newcomers from nearby lands, she casted a very strong ancient Gratultyn magic. One that is similar but incomparable to the barrier that hid White Woods. Over time, people from outside and inside the barrier forgot about each other's existence. Until thirteen days ago, on the night of May the third, Lord Grindel broke the barrier. It was supposed to be a secret but recent events require me to tell you the truth. You see, your world and their world (he referred to Dewi and Omar) are the same. But I'm afraid I have to tell you because people are coming. The Fifteen are still investigating on Grindel's actions. But for now, Sage Master Alden himself had instructed me to inform you. The whole world knows. And there are people coming. I can't tell you more. But perhaps, your prisoner could. Nathan and Jake, do get back to White Shore. You'll need lots of defences on the waters, if these newcomers are not friendly people. I'll come again soon, I have to check on something'

With that, Nvago left. Nathan and Jake got up to go as well. Darleen too.

'I need to check on the academy' Lillain said and left. One by one they separated, leaving Edward and Flyangel wondering when their problems would ever end.

ON THE NIGHT
OF 3RD MAY

*Before you start reading the next
chapter, finish what you're supposed
to do first. Done? Carry on!*

The night of Talents Day. The sky lit up very brightly. From the furthest ocean line visible to the human eye up to the sky, lights and translucent silk-like substance lit up rhythmically. Whoever was near the source of power could hear loud blasting magic. Lord Grindel was standing in a clearing in one of the forest districts. His arms shot up into the sky. Ray of light shone upwards from both hands. What used to be the sky was now a translucent forcefield breaking apart. The forcefield stretched in all directions covering the whole entire area of Southernere, the two small islands and a few kilometres of the ocean. The forcefield lit up every few seconds in reaction to Grindel's magic until it just stopped. In a spherical motion, the forcefield disappeared all the way down.

Master Nvago emerged from among the trees,

holding two metal bracelets in one hand. Grindel was about to strike but then the bracelets flew out of Nvago's hand and locked themselves on both of Grindel's wrist. He couldn't move. Lady Feramein appeared instantly in front of him. A swirl of water near her took the form of another beautiful young girl. She had scale-like light green skin, light blue eyes, a pair of translucent light green wings on her back, and her supposedly green hair looks like it's a part of her light green head. She was covering most of her skin with a light green silk dress, but the dress also seems to be a part of her.

'How long Nvago?' Feramein asked.

'Five minutes' Nvago replied.

Feramein focused her energy on exerting a powerful force on the sky. She was attempting to reform the barrier. Grindel started laughing.

'You're gonna waste your time. After five minutes I'll be strong enough to break out of these and you'll be sorry' Grindel said. The green girl flicked her hand, a flow of water came out of her hand and surrounded Grindel from all angles.

'You got ten minutes. I got you' the girl said.

'Sweet young Arabelle. You think you are powerful enough to stop me?' Grindel teased the green girl, Arabelle. Although they couldn't see each other, Grindel was still being annoying.

Lady Arabelle, protector of the Field of Petals and lady of Westeria, keeper of growth, flowers, and woodland. She is only eight years old and being the talented daughter of Lord Tavier, protector of the Kingdom of Fairies and lord of the East Region, keeper of magical creatures, she became the youngest high master to receive the honour of owning a position among The Fifteen.

'I can't stop you alone, not yet. But Feramein can' she said.

'People keep telling me that. Well I have the same answer as you, not yet. But soon, I can' Grindel said confidently.

'Not on my watch' Nvago said, stepping closer to the water surrounding Grindel.

'Save your energy old man. Your time is almost up, you won't be my problem anymore' Grindel said, rolling his eyes. The tension between those two is obvious that their history together goes way back. Only five minutes had passed and what felt like eternity just became longer after Grindel started whistling.

'Do you need my help?' Arabelle asked.

'No, she can't accept any help. This ancient magic is very complicated that a single disturbance will disrupt everything. She has to do this alone' Nvago said. But both of them were already feeling very uneasy. Feramein was struggling but there was nothing they can do to help. Grindel was enjoying himself even though he was doing absolutely nothing. Another minute passed and Feramein stopped. All the light rays disappeared and she fell to the ground instantly. Nvago and Arabelle went to her aid.

'You see that Nvago, she clearly isn't as powerful as her predecessor. That is why I will be able to overpower her raw talent anytime soon' Grindel smirked.

Ignoring Grindel, Nvago focused on Feramein.

'Fermein, we need to bring him back to Gratultyn now or he'll break free. There's nothing we can do now except inform Alden' Nvago said. Feramein accepted both of their hands and stood up. She nodded her head in agreement. They readied themselves around the swirling water. In a few minutes, the enchantment will be broken and Grindel will be free. But everything went wrong. After Arabelle stopped the water, Nvago and Feramein were very ready to force-grab Grindel as the bracelets fall apart. But what happened was, Grindel had been saving a powerful blast inside him. As soon as the bracelets fell apart a powerful forcefield sent all three masters falling backwards. When they recovered, Grindel was gone.

Somewhere in a different realm, Arabelle, Feramein, and Nvago were waiting in front of a set of large magnificent golden double doors in a vast long hallway of different rich stones built in together. A smaller entryway at the other end. Huge grand windows that can never be opened lined on each side equally. There were a few other people as well. And they were also waiting. Sudden footsteps from behind and they turned to see a few more people and different creatures walking towards the large doors.

'Father' Arabelle said, briskly walking towards a

man who looks a bit like her but not like her at all. He has completely normal white skin and a medium length brown hair. Lord Tavier.

'Arabelle, are you alright?' he asked. She simply nodded and gave him a quick hug.

The large doors opened and two golden humanoids invited everyone in. It was a cozy circular room. The floor was carpeted. Red colour with designs. The wall was made out of a type of rich stone, tanzanite. The room gives off a magical aura because of that. But there are no windows. Aside from that, there are many magical objects placed on floating stands that look like pillows. And other knight or soldier statues that were made out of different materials that can never be found in the main realm. A large round table with a large hole in the middle was placed in the centre of the room. Fifteen chairs arranged just nicely around the table. Lastly, an archway that leads nowhere in the wall opposite to the doors. There were already two men and a lady occupying three chairs. One very old man, probably in his hundreds, in front of the archway, and the other two on each side. They stood in respect to everyone entering.

'Please have a seat masters of Gratultyn' the one in front of the archway spoke. He was the leader of The Fifteen, Sage Master Alden, protector of Sage's Keep and Gratultyn, keeper of Gratultyn lineage and magic. They all sat. Only one chair was left unoccupied. Most of them were too uncomfortable to even look at it. But Alden called this meeting specifically for that matter.

'Terrible times masters, never before has a member of The Fifteen break our sacred laws' Alden said. 'As you can see, we are missing one member of the council'

Eyes turned to the empty chair.

'Earlier this evening, Masters Nvago, Feramein, and Arabelle tried to stop Master Grindel but he had prepared tricks up his sleeve. Hence the mission was not a success'

A short pause. Arabelle sank in her chair feeling disappointed with herself.

'The Tyn has gathered information from the main realm that Grindel is currently spreading Southernere's existence everywhere around the world' the old man beside Alden said. Sage Marlan, sage master's apprentice, protector of The Tyn, keeper of knowledge. The Tyn is a grand library also known as Sage's Library, where members of The Fifteen and related members go to to gain knowledge, but mostly to find information. The Tyn operates like it has a mind of its own. Lots of magical things can happen there. And it has minions that work to safeguard it and enforce its rules. Marlan being assigned as its protector has suzerainty over the minions so he tends to get information faster than the rest. Though Alden still has his ways of knowing first, no one else knows how. The Tyn's minions are invisible creatures. No one knows their actual appearance as they never reveal themselves. But what everyone knows is that they are small, like the size of a wild fairy. Since they are invisible, when they go out into other realms, no one will ever know when they're around. That helps them gain information very easily.

'And from that my seekers reported back that a few human nations are already planning their journey to Southernere' the lady beside Alden said. Sage Alisa, protector of Kingdom of Sages, keeper of masters and seekers. Seekers are Gratultyn's interrealm soldiers or spies. They are spies that work internationally, or in this case, in all the realms. Seekers live everywhere, operating undercover, living among different nations of different creatures, pretending to live a normal life. Once they gather intel, they'll report back to Alisa and proceed to be assigned their next mission. In this very situation, three seekers have reported back.

'The British Nation, The Dutch Nation, and a few bands of Malay and Indonesian pirates are making their way' Alisa said.

Everything was happening so fast.

'Our main focus now is to apprehend Grindel and bring him in for questioning and further actions. I'll use the archway to inform you again anytime we receive intel of Grindel's whereabouts. Council is dismissed' Alden said. The archway in the room is made out of unique magical resources that contain a powerful force to transmit messages to all the realms. With Alden's powers, he can control whom he wants the message to be delivered to. That is also how every member of The Fifteen received information about the meeting. The council members dispersed.

THE NORTHERN
KINGDOM

The next few days passed by very quickly and now the whole world has known the appearance of a new island somewhere in the Southern Ocean. Lord Grindel had just finished exerting his magical influence in a small village in the corners of the Soviet Union. A mysterious presence people were saying. No one knows anything except the thought of a new land instilled in their mind. Some say they saw a man in black, a stranger. But then he just vanished without a trace.

Two masters, members of The Fifteen, Lady Feramein and Lord Tavier, visited the village. It was odd for the villagers to receive guests continuously. They were more curious about these two. Their bright clothes are not from around here. As they entered one area hidden from the public's view, a villager was there waiting for them.

'Lady Feramein, Lord Tavier' the man bowed in respect. He is actually a seeker tasked to look out for Grindel in this village.

'There's no need for that here' Tavier said.

'He was here wasn't he?' Feramein asked.

'Yes milady, about three hours ago. Then he just vanished' the man said.

'Thank you' Tavier said, and they walked away.

They went further away from the village until they came across a field with a few trees. The snow was thicker here. So to look out for footprints left three hours ago is not possible. But Feramein and Tavier were determined that Grindel was here. Tavier clapped his hands together and pulled them apart immediately. An almost invisible line of magic opened up in between, forming some sort of magical barrier or portal. He let it go free onto the soft snow and they both stepped into it.

Dark. Rocky terrain. Warm and foggy. A constant horrid smell. That is how the atmosphere is like in the Northern Kingdom. But even for such an unpleasant place, there is a small area where harmless creatures live peacefully with the trees. And that is also where Grindel likes to spend most of his time whenever he's here. Tavier was about to do the same magic to allow them to teleport but Feramein stopped him.

'Remember Forges of Beasts? Grindel could have

done the same to this place. For all we know, every step is a possible curse' she said.

Grindel is a master of tricks, mischief, and curses. It's not a surprise if he likes to put lots of booby traps, even magical ones.

Due to that, they were now more focused on the actual distance from where they are to the peaceful area. It was quite a distance. Downhill, there's a narrow bridge that goes over a dark abyss that runs like a river cutting its way across the land. Then they will still have to go through a field of giant skeletons of creatures that no longer exists. And it's also a must to expect harmful creatures to come out of nowhere randomly and attack.

'Let's go' Tavier said and led the way carefully.

They passed some huge boulders and saw something slither away. It was nearly invisible, the creature blended in with the rocks very well. Knowing nothing good will come out, they just carried on walking cautiously. A few more of the same creature slithered away. That's when they realised, these creatures are just doing what they do on top of a much larger creature. The ground started to move. Tavier grabbed Feramein's hand and they ran as fast as they could, trying to keep their balance as the ground slowly turned into a slope. They reached the edge and jumped onto the rocks below. Fortunately it wasn't so far and the rocks were smooth. But their threat has just appeared. The previous rock they were on was now a giant snake with stone-like scales and very black eyes. It stared at them, waiting for them to make a single movement. The little creatures, also like a snake, but tiny versions, slithered all around the giant snake's body.

'That's a varbala' Tavier said.

Lord Grindel is the keeper of beasts whereas Lord Tavier is the keeper of magical creatures. In terms of bestiary knowledge, Grindel is the first, Tavier is second place. Hence the reason why he knew most of the beasts they might encounter. A varbala is a snake with scales of stone and black eyes that look like shadows trapped. Since it has stone scales, it's movement is very slow due to the mass. That makes it very excruciating if anyone gets bitten by it.

'Varbalas are never alone' Tavier said.

Feramein tried to control it since it was mostly stone but nothing happened.

'And no elemental magic will do them anything, run' Tavier said.

He grabbed Feramein's hand again and they ran downhill. The varbala moved to catch. The rocks broke apart under its mass and the impact sent the two masters flying forward. Feramein spread her arms open and water came out of nowhere in front of her, making a continuous flow. They fell into the water before they could injure themselves on the rocks. Feramein and Tavier swam according to the flow and soon their legs transformed into mermaid tails, changing their clothes as well to suit the appearance. The varbala wasn't far behind. It had already started biting on the water. Thanks to the mermaid tail, both of them moved very fast. Below, the rocks were moving even though the snake hadn't reached them yet. The rocks rose to reveal two other varbalas. Feramein directed the water in another direction just in time before they could hit the jaws of the varbala.

The peaceful place was very close now, but it won't be peaceful any longer based on the massive threat they're bringing towards it. The water stream ended and they fell onto a leaf of a tree. Their tails changed back to legs and everything else back to the way before. But the threat is still onto them. As the three varbalas stared hungrily at them, one of them moved to attack. But an invisible forcefield that protects the green area deflected its bite. Feramein let out a short laugh in relief. Suddenly, the leaf they're standing on started moving. Now that they were close, they realised that the trees are all very large in size. No wonder the leaves could fit them both on top. But not all the leaves are actual leaves. Like the one they're on is actually a leaf-like creature. All green, soft on its sides (like a leaf), at the top where the stalk is supposed to be is its head with a pair of very thin green antennae sticking out above its tiny light green eyes. Underneath, it has three pairs of thin light green legs, crawling wherever there is food. It feeds on leaves and smaller creatures that roam the same area.

'This is a giant phylliidae, they exist in the main realm but a little bit different and much much smaller' Tavier said.

'Is it safe?' Feramein asked cautiously.

'Yes, it disgusts flesh, specifically ones that have lots of blood. Best not to turn into a mermaid in front of them'

Feramein smiled at his joke.

'Right, let's find Grindel'

They both waited for the leaf to reach nearer to the ground or at least a way for them to make their way down. Before they could make it to the ground, all the phylliidaes suddenly turned their attention towards them.

'You said they don't care about us'

'They don't' Tavier replied in confusion.

'This must be Grindel'

The laughter of a familiar voice could be heard below. It was Grindel. He was also clapping.

'Yes indeed it's me. I command them too. You see the difference between me and you is, you are in my place now. You don't have the upperhand'

Grindel laughed.

'I got you back. You said that to me when I was in Southernere'

'I didn't'

'Well something like that. Now I am returning the favour. You don't have the power to stand against me here'

'Grindel, you have broken the laws of The Fifteen, you are to stop this nonsense and follow us back to Sage's Keep' Tavier said.

'And why would I do that?'

'He won't listen to kind requests' Feramein said, rolling her eyes.

'I think I should enjoy this moment first'

A disgusting looking creature made its appearance, crawling in a straight line like a caterpillar. Except that it's large, even bigger than the leaves. It's green and orange in colour, and has fat tiny legs. Just like the caterpillar, it has no bones in the body, it moves by squeezing muscles in sequence in an undulating wave motion. It's face is exactly like the caterpillar but enlarged. It crawled up to Grindel's side and looked up. It was a scary sight. More of them crawled up to Grindel's side.

'My caterpillar friends feed on the leaves, but they wouldn't mind flesh sometimes. They would eat me too, if I'm human' Grindel said. Feramein conjured fire on her palm.

'If you kill my creatures, I send everything after you'

'Who said anything about killing them?' Feramein said and sent the fire at Grindel. Grindel caught the fire in his hand and vanquished it. He can't send it back with the risk of burning the forest. Instead, he ordered the caterpillars to catch them. The caterpillars began crawling and climbing the trees. The phylliidaes started running for their lives. Feramein summoned another fire but Tavier stopped her.

'They just need the right motivation' he said as stalks of leaves shot out from within his sleeves. They grew longer and made their way to the caterpillars which got distracted immediately.

'Huge mistake' Grindel said. He set the leaves on fire. The fire travelled up the stalks towards Tavier. Tavier magically cut the stalks before the fire could reach him. With their temptation gone, the caterpillars were extra mad. Tavier did his last trick. He spoke to the caterpillars in their language which mostly sounded like blowing breath. Instantly the caterpillars turned their attention to Grindel.

'What did you do?' Feramein asked in confusion.

'Like I said, motivation. They're angry that their food was burned so I just gave them a little push towards the person that caused that' Tavier said, smiling like the intelligent person he is.

Grindel however wasn't done. After one frustrated breath he transformed into his natural form. An artazer. It has the body of a lion, the head of a bear, and a very sharp tail. It is covered in sparkly scales which are surrounded by ongoing currents. The most majestic part of an artazer is its wings and claws sticking out of all its paws.

'I'll get you myself!' Grindel bellowed.

As all the creatures ran away, Feramein glided towards the ground before Tavier could stop her. She formed a long majestic stick from the air and banged it on the grass. Grindel's currents were deflected by the force. He roared and charged at her. She spun the stick in her hands and pushed the tip in Grindel's direction. But Grindel broke the forcefield barrier

Feramein intended to create and his currents went wild everywhere. The trees started catching fire. Tavier jumped down and rolled to the side just as one of Grindel's currents struck. Feramein dodged just barely before Grindel went past her slamming into a tree. A tree branch fell.

'Feramein, you can't fight an artazer just like that. Let's go while there's still a chance' Tavier said.

Feramein stubbornly stood her ground. Grindel was already turning around to face her again. Feramein banged her stick on the ground and the roots of the tree behind Grindel sprung out of the ground around itself and tied up together, trapping him inside. But Grindel's currents burned them. The fire spread quickly into the ground, back up its trunk until every last corner of its branches and leaves were burned. Tavier did not wait for another attack, he grabbed Feramein's hand and pulled her away. She dropped the stick and it dissolved in the air back to being the particles it originally was. With Grindel now free from the trap, he was a few metres away from catching up to them. Tavier tried to create the portal but nothing happened.

'We have to go the long way back' Tavier said and brought themselves out of the forest. The grass changed to black sand and the trees changed to rocks. It was almost pitch black. They were probably underneath the varbalas who had gone back to sleep. The passageway became narrower as they progressed. It was total darkness. The thought of Grindel not far behind and the varbalas crushing them as they moved were very disturbing. They continued on through the dark passageway slowly and carefully. Until one point, Tavier was sure they were close to where they spawned upon entering this realm.

'I believe we're close'

Tavier clapped his hands and brought them apart. The portal appeared and they went through.

THE ARRIVAL OF THE BRITISH NATION

Before you start reading the next
chapter, finish what you're supposed
to do first. Done? Carry on!

The Indonesian ship was nothing compared to the massive ships of The British Nation. There were six of them. Although it was nighttime, the darkness was not a problem for King Nathan and Prince Jake. First thing they noticed was that some of the ships are the same compared to the rest. These ships are part of the Royal Navy, while the rest are privateer ships. The flags of the United Kingdom and the Royal Navy wave proudly in the wind. The moonlight making reflections in the water made the ships look more intimidating. There were many people looking professional in red coats carrying a long unknown object on board the Royal Navy. And the way the people speak English is very sophisticated. But the people of White Shore were not that amazed because they've seen Trisnarim's ship, the Guardian, more grand than these. White Shore's soldiers and knights lined the shore as smaller boats approached. Men in red coats carrying those objects seem to be taking orders from a man in a blue coat. King Nathan and Prince Jake stood with the soldiers and knights, looking out for any suspicious activities.

'Greetings, I am Captain Charles Ericson of the Royal Navy. We are the Australian fleet led by Blue Moon' the man in blue coat spoke.

No people of Southernere can understand the second part.

'We come in peace. May I know who I am speaking with? And how can I address you sir?'

'Greetings Captain Charles Ericson of the Royal Navy. I am King Nathan of White Shore and this is my brother Prince Jake of White Shore. You can address me with your majesty. And before I continue, I would like to ask your business here' Nathan said.

'We seek a new place to grow and perhaps both our nations could live in peace' Charles said.

'Well then, I welcome you to Southernere'

They moved aside allowing the captain and some of his men to step foot on shore. One of the boats returned to the ships to call the rest.

'What's your strongest unit?' Charles asked.

'White Shore's strongest? I'll have to say the masters' Nathan replied. Jake wasn't comfortable with his brother answering the questions, but he just let it slide. It was quite weird for a newcomer to ask all those questions.

'Do the masters have weapons like this?' Charles held up the object one of his men was carrying.

'No, what does that do?'

'Oh, you don't know what's this?'

Charles sounded genuinely surprised, but there's also a hint of relief in his voice.

'No, never seen that before'

'Let me show you' Charles said confidently. 'Clear the area please'

He aimed at a nearby tree. They all waited until a loud sound was emitted followed by white smoke. The people of White Shore who were there either flinched or attempted to duck.

'That's a very dangerous weapon' Nathan commented. He and his brother could see the difference it made even though small to the tree.

'This is a rifle. But it's nothing compared to mine' Charles took out a smaller one.

'It may be small, but it's faster'

He aimed at a different spot on the tree and shot.

'That's amazing' Nathan said.

'Please don't do that again or you'll have to apologise to the tree' Jake said.

Charles reacted in a way showing that he thinks that was a crazy comment. He glanced at his men who were all sharing the same thought.

'Is what my brother said funny?' Nathan asked. The seriousness in his tone surprised Charles as well. He was even more pissed that these people with only swords as weapons dared to stand up to him even after he had shown the amazing power of the guns. But his overconfidence got the better of him.

'You've seen our weapons, the power we hold, and you think you can make me apologise to a tree? Are you threatening me? With a sword?'

By now White Shore's soldiers and knights were in a stance ready to draw and fight.

'Who is threatening who now? Stepping foot onto a land that doesn't belong to you after being welcomed and then threatening its people' Nathan said. Charles put his hands up like in surrender.

'My apologies, my mistake. It's just, we're not used to the practices of your people. We set course here days ago, thinking that this is a new empty land'

'That's alright. Come, to the palace. I'll notify King Edward of your arrival. Combination has more accommodations than White Shore'

For a quick second, Charles glanced at one of his men and then followed Nathan.

'What is this land? How did we not hear about it before? And why do I get the impression that you're all living in medieval times?' Charles asked Jake who was walking just a little bit in front of him.

'Sorry what? I can't remember three questions at once, captain' Jake said. Charles was pissed. But Jake was too. He wasn't happy with the way this newcomer acted earlier. He is a huge threat.

'First question, what is this land?'

'Southernere'

'That's it? No explanation?'

'How am I supposed to explain the name?'

'Like, how did it come about? Its history?'

'Long story. Wouldn't have enough time for your other questions'

Charles sighed.

'Right. How did we not hear about it before?'

'You're asking something that I don't know myself'

It was a lie. Master Nvago did explain briefly earlier.

'Why is everything medieval?'

'What's medieval?' Jake asked although he didn't care.

'Like during the times of the Roman civilization. The weapons and perhaps a little bit of the way people here dress' Charles noticed the very few people walking about in the streets. The most intriguing are the ladies wearing fully-covered clothing.

'Fascinating' Charles said to himself. Perhaps the Ottoman Empire never ended, he thought.

A few minutes later they arrived at the palace, by which time word had been sent to Combination.

'How many cities are there?' Charles asked. They were already sitting awkwardly in the lounge.

'Why do you ask such questions?' Nathan replied. Charles was silent for a second.

'Out of curiosity' he said.

'King Edward will be arriving in about half an hour. In the meantime, would you like a place to rest or do you prefer your ship?'

'Yes please, do you have enough for my men as well?' Charles was delighted to hear that.

'We can accommodate only a few because the other guest houses are occupied' Nathan said.

'That's alright, it's already a marvel that you have guest houses ready anytime for visitors'

'People and animals travel all around Southernere. Guest houses are very important'

'Fascinating'

Captain Charles was provided with a comfortable guest house to stay in for the time being. Some of his men, the higher rank soldiers, have their guesthouses close to his. Each house has about three men sharing the space. The rest stayed on the ships. Shortly after settling in a servant came in to see if Charles needed any more assistance, but Charles was too shocked to answer immediately.

'You can talk?' he gasped, staring at the beaver servant standing in the doorway.

'I know where you come from, you are not accustomed to my kind, but you have nothing to worry about. Do you need anything else sir?' the servant said.

'N-no' Charles said and the beaver left.

Later on, Charles was having conversation with a few of his men in one of the guesthouses.

'There's something strange about this place. I don't believe in magic but it seems like that's the idea we're going towards' Charles said.

'If it's real then their magic could be a threat to us' one soldier said.

'I believe our weapons are a greater threat to them. My concern is the animals. When the king mentioned that people and animals travel I didn't expect it to actually mean the animals travel. That means they have greater strength'

'Whatever creatures that lurk in the water' another soldier shuddered, thinking about the ocean.

The soldiers waited for Charles as he went deep in thought. Finally, he decided.

'Call the rest of our man, we take this small city tonight'

THE RED COATS
TOOK OVER

*Before you start reading the next
chapter, finish what you're supposed
to do first. Done? Carry on!*

The ships of the Royal Navy were harbouring so close to the docks. But before the White Shore soldiers could suspect anything, they fired their artillery. There were explosions. The people living near the bay ran out of their houses screaming. Fire was created from the explosion and it started to spread very quickly.

At the palace, King Nathan and Prince Jake, accompanied by the royal guards, were about to head out and investigate. But Charles and some of his men were already blocking their way. Charles has his revolver pointing at Nathan.

'Your reign is over Nathan. Admit your defeat and I shall set you free. The royal family would be pleased that I have found for them another country under the British Empire' Charles said.

Nathan remained silent. But his guards drew their swords. Unfortunately, Charles shot one of them in the head. A pool of blood was formed where he fell. Charles' men pointed their rifles at them.

'What have you done?! Why are you doing this?' Nathan cried in disbelief.

'If you don't have great power, you are not fit to rule this world'

They could see the evil glint in Charles' eyes.

'Terminate all of them' he said. The soldiers took their shot but Nathan had formed a shield between them. The bullets went through the shield and turned to dust. Charles' eyes widened.

'You talk about great power, now let's see how you handle this' Nathan said. The soldiers shot at him again but his shield was still there. Charles was already retreating slowly, leaving his soldiers in front to fend for themselves. By now, Nathan has figured out the speed of the bullets when being shot and he prepares for the next shot. The soldiers shot again but this time, Nathan caught every single one of them and returned it back to its source. Some of the bullets pierced through the soldiers and some damaged the rifles. Charles was already running out of the palace. White Shore soldiers charged at the remaining soldiers with their swords. Nathan and Jake pursued Charles. Some of Charles' men were outside and they were very ready to take their shot and the king and prince. Nathan stomped his foot and the earth trembled. He sent the ground where they stood upwards, shooting them into the sky. They continued on with their chase and saw Charles metres ahead. Suddenly, a rifle shot was heard and Nathan fell and rolled on the ground. Jake got down immediately and took cover behind an empty carriage. He looked upon his brother breathing heavily. He tried to look for the area where he was shot but he couldn't see from that angle. Nathan tried to move.

'Nathan, don't move. Stay low, I'll see what I can do' Jake whispered loudly. But Nathan still moved. He brought one arm up, magical sparks left his hand, and another shot was heard. Nathan was now completely still.

'No!' Jake hissed furiously. A few seconds later, the soldiers in red coats surrounded him.

'Surrender or face the same fate' one of them said. Jake raised his hands in surrender. Charles was there again. He observed Nathan's dead body and smirked.

'You have magic. So that's your power then. But you are still defeated' Charles said. He stepped up to Jake's face to get on his nerves.

'I used to love magic when I was a child. But over time, we learn that there's no such thing as magic or superpowers. And now, faced with magic, science is the more dominant power obviously. I have no regrets losing my belief in magic. I got to kill someone with magic' Charles laughed at the end. Jake couldn't take it anymore, he lashed at Charles but the soldiers hit him in the side with their rifles and pulled him back. Charles brushed his coat with his fingers and grinned.

'Take him to my ship and make sure he can't escape' Charles said. Four soldiers proceeded to escort Jake away.

'Captain, what about the rest of the city?' one soldier asked.

'Kill anyone who stands in your way. And make sure no one leaves the city. I shall address the people tomorrow, this city is now under the rule of the British Empire'

THE SUDDEN
CHANGE

*Before you start reading the next
chapter, finish what you're supposed
to do first. Done? Carry on!*

While King Nathan and Prince Jake were about to meet Captain Charles Ericson for the first time, King Edward and Queen Flyangel were descending to the dungeons to speak to an old enemy.

'How has she been?' Edward asked the guard on duty.

'As per normal your majesty' the guard said nervously. He wasn't expecting the king and queen to be there at all. Although it's the same building, Edward rarely visits the dungeons.

'Thank you Chad' Edward said and headed deeper to where the prisoner was.

The guard smiled dreamily. His majesty knows my name, he thought.

Lizyati sat in her cell facing the stone wall. The

door of her cell was blocked by a table with the holy book on top of it.

'I could hear your footsteps from the moment you entered' Lizyati said.

Edward and Flyangel did not reply, they waited to see if she had anything else to say.

'You want something from me' Lizyati continued.

Edward and Flyangel glanced at each other.

'We just want to ask some questions' Flyangel said.

'Hmm, not to free me?'

'You are aware of your sentence. Freeing you will only provide more disasters to Southernere' Edward said.

'Well, but you do need my help' Lizyati continued playing her own game of testing everyone's patience. She finally turned to face them. Her face seems more dangerous in the dark.

'We were given the idea that you might have something to do with Lord Grindel breaking the barrier that separated our worlds' Flyangel said.

Lizyati cackled.

'Set me free and I will help you' she said.

'This is a waste of time' Edward turned to leave.

'Eddie wait' Flyangel stopped him.

'Don't negotiate with her' he said.

'I just want my freedom back' Lizyati said, smiling profoundly.

'With that behaviour, there's no way you're getting it back!' Edward said.

'Awww' Lizyati teased.

Edward left the dungeons immediately.

'Eddie!' Flyangel ran after him. 'She is like that, you can't change her, I can't change her, no one can. But we need information'

Edward cupped her face in his hands.

'I love you angel. But we gotta move past that. No giving in to the enemy. We don't need her information. We'll manage like we always do' Edward smiled reassuringly.

Flyangel kissed him tenderly. She pulled back and gasped.

'What is it?' Edward asked alarmingly.

'I feel weird in my tummy. Like magic swirling around'

Edward smiled.

'It's only been more than a week and our baby is ready to show his or her presence' Edward said. Flyangel kissed him again.

'Your majesty' Bobby's voice suddenly spoiled the mood. 'Oh, I'm sorry your majesties'

'Nothing to apologise for Bobby' Flyangel said.

'I received word from White Shore, there are newcomers, a large number of them' Bobby said.

'I'll go' Edward said.

'I'm coming' Flyangel said.

'No, my lady with her baby needs to stay' Edward said.

'I agree with the king, your majesty' Bobby agreed. 'Don't worry my queen, I shall go with him'

Edward and Bobby took their horses and

proceeded to White Shore first. Another group of servants and soldiers will be proceeding with a few carriages in case they need to bring some people back to Combination.

More than halfway through the journey, sparks of magic could be seen in the sky moving above the trees. Edward and Bobby stopped to observe. The sparks started going down towards them.

'Take cover your majesty' Bobby said, drawing his sword.

'No Bobby, that's an emergency message from Nathan' Edward said.

The sparks dropped to Edward's eye level.

'Edward, it's too late for me, but you still have time. Do not enter White Shore. Do not underestimate these people. They have weapons faster than magic. Stay strong brother, for Southernere' Nathan's voice said. Everything went silent and the sparks vanished. There's no need for further explanation. Even without Nathan's voice, the sparks had given Edward a feeling of what had happened, including the passing of Nathan.

'White Shore has fallen' Edward told Bobby in a distressed tone. 'And… Nathan is gone'

Bobby sheathed his sword and got down from his horse.

'Bobby, we need to go now' Edward said. A tear rolled down his right eye. Bobby was silent for a while, trying to calm himself down.

'Yes your majesty' he said, getting back on his horse.

'Don't worry Bobby, for every problem there will be a solution'

They turned and headed back to Combination. Along the way they met up with the second group. Edward explained to them what had happened and they all went back.

It was already 2 in the morning but the royal council was having a meeting.

'Alright everyone, I need you to wipe those sleepy faces off, I'm afraid I have grave news' Edward began. Flyangel was beside him for support. She had already been briefed of what's happening. Edward glanced at the faces that were in the meeting room. His wife, Bobby, Dewi, Masters Lillain, Mousy, and Kitty, and Sir Everos. One seat was empty. The late Master Asher used to sit there.

'We will have more time to plan later, now we need to conduct emergency evacuation'

At the words emergency evacuation, the rest of them have their eyes widened in horror.

'What has happened this early morning?' Mousy asked, sounding more like a complaint.

'Foreign force had taken over White Shore, King Nathan is dead. I need all the civilians to be evacuated' Edward said. 'Master Lillain and Sir Everos, you will guide the western districts. Masters Mousy and Kitty, you will guide the southern districts. Captain,

Bale, and Oliver will be helping us to guide the forest districts. Queen Flyangel, Bobby and myself will guide the rest. Everyone is to proceed to White Woods. Now let's move!'

They left the room. Annie and Laura were standing outside, waiting.

'Laura, send word to all the other cities' Edward ordered.

'Yes your majesty'

'Annie, kindly inform Jayden (one of the castle guards) to ensure the king's guards and the soldiers have proper rest for tomorrow. And you must evacuate the castle as well before dawn'

'Yes your majesty'

They proceeded to complete their important tasks. All around the city, everyone was evacuated. The king's guards and soldiers were alerted. Some of them had to sacrifice their sleep to be on duty. Those in the west were being guided towards Barenge. Those in the central and the south were guided towards Silverside. Queen Flyangel guided the rest towards White Woods. King Edward and Bobby stayed behind with the army to defend the city. They were divided into smaller squads and took turns to sleep. And it was not long later that dawn arrived. Bobby was assembling the squads together in the training field of the Encampment District as Edward was about to give them a formal briefing. Members of the council had completed their tasks and were there to help. Some other important people, friends and family, like Captain, Bale, Oliver, Omar, and others were there as well.

'Council, report' Edward spoke to the council first.

'Barenge is too small for our people, sire. Queen Darleen however had accommodated a few empty rooms in the castle for some. Many of the citizens were kind enough to share their homes. The rest are in tents' Master Lillain and Sir Everos reported.

'Our Southern people are sleeping in tents outside the wall of Silverside. King Harold is sick and Princes John and James were concerned that he might infect more people if they were to bring them inside. But they were very helpful in providing the tents' Masters Mousy and Kitty reported.

'White Woods is very small. We didn't have tents. So our eastern people are sleeping in the open' Flyangel reported.

'The forest animals also have taken refuge there...' Captain reported but at the end his voice changed. He sounded more like a chipmunk trying to speak English in a human voice.

'What is that Captain?'

(Chip...) Captain sounded completely like a chipmunk.

(Meow...) Kitty made a sound, but all that came out was his cat language.

Edward wasn't the only one who was shocked and confused. The animals were equally the same.

'Sire, all the squads have assembled' Bobby came up to Edward to report.

'We'll need to talk more about this later' Edward said and then turned to brief the army.

'Attention! His majesty has a few words' Bobby announced loudly.

'King's guards, squads, soldiers, there is a new threat coming to us. We don't know when, but it will. White Shore has fallen and King Nathan has been killed in action. I need everyone to be on high alert at all times. Until we can push this threat away, no unauthorised persons shall enter Combination. All of you have been assigned into shifts depending on your squads. There'll be four shifts per day, consisting of six hours each and five squads per shift. Lastly, don't underestimate this new enemy. Get to work' Edward addressed.

'Sir!' all of them shouted in unison.

THE CAPTAIN'S
SECRET

*Before you start reading the next
chapter, finish what you're supposed
to do first. Done? Carry on!*

As dawn came, the people of White Shore were being forced out of their homes to gather near the docks. The area was massively ruined. There was no more fire. But there was still smoke rising from ashes. Bricks and wood scattered around the demolished buildings. The majestic view of the ocean glistening in the soon to be sunrise was disrupted by the glorious enemy ships docking the bay. Captain Charles Ericson stood proudly on a pile of bricks and stones, his back facing the ocean. A soldier came to report.

'Sir, all the people have been accounted for excluding those that tried to run away. Those who attempted has been shot on sight. All military troops have been killed. Currently total count is twenty-seven, excluding the women and children'

'Go and count the women and children as well you idiot. And the animals!'

The soldier proceeded to count.

'Greetings, people of…' Charles began his speech but he had forgotten the name of the city. He turned to his men who reminded him.

'White Shore. Greetings people of White Shore. Your king is dead. You have been lacking in civilization and not to worry, we are here to help your nation move forward. You are now under the rule of the British Empire. Men will report to the lieutenant in charge, Lieutenant Greenwood, for community service. That's mandatory. Anymore instructions will be given by the lieutenant. If any of you wish to leave this city, report to the lieutenant or myself. If any of you are caught trying to leave without permission, you will be punished. You are dismissed'

'Sir, total count is eighty-eight. Thirty-five women and sixteen children. And… ten animals' the soldier reported back. Charles nodded and walked back to a rowing boat.

'Take me back to my ship' Charles told the soldier who was tasked with rowing the boat back and forth for Charles.

Soon he boarded his ship. The biggest of them all. On board the deck were some of the crew, first mate, second mate, watch leader, and a few soldiers.

'Bring the prisoner to my cabin' Charles told one of the soldiers.

'Yes captain'

The captain's cabin was very cozy. Everything looks expensive too. The captain's table, chairs, and some furniture with wood are made of elm wood. Soft carpet covered the area around the study. The bed has a clean white mattress with blue design. The window at the back captures a magnificent view of the ocean and the other ships around. Charles was just sitting down at his study table for a few minutes to rest when there was a knock on his cabin door.

'Come in' he said.

The soldier came in with Prince Jake.

'Sit down' Charles signalled Jake who sat without question. Then he dismissed the soldier.

'Now, what can you tell me about the people in this land?' Charles asked.

Jake was silent for a few seconds and then he rolled his eyes. That made Charles snicker.

'The only reason you are still alive is for you to be my guide to this strange magical land. If you refuse to cooperate, I will have to kill you'

Jake stared darkly at him for quite some time.

'Is your kind always this merciless?' Jake said. Charles snickered again.

'My people are following orders. If your kind know what loyalty means, you would understand. And between you and me, they don't need to know that I'm the one who decided to do this without the king's authorisation'

'So you're a traitor. Talk about loyalty' Jake scoffed.

'Is it not loyal to succeed in the progression of my nation?'

'Succeeding on false orders is definitely not'

'The men need not know that, as long as it stays that way, there will always be honour'

'You are hungry for power. But yet again, if your men doesn't question your violent ways then perhaps your people are generally violent after all'

Charles leaned back on his chair, rethinking the conversation. After a while he called the soldier to come in.

'Did you hear what we were talking about?'

'No sir' the soldier replied.

'Take him back to his cell'

Jake stared at him unsure whether to be confused or angry as the soldier pulled him away. He also wondered if he should say something to Charles' men, and whether they would believe him or not. One thing is clear, this man is not acting for whoever he claims to be loyal to. He is acting on his own agenda. And all of his men are blindly following orders. Which reminds Jake of the soldiers, king's guards, and any armed forces of Southernere. They were also following orders. There have always been righteous orders by the good people. But what if there were bad ones? Will the forces of Southernere still follow them?

THE MARCH ON
WHITE SHORE

*Before you start reading the next
chapter, finish what you're supposed
to do first. Done? Carry on!*

It was very difficult now for the council to communicate with one another because the animals could no longer speak with human voices. They do understand what's going on but everytime they open their mouth to respond, all that comes out is their natural animal sound.

(Squeak…) Master Mousy squeaked.

'I think the only person that can help us understand this is Master Nvago' Queen Flyangel said. They all nodded in agreement.

A squad of soldiers that had been patrolling the north came up to King Edward. A terrified looking woman and possibly her daughter was with them.

'Your majesty, we found this lady and her daughter. They claimed to have come from White Shore' one soldier said.

'Your majesty, please help us, White Shore has been overrun by the newcomers. They wear scary looking red coats. Most of us have been killed trying to escape. They have weapons even King Nathan's magic couldn't stop them. Me and my daughter are the only survivors. The rest I believe are held captive in the city' the woman informed desperately.

'I thank you for the information ma'am, and my council and I will plan the proper strategy, my men will take you to a safe place' Edward replied reassuringly.

The woman nodded her head, calming down.

'Are we going to attack?' Master Lillain asked after the woman was gone.

'No, we'll wait first. Today we'll strengthen our defenses. Tomorrow, we will bring the troops to White Shore' Edward said.

The day passed by very quickly. Until nightfall, there has been no attack. But they have managed to build traps and set up places for ambushes. The magic-abled were practicing their magic. Given the warning the woman gave, if Nathan's magic couldn't stop their weapons, they have to play smart. King Edward was sparring with Master Kitty. Queen Flyangel with Master Mousy, and Master Lillain with Bobby. Although they couldn't communicate with the animals, that doesn't prevent them from understanding each other. Edward let out water from between his fingers and sent them rushing at

Kitty. Being the fastest runner among them, Kitty ran around the water at very high speed, trapping it for a few seconds, and then stopped for a rest at the side. The water was now twirling like a tornado and Kitty tried to send it towards Edward. But the water wasn't obeying his command. The water tornado started terrorising the area. Edward gripped onto the force just in time before it could cause any injury to anyone. He toned down the speed and sucked the water back into his hands. He looked up to see everyone looking worriedly. If the masters themselves can't handle magic, how can they use it as a weapon.

(Meow...) Kitty meowed. Somehow Edward understood him. Kitty was saying that he tried to control the tornado confidently as per normal, but it didn't work. It's a wonder just like how the animals suddenly couldn't talk either. Understanding that gave Edward an idea.

'I think I know how we can talk to each other. Can we do mind reading?' Edward suggested.

'I'm sorry to break it to you, but Gratultyn magic doesn't work anymore' Master Nvago's voice came out of nowhere. As usual he came out of nowhere leaving people wondering where he came from.

'Master Nvago! We have many questions' Flyangel exclaimed eagerly.

'I can see that' Nvago replied amusingly.

(Meow...) (Squeak...) Mousy and Kitty sounded angry and sad.

'I'm afraid that will be permanent for now' Nvago said, understanding their frustration.

'Why?' Lillain asked.

'Fearing the worst, Gratultyn has fallen' Nvago's comment on that sent them gasping in horror.

'Yet again if that was true, places filled with Gratultyn's magic in this world would perish, but the Valley of Sorrows still stands strong, frozen from the seed of Gratultyn's magic. White Woods' invisible barrier is still there...'

At the phrase "frozen from the seed of Gratultyn's magic", Flyangel smiled, knowing that she was the one that caused it.

'I believe something has happened in Gratultyn. There had been a long week of civil war there but I thought it had ended. Now I myself can't return. My Gratultyn magic is not working. Just the magic that I'm born with that works' Nvago continued.

(Squeak...)

'So you're saying that whatever that is already there will be there, but whatever magic that is not natural, it's no longer there?' Lillain asked, but she sounded confused herself at the last part.

'Yes. That is why you can't communicate with one another. Because animals naturally don't talk in human voices. But I believe if you really have to practice Gratultyn magic again, you need to go to the heart of the Valley of Sorrows. That was where Majuza used to spend her days. Flyangel knows where it is, she's been there. But it's too cold to go there without proper gear. And with the current situation, I believe you have a threat in the north'

'Yes. And Nathan was killed by them' Edward said. They all went silent for a few seconds.

'We didn't even get to give him a farewell' Flyangel said angrily.

'Since my inability to return home might be a reason I have to interfere with your affairs, I shall help you. But you will lead me, I can't be making the decisions, I'm just a master' Nvago said.

Edward proceeded to update him on the plan. When dawn arrives tomorrow, they will march towards White Shore.

As usual, the night passed in a hurry. Ten squads have been combined together. An army of 120 men, mixed soldiers and king's guards, will be marching towards White Shore. King Edward, Queen Flyangel, Bobby, Master Nvago, Masters Lillain, Mousy, and Kitty, Captain, Bale, and Oliver will be leading in front. Sir Everos and Dewi will stay in Combination to ensure everything stays normal.

Just as they left, Alphaga came with a few other Outlanders.

'Sir Alphaga, you came at a bad timing' Sir Everos said.

Alphaga looked at him sideways.

'Don't call me sir' he said. 'Where is Edward?'

'King Edward you mean?' Everos said again.

'Don't test me knight' Alphaga said.

'What are your intentions Alphaga?' Dewi asked.

'Some of the Outlanders are seeking new homes in the Inlands' Alphaga said, referring to the people that came with him. 'And something strange is happening in the Outlands'

'Wait a minute' Dewi had just realised something. 'How are you still talking? Master Mousy and Kitty couldn't!'

'Yes, that's the strange part, many animals can't talk. But for my case, not many people know this, I'm not naturally a rabbit'

Sometimes Dewi wonders who turned this adorable rabbit evil. He was so mysterious and scary before, now he's just innocent. And what he said sounds funny.

'I am a human. But I'm born with shape-shifting powers, and I love this form. So I've stayed in this form all my life'

'You mean to say out of all the forms you decided to stick with a pink rabbit? How did that make you evil?' Dewi laughed.

'Not funny' Alphaga scowled. Dewi put her hands up, showing that she meant no offense.

'I have matters to discuss but I sense there's something greater here' Alphaga continued.

'There's a new threat. People from where I came from' Dewi said.

'And King Nathan's been killed by this new threat' Everos added.

'People from where you came from' Alphaga repeated Dewi's line. 'Have you tried asking Lizyati?'

'King Edward and Queen Flyangel had' Everos replied.

'But she didn't cooperate' Dewi finished his sentence.

'Or how about you? You came from there as well' Dewi was a little bit offended.

'No offense' Alphaga said.

'I've been here for more than twenty years, I tend to forget how even my own race is like'

'Want me to help?'

'With what?'

'Questioning Lizyati'

'What? With your violent methods? Please no' Dewi rolled her eyes.

'She's your enemy too. Surely you don't care'

'No, wait till Edward gets back. And besides, she's been brought to White Woods'

'Well then, don't mind us, we are going to stay in the castle until Edward gets back' Alphaga hopped away, leading the Outlanders to the castle. Dewi and Everos were left feeling frustrated.

THE ATTACK ON
WHITE SHORE

*Before you start reading the next
chapter, finish what you're supposed
to do first. Done? Carry on!*

Someone knocked on the captain's cabin door with great haste. Captain Charles Ericson opened the door to find one of his men, his face full of worry.

'An army has formed up outside White Shore captain. Estimated to have more than a hundred men'

Charles pushed past him to go on deck to see for himself. Although it was quite far, he could see movements in the trees on the outskirts of the city.

'Alright, let's show them what we have' Charles said, climbing down to the rowing boat. A horn was blown from the captain's ship, signalling the soldiers on land to prepare for battle. The soldiers hurried off to get their rifles as the innocent citizens ran back to their homes. There was no warning, King Edward's men had already begun charging into the city. They were very confident knowing that they outnumbered the enemy. There were only forty men in red coats on land. Including the privateers, they have fifty. But they were equally confident to defend themselves. The soldiers stood in a straight line, side by side, on all entryways where Edward's soldiers were coming. They have their rifles aimed. The privateers split themselves and pointed their revolvers. Charles reached the shore just as his men began firing. Edward's men began falling one by one. Those that survived the first round didn't survive the next. Edward and the others stared in disbelief. But Master Nvago knew what's coming. He was just restraining himself. He was only there to follow and not to lead. He was conflicted because some members of The Fifteen concluded even advising is interfering. Seeing more men running to their deaths made him want to say something. But Edward had already done it. Upon seeing that many deaths, he had ordered his men to find cover. Charles' men reloaded their rifles and revolvers and started moving forward, intending to slowly push the enemy back out of the city. Charles was very satisfied with the results, grinning the entire time. Then the ground started to tremble. From the tree line, the ground broke apart, making its way through all the entryways, pulling the dead soldiers underground, and charging at Charles' men. Charles' grin was gone. His men broke formation and started retreating. But the disaster was much faster. The ground broke apart even more and devoured Charles' men. Out of four entryways to the docks, two of them were now completely free of Charles' men. The remaining that survived were either they held onto parts of buildings or they were fast enough to dodge.

'Nice work Lillain' Edward complemented. He turned to Bobby. The king's guards stood behind him, waiting for their turn.

'They are still recovering, Master Nvago will be appearing and disappearing around them, the moment he does, you'll be leading the entire army forward'

'Yes sire' Bobby said. He turned around to energise his men. And on cue, Master Nvago surrounded himself with mist and he disappeared.

Charles' men were now around him, trying to calm down.

'They're just witches, demons who are supposed to be burning in the depths of hell. Keep that in mind! Continue your fight!' Charles exclaimed. 'Lieutenant, get yourself together'

Lieutenant Greenwood, one of the bravest men Charles had ever met. But he couldn't blame him, David Greenwood has a son, a cadet on board one of the ships. If he dies, who will take care of him in the hands of the enemy.

Mist surrounded them all of a sudden. There was a small amount at first but it became thick very fast. Nvago appeared, scaring some soldiers. Charles shot at him. But he had disappeared. Nvago appeared elsewhere. Charles shot another round. But Nvago was nowhere to be seen again. The mist cleared up and the king's guards and soldiers were already so close.

Charles' men have not enough time to aim, Bobby and the king's guards have already attacked, disarming them, and putting them on their knees. Charles could take a shot, but only one round. He wouldn't make much difference. He got on his knees voluntarily, placed the revolver on the ground and put his hands up in surrender. King Edward, Queen Flyangel and the rest of the council had caught up to them.

'So you're the force that tried to take over Southernere' Edward said.

'And killed my brother' Flyangel added angrily. She tried to force choke him, but nothing happened. She changed her mind and used water instead. Water exited her hands and surrounded itself around Charles' neck. Edward's hand suddenly grabbed her wrist, she was taken aback. The water fell, wetting Charles and the area around him. Edward and Flyangel made eye contact. Edward shook his head lightly, meaning this is not the time for that.

'Where's Prince Jake?' Edward asked.

Charles didn't respond.

'Bobby, take him to the palace cells' Edward said.

'Your majesty, what about the rest of the men?' one king's guard asked.

'Them as well. I'll question them later'

'Please don't harm my son, he's innocent' Lieutenant Greenwood pleaded.

'No one shall be harmed as long as no one tries to hurt anyone' Edward reassured.

They gazed upon the ships of the Royal Navy.

As they thought gratefully that the battle was over, the ship's horn blew again. The crew on board the ships were seen scampering around the deck. A few climbed the masts. Others went below deck. The sound of artillery instilled fear in most of them. The privateer ships started moving, turning around for a better angle. The Royal Navy ships also moved. And that's when they saw what they were firing at. Three ships with large black sails are attacking them.

THE MALAYAN
PIRATES

*Before you start reading the next
chapter, finish what you're supposed
to do first. Done? Carry on!*

The ships are a little bit smaller than the navy but they have bigger crew, so they were operating very fast. Cannons were fired. The new ships managed to sink one privateer ship. Some of the crew on board had jumped off before it sank and were now swimming for their lives. The crew on the new ships were not giving them any chance. They shot their revolvers at them before they could escape. Not long later the other privateer ship also went down. The new ships were taking lots of damage but the crews' agility were maintaining the ships' condition. However, one of the new ships was already burning. It was going down soon. They started firing grappling hooks onto the navy ships. Some of them were already getting on board. Rifles, revolvers, and swords were used for attack and defense.

'Should we do something?' Queen Flyangel asked, although she was enjoying the scene.

'Let them fight, they are all from the same world' King Edward replied.

The crew of the new ships are very aggressive. But those on land can't really tell much of their behaviours or appearances from quite a distance away. The navy doesn't have that many people on board their ships, hence the navy crew surrendered immediately. After a few minutes, the ships that were still stable started sailing towards shore.

'They're coming at us' Master Lillain said in disbelief. 'And not one of us has the ability to stop a ship, not without Gratultyn magic'

Edward gazed upon the water, moving according to the ship.

'Angel, help me with this' he said. He used his powers, digging deep into the water, feeling every water particle in the bay. Flyangel joined him. Together, they controlled the water in the bay. Water started resisting the movements of the ships. The crews were shocked and confused. With a final push, Flyangel exerted cold and ice into the water, stopping the movements of the water particles, and freezing the entire bay. The ships' bilge were destroyed. The rest of the ships slid down the frozen waves and soon came to a stop. Everyone on the ships looked down at the frozen bay, wondering what had just happened.

'I didn't know the seed of Gratultyn is still in you' Edward said, amazed.

'The seed of Gratultyn can never fully disappear once you've eaten it, even if you've been protected from death' Master Nvago said, appearing out of nowhere as usual.

A few people on the closest ship, the captain's ship of the Royal Navy, climbed down. They were not dressed smartly like the British soldiers. They wore random clothes. No uniform. Their appearances are wild, dirty, and aggressive. They have brown skin. Some are similar to the Indonesians, a few are lighter, but most are darker brown. Edward and the rest remained at the docks, not intending to make the first move. Edward wants to see who these people are and how they are different compared to Charles' men. The brown men made their way to the shoreline.

'Who are you? And why have you come?' Edward asked. But they don't seem to understand a single word.

'I think we need Dewi for this' Flyangel said.

'Never mind, they are Malay pirates. I can translate for you' Nvago said confidently. He stepped closer to them.

'Apa sebab datang sini?' Nvago said in Malay perfectly. He doesn't sound foreign or weird at all. (Why did you come here?). The pirates looked at each other, impressed.

'Mana kami mahu pergi, terserah kami. Kami lanun, dan seperti semua lanun, kami nak harta karun. Itu sahaja' one pirate said, he seems to be the leader.

(Where we want to go is up to us. We are pirates, and like all pirates, we want treasure. That's all).

'They're saying that they're pirates, they can go wherever they want, and the only thing important to them is treasure' Nvago translated for Edward and Flyangel.

'Tapi sekarang apa ini? Sihir? Kapal kami sudah binasa. Semua kapal binasa. Kami nak kapal baharu, dan harta, baru kami akan pergi dan tidak ganggu lagi' the pirate continued.

'But now what is this? Magic? Our ships have been destroyed. All the ships are destroyed. We want new ships, and money, then we will leave and never return' Nvago translated.

'That's not a hard request' Edward said, smiling. The pirates eyed him suspiciously.

'Nvago, ask him if he doesn't mind us checking the red coats' ships?' Edward said. 'And also the crews will be given to us'

'Raja Edward tanya jika beliau boleh lihat semua kapal orang putih dan orang-orangnya jadi banduannya'

The pirate leader thought for a moment.

'Boleh' he said.

'He said can' Nvago said. Edward smiled, grateful for a peaceful exchange even though with a pirate. But people of Southernere don't really know what pirates are like, there were no pirates in Southernere before.

Edward, Flyangel, and Nvago went to search the enemy ships. Bobby led a few men to gather wood for the ships. Fortunately, there is one Indonesian builder who survived the British attack. He used to be a part of Rajah's crew. With the help of Masters Lillain and Mousy, they started building the ships. Edward and Flyangel were so relieved to find Prince Jake alive in Charles' ship.

By the end of the day, the frozen bay had started melting. The dead bodies had been buried. Three ships had been built. Just like the fallen ones. The pirates transferred their sails to the new ones. All that's left to settle was money. The pirates also wanted money. In Southernere they use random items for trade. The most valuable items would be the iron and jewels. But that's the part Edward wasn't sure whether the pirates will accept the gift or not. Edward presented both options. After a few minutes of thinking, the pirate leader decided to take both. They had refreshments for a few hours. The pirates sang songs in their own language. And by midnight, all the ice in the bay had melted. The pirates were on their way back to wherever they came from, or like they said go to wherever they want to go. Everyone waved as they sailed away. Edward actually likes them a lot.

'I wonder why you guys don't seem to like them' he said to literally everyone.

'King, sorry to interrupt' someone with a timid voice and a different accent said. Among the small crowd, a foreign person, an Indonesian was trying to talk to Edward.

'Yes?' Edward asked, smiling. He was still very happy from the victory and the joyous evening.

'Wait, what are you doing here my friend? I thought you're with them?' Nvago asked, referring to the pirates.

'No, no. I am alone, I am not from their gang. I pretended to be so that I can come here. I wanted to come with Omar but I was too late' the guy said.

Everyone was waiting for his reason. Though they have to admit, his English wasn't good.

'I want to ask, is Dewi here?' he asked.

'Dewi?' Lillain asked, surprised.

'How do you know Dewi?' Flyangel asked.

The guy was blushing.

'I love her'

FAREWELL FOR NATHAN

Before you start reading the next chapter, finish what you're supposed to do first. Done? Carry on!

King Edward and Prince Jake have decided to turn White Shore into an outpost. Training grounds, barracks, forest training grounds, water training area, shipyard, the palace for the leader or commander, new building for holding prisoners, and more. The plan was a good plan. Everyone started packing the next day for their return to Combination. The apprehended British soldiers and associates will be brought to Combination. The citizens of White Shore will be moving as well. Only Bobby and half of the army will be staying behind for the outpost project. Builders among the citizens also stayed behind.

King Nathan's body was found in the palace alongside some dead White Shore soldiers and British soldiers. They brought him back as well and buried the rest.

Their return to Combination got them busier. There were a lot of things to be completed. Firstly, the new prisoners are locked up in the castle dungeons. Secondly, King Edward and Queen Flyangel welcomed the Outlanders who came with Alphaga and wanted a new life in the Inlands. And they also found out about Alphaga's secret and how he could talk. Thirdly, the citizens of Combination returned to their homes at last. The districts are once again filled with signs of life. Fourth, the prisoners that were transferred to White Woods are being transferred back to Combination. Fifth happened on the next day, King David of Arstar arrived in Combination after receiving an urgent letter from Queen Darleen of Barenge. She had informed him the moment a portion of the citizens of Combination arrived at her city. He helped with whatever they needed to do, later on stayed a while after Nathan's farewell and then left for his home. Sixth, which is totally unrelated to what's important, the Indonesian guy reunited with Dewi. Dewi had never mentioned him before, but at the sight of him, they both ran and greeted each other excitedly. Dewi had tried to forget her past ever since she got here. But some things are just unforgettable. And this guy here, Aditya is his name, he was her first and only teenage lover, before she disappeared from her friends and family. And seventh, they organised a farewell for Nathan at the castle. Lots of chairs had been placed in the ballroom facing a platform with a table on top. King Nathan's casket lay on the table.

The ballroom was filled with people in a matter of minutes. The royals, relatives of the deceased, and important people sat in the front rows. The rest are filled with commoners. There wasn't enough to fit that there were still many standing outside in the main hallway. Queen Flyangel went onto the platform to speak.

'We are gathered here today, because of our own will to pay the highest amount of respect for the passing of our beloved king, King Nathan of White Shore. A son, a brother, and a friend. And his efforts will continue to provide assistance to all of Southernere. We wish this farewell to you as a reminder for us as well, that we will be in your place one day. And your spirit will always stay with us. Farewell my brother, Nathan' Flyangel said, a tear rolled down her cheeks after she spoke the last few words. She stepped down from the platform. Afterwards was the individual respect. One by one, families together, or one person alone, take turns to go up front and stand in front of Nathan's casket as a sign of respect. As the ballroom cleared up, the people outside went in for their turn. At the end of the day, King Nathan's body was buried alongside King Henry's and Queen Dorothy's grave in Alhora cemetery.

DEWI'S WEDDING

*Before you start reading the next
chapter, finish what you're supposed
to do first. Done? Carry on!*

On the 20ᵗʰ of April, 3 days after the short battle in White Shore, and also the last day of winter, Dewi's wedding was about to happen. She had 2 days of catching up with Aditya and she has never been more sure in her life. She's ready to marry him. Although she was already above forty, Aditya as well, that is not stopping them from finally settling down with a partner. The wedding was to be held at the castle. Her wedding isn't going to be like any wedding in Southernere. Her wedding is going to follow the rules of her religion. Her father, Omar, will be the bride's guardian (or better known as "wali") and marriage officiant. There will be two male witnesses among Dewi's relatives to witness the marriage words (better known as "ijab qabul") that will be spoken by the groom. The wedding was not that big. Dewi refused Queen Flyangel's offer to inform the whole city. Dewi only wanted her relatives and close friends to be present in the ceremony.

Just an hour before the wedding, Flyangel and Master Lillain came into Dewi's room to check on her. She was standing still facing a tall standing mirror. A handmaiden was helping her get dressed. A very beautiful long white dress covered in glitter fits perfectly. The handmaiden was finishing the last few touches on the headscarf. A white headscarf as well, longer than the others. The ends of it were stylishly pinned to different parts of the headscarf making the whole appearance majestic. Dewi had put quite a thick makeup on with cherry red lipstick. But it wasn't bad in any way, she was very beautiful.

'I'm so happy for you!' Lillain said excitedly. The ladies squealed with delight.

'By the way, I have dresses picked out for you guys as well. Put it on!' Dewi said, pointing to two dresses and headscarves on her bed. Flyangel and Lillain gasped at how beautiful it looks. They both went into Dewi's walk-in closet to try it on. A few minutes later they came out like fasion icons arriving at their own show. Flyangel wore a light blue dress with a little bit of very light purple colour. The shape of the dress was perfect for Flyangel because it even matched with her character. Her headscarf was light blue. Lillain has a light green dress on with a little bit of very light blue colour. The shape of the dress also perfectly matched Lillain with her character.

'Now I'm ready' Dewi said, smiling widely, looking

at her friends so adorable. The ceremony was held in the ballroom. But they only used up a small space. Dewi sat on a chair away from the crowd that has gathered. The crowd gathered around in a circle, facing the centre where Omar and Aditya were sitting facing each other.

'Can we begin?' Omar asked everyone. They all agreed and Omar proceeded. He held out his hand for Aditya to hold (like shaking hands but without the action of shaking, better known as "salam").

'Aku nikahkan dikau dengan puteriku Dewi Binte Omar dengan maskahwinnya sebentuk cincin emas' Omar said while holding Aditya's hand. (I marry you to my daughter, Dewi Binte Omar, with the dowry as one gold ring).

Aditya repeated the words without removing his hand.

'Aku terima nikahnya Dewi Binte Omar dengan maskahwinnya sebentuk cincin emas' Aditya said. (I accept the marriage of Dewi Binte Omar with the dowry as one gold ring).

Omar turned to the two witnesses to ask if Aditya has said the words correctly and properly.

'Sah?'

(Officially legal?)

'Sah' the two witnesses said. And all of Dewi's relatives cried with joy. Omar and Aditya pulled their hands away. Dewi and Aditya are now officially husband and wife. Aditya proceeded to where Dewi was sitting and gave her a kiss on the forehead. Dewi replied with a long hug.

Afterwards there was a wedding reception in the castle main gardens. A buffet of Indonesian cuisine specially made by Dewi's friends and relatives. They dominated the kitchen and taught the royal cooks how to make the dishes. There were a few plates of grilled fish, each with different sauces and flavours, sate, meat cut into small pieces on a stick. The meat were mostly beef and chicken. The Indonesians have a big farm in between SHAW Academy and Forest District 1. That's where they breed and care for their cows, chickens, and sheeps. Some of the farm animals were brought here by them when they arrived. But most came from the wild plains of Alhora. And since they're from the wild, unlike the animals in Combination, they do not understand English to communicate with the humans.

Aside from the grilled fish and sate, there was also fried chicken, marinated in very delicious spices. The whole event was a success. Everyone enjoyed the food especially.

THE UPRISING

*Before you start reading the next
chapter, finish what you're supposed
to do first. Done? Carry on!*

U p north, Alphaga was having a hard time
controlling the Outlanders. They were after all
former avengers and enemies of the Inlands. And they
were never happy with Alphaga's actions of making
peace with the Inlanders. And a lot of them are already
thinking, it's time they fight back. They are Majuza's
avengers, they are meant to avenge her and not sit back
and make peace with Majuza's enemies. Maracala was
a better leader. From the moment Alphaga stepped
up to lead until now, those who disagreed with him
had slowly turned the people against him one by one.
And now, the rebellion is very strong. Alphaga's latest
return from Combination the night after a meeting
with King Edward sent him in shock when he saw
his loyal followers' heads stuck onto spikes, outlining
the perimeter of their base. The Outlanders' new
base is a few kilometres away west of Flyra's Stand
(Morgan's former kingdom). The rebel leaders stood at

the entrance staring aggressively at Alphaga. Among them were Lydia and Pertum.

'Why?' Alphaga asked simply. He knows the answer to it, but he was still in disbelief.

'Because we are avengers, not forgivers' the guy standing at the most front said, he was definitely the leader.

'Ciaran, don't do this' Alphaga said, he was very tired to deal with this right now. Ciaran, was never an important person to Marcala, but he was certainly very loyal to the cause, and the reason the cause was created, to avenge Majuza. Ciaran, a very nice looking dark-haired guy. A nice person as well, only nice to fellow avengers. But never nice to the enemy. And now, he sees Alphaga as the enemy.

'Oh I do. You know I will' Ciaran said.

'We have a common enemy now. Inlanders and Outlanders must unite'

Some of them reacted in disgust at Alphaga's words. Alphaga then realised that he was completed surrounded. There were people in the trees as well, hiding, waiting for the right time to attack.

'Listen to him everyone, can you believe it? The one and only Alphaga said we must unite!' Ciaran mocked him. Everyone reacted in disgust again and laughed.

'Nobody, nobody makes peace with Majuza's enemy. Nobody makes peace with those city rats!'

Everyone shouted loudly in agreement. Then they went silent again, waiting for Ciaran's next comment.

'You don't understand…' Alphaga tried to speak. But Ciaran was too powerful as an influence already. The people were not happy to hear Alphaga speak.

'No, no! You don't understand! Aren't we still being treated like we used to? An Outlander, a vicious Outlander! We will never be more than a villain!'

Everyone shouted again.

'We must never forget our main reason why we are all here. Who do we fight for? Who do we stand for? Who?!'

'MAJUZA!' the people shouted together in unison. Their voices were so powerful, that the ground seemed to tremble a little. The wind blew past Alphaga into the trees. And the rebels started stomping their foot and punched their arms into the air as they chanted Alphaga's name. They were waiting excitedly for Ciaran to kill him and put his head on the spike together with the others where he belongs. Ciaran stepped closer to Alphaga. And every step he took, the people cheered. Alphaga's heart was now pounding. He has never been this nervous in his entire life. But he wasn't going to back down without a fight. He conjured fire on his bunny ears, lighting up the clearing. The people around oohed and aahed, anticipating an epic fight, one where Alphaga dies.

'You want to do this the hard way' Ciaran said.

'It will be hard for you' Alphaga replied. Ciaran was not happy with that. He sent all the wind towards Alphaga. The fire on his ears died. And Ciaran drew his sword to strike. But Alphaga was fortunate to be a rabbit and small. He hopped away quickly and conjured fire again. This time he immediately sent fireballs at him. Ciaran deflected a few with his sword. But there were ones faster than him, he managed to dodge all but one. The fireball burned his left ear. Ciaran swiped his left hand at his left ear, wiping the fire out. He glared at Alphaga angrily.

'That's all you can do. Fire. Gratultyn magic is not working anymore to save you. So just stop this crap and just die' Ciaran said.

'No'

Alphaga sent more fireballs at him. Ciaran dodged all of them and sent the wind towards him. Alphaga hopped around as the wind chased him. Ciaran turned the wind into a man-sized tornado. Alphaga let out a fiery explosion. Ciaran managed to summon all the wind and the tornado in time to block of the fire. Some of the rebels got burned alive. The trees around were burning. While the rest had taken cover. No one was looking. Now was Alphaga's chance to escape. Alphaga transformed into a pink bird and flew up into the sky just before Ciaran wiped the fire in front of him. Long journey ahead, his next stop was Combination. He has to inform King Edward or there will be more chaos.

THE REBELS
TOOK OVER

*Before you start reading the next
chapter, finish what you're supposed
to do first. Done? Carry on!*

Morning of April 19, Alphaga was flying over Barenge. And the thought of the Outlanders attacking this small city first since it's the closest made him uneasy. So he flew down and transformed back into a rabbit. There were only a small number of musketeers. He remembered the first time he helped conquer this city with Lord Morgan, Marcala, and Princess Erieka. There were a lot more armed men back then. There were a lot of deaths on that day. Now he felt responsible to prevent that from happening again. The musketeers recognised him immediately but they didn't try to stop him, because they know he is now the representative for the Outlands or so they thought before the uprising.

'Is Queen Darleen around?' Alphaga asked one of the musketeers.

'Yes, she's in the stronghold' he replied.

Ever since the first fall of Barenge, the castle was no longer a castle. When King Edward helped rebuild the city, the castle was changed into a stronghold.

Alphaga made his way up a flight of stairs and stumbled upon Darleen at the landing.

'What are you doing here?' Darleen asked, feeling annoyed but tried to hide it as best as she could. Even though they had made peace, Darleen had never forgiven the avengers for being the reason she lost both of her parents and her sister. So the grudge is still there.

'I came to warn you and offer my assistance' Alphaga said.

'Why?'

'Because my people have risen up against me. I believe they're making their way here now. We need to tell Edward'

'No!' Darleen said immediately after he finished his sentence. 'Edward has so many problems to deal with right now. I don't want to bother him. We will defend the city on our own'

They both nodded in agreement.

'Alphaga, thank you' she added.

They both went to do whatever they can to defend the city. Darleen met with her musketeers and planned out their standing positions and strategy. Alphaga gathered the few citizens, including the women, except the children, and taught them basic fighting skills. In the evening, the people were ready. Following

Alphaga's advice, Darleen and her troops dug out a small trench around the city. And then they waited. Darleen stood outside the stronghold with Alphaga and the musketeers, while waiting, they recapped the strategy and escape routes. The square was once called Unity Square. Now it's just a small gathering area for the citizens. The citizens were in their homes, ready to defend their family against the rebels.

Soon, the sun was setting and just as they thought the rebels were not going to attack today, the combined voices of people roaring with pride reached throughout the city.

'Okay, position everyone' Darleen said. Everyone got into position. Alphaga went off towards the trench. It was all part of the plan. In the trees, he could make out figures moving. Suddenly, everything happened so fast. The rebels started charging into the city, they were coming from all directions. But fortunately because of the trench, it wasted their time a little. Alphaga focused on his powers and conjured lava. The lava flowed from his feet into the trench. This lava was magical, so its speed wasn't slow as normal. It covered the whole trench within a minute. Some rebels made it out on either side but others screamed as they got burned alive.

'Fire!' Darleen commanded. The musketeers released their arrows into the air. The arrows hit the rebels who survived and those who are already burning in the lava. A few who made it past the trench charged into the square. Darleen released her arrow at one of them. Another was shot by a musketeer. And the third, Darleen smacked her face with her bow. It was far from over. There were so many of them, avengers, Outlanders, Ciaran even brought beasts, all of them are now rebels. Alphaga knew his lava wouldn't stay for long. Ciaran will soon ask a Winterain to wipe it out. He hopped back to Darleen's location.

'The forces are too strong. They even brought beasts along. We need to evacuate immediately' Alphaga said in a hurry.

'No, just evacuate the people. Head west, cross The Waterfront River, there's a small town called West Coast' Darleen replied. 'I will defend this kingdom to my death'

'You're not thinking straight'

'That's an order!' Darleen exclaimed. There's no changing her mind now. Alphaga proceeded to evacuate the citizens.

'Go with the rabbit' Darleen told her musketeers.

'We stand by you till our deaths my queen' the musketeers said together.

Alphaga led the people to the west side of the city. Not everyone wanted to follow him. Some, just like Darleen, wanted to stay and defend their homes. Those with children followed. Alphaga cleared one part of the trench from lava for them to escape. There were not that many rebels on this side. Alphaga and some of the people killed them with ease. And they continued on west.

As soon as a rebel Winterain wiped the lava out, the rebels rushed into the city. Darleen and the musketeers released their arrows killing some of them. The rebels broke into houses, lit them on fire, and killed the remaining people. They all eventually closed in on the square. Darleen and her musketeers had already gone inside the stronghold and barricaded it. The beasts were commanded to break it down. Outside, the rebels taunted whoever survivor was inside. They threw fireballs and strong wind through the openings. Darleen and the musketeers were safe from them. But the barricade was coming down. Every step closer to destroying the barricade, the rebels cheered.

'I'm sorry Barenge had to end like this my friends' Darleen said.

'I am proud to have served you my queen' a musketeer said, the rest agreed.

'For Barenge!' they exclaimed in unison.

The barricade went down. The rebels charged in. The musketeers' arrows killed some. But as swift as the arrow flew, the rebels killed them with their swords and powers. Rebels attempted their way up the stairs towards Darleen's position. Darleen's arrows pierced through them. More charged their way up taking cover behind a glowing bear. Darleen shot her last few arrows at it. As the bear reached her level and a rebel came out of cover, Darleen's final arrow brought down the beast before the rebel struck her with a sword. Darleen pushed the sword back with her bow. The rebel pushed on her attack and Darleen successfully blocked every strike with her bow. Seeing no more arrows, the other rebels came out of cover. Darleen knocked the sword off the first rebel before another rebel struck her in the hips. She cried out in pain. She strained to turn around and face the others. A sword came at her which she blocked with her bow. The sword completely cut the bow since it has taken lots of damage before. The rebel proceeded to stab her in the chest. Darleen gasped and she gave out her last breath.

1ˢᵀ OF SPRING FESTIVAL

*Before you start reading the next
chapter, finish what you're supposed
to do first. Done? Carry on!*

2 1ˢᵗ of April. It's the 1ˢᵗ of spring. Not knowing about the uprising and the fall of Barenge, citizens of Combination were very excited for the day ahead. From one end of King's Road to the other, decorations were put up. Festival banners, flowers, and everything related to spring. The Business District and the Merchant's District contained market stalls temporarily set up just for the festival. The vendors sold different types of flowers, cleaning items, and everything about plants. People strutted about the streets and chatted with one another.

The highlight of the festival would be the street show in the Business District. Sprites and other performers have volunteered to showcase their nature abilities or their love for nature. King Edward, Queen Flyangel, and Prince Jake will be coming to the show.

And that excites everyone even more. Two famous Sprite masters will be performing, Masters Lillain and Mousy. All the more reason to be present for the show.

Newly married couple, Dewi and Aditya, were strolling around the Merchant's District, looking at the beautiful dresses and suits they have for sale.

Captain, Bale, and Oliver were putting up a show specially for the forest animals in Combination Forest. They had invited Master Kitty to be their guest of honour, who will also be showcasing his Ardni skills.

Sir Everos, the Knights, and Bobby, and the king's guards were less tense today. Edward forced them to loosen up. 1st of spring only happens once a year. But they were still patrolling the streets, it's just that they can go shopping or enjoy the show if they want to.

The city has not been this festive in a very long time. Even nature looks more calming and magical.

The forest districts were very busy, animals leaving and entering their homes in the ground and the trees. The leaves swayed gently with the slight wind. The sun shone brightly, sun rays passed through the openings around the branches and leaves, touching the soft green grass. The downside of it all was that the animals couldn't talk in human voices. So only animal noises were heard. The animal show was starting in Combination Forest, Forest District 1. Captain went on stage to welcome the animals. The first performance was by a friendly squirrel named Misha. She brought dead leaves with her. As expected, the audience witnessed her bringing the leaves back to life with her powers. They all clapped as a sign of respect and appreciation. Next was Oliver. He put up an amazing show. All around the clearing, he blossomed flowers from the grass. Some he made grew to be even bigger than humans. They exploded, giving out fragrance everywhere. Everyone was awestruck, they clapped vigorously. Last was Kitty. Taking advantage of the fragrance still in the air, he summoned the wind to blow them around. The magical essence in the air blossomed even more flowers. Controlling the wind further, he made the flowers come out of the ground and floated gracefully in the air. Everyone clapped and cheered incredibly. They were very impressed. For someone who isn't a Sprite but can give such a wonderful performance.

Over at the city square in the Business District, the Sprite show mainly by the humans was about to start. The show host welcomed a performer on stage. A smart-looking young gentleman. He held out his hands and flowers blossomed out of it. He sent them gliding up and back down into some of the audience's hands. Next was a white deer. She formed dirt out of nothing around her body and grew plants and flowers on top of it. Different acts performed and the audience was having a very good time. Then it was time for Masters Lillain and Mousy's performance. Lillain, as usual, loves magic that shouts "dramatic". She made the ground tremble. The trees that were already around the square slowly grew taller. Mousy sent the leaves floating around the square. And Lillain grew more leaves from the naked trees. They may not understand each other now, but they do understand how to show a good performance. Above all, Lillain and Mousy know it would have been better if they could control the other elements and Gratultyn magic. The audience applauded. It was a beautiful closure for the show.

As the two masters headed downstage, a large number of animals stampeded into the square, heading towards the southern districts. Most people and animals did not know what's going on but they just joined them without question. Chairs and other objects went out of place as they pushed one another. Edward, Flyangel, Jake, the two masters, some soldiers, and a few other people were the few people left. But something was definitely not right. Suddenly two soldiers ran into the square in panic.

'Your… majesties!' one said but was out of breath.

'The Outlanders are attacking!' the other helped finish the sentence.

'Soldiers, gather the men. Inform Bobby as well' Edward told the soldiers who were already in the square. The soldiers ran off.

'They must be attacking from the forest districts and SHAW Academy' Flyangel said. Lillain immediately ran off to the direction of the school. Mousy was a little slow to catch, but she ran after her as well. Edward noticed the few civilians left in the square.

'Brave men, I need you to help me evacuate the city. Bring them south' Edward said.

'Bring them to White Woods. We don't want to disturb Silverside again' Flyangel added.

Just then, Dewi and Aditya came looking curious.

'Oh Dewi, we need to evacuate the city immediately. Bring everyone to White Woods' Flyangel said.

'Yes your majesty' Dewi replied. She and Aditya led the civilians away. Edward, Flyangel, and Jake then proceeded to SHAW Academy.

The rebels had swept Forest District 3 and were now pushing inwards towards Forest District 2 (where SHAW Academy is) and Village District 5. It was fortunate that most people were at the festival, so there were very few casualties except of course the animals. It was a school holiday as well so there weren't any students at the academy. Just workaholic masters and teachers who were now bravely defending the school. Ciaran pressed on the attack on the academy and Lydia led the attack on the village. They were getting closer to the Town Park which is the centre point in between the Business District, Merchant's District, Village District 4, and Village District 5. As innocent people scurried away, king's guards and soldiers marched their way up northwest.

Over at the academy, Ciaran had burned down parts of the school. But the masters managed to control the charging rebels holding them stationary. Ciaran sent his deadly man-sized tornadoes all around the school field. Sprites brought up the ground creating a wall between them and the wind. Helazes enlarged fire around them. Ardnis took control of the wind and sent them back. And Winterains added water into the wind creating a waterspout and as they controlled the water, they managed to make the wind follow suit. Different powers were used. No Gratultyn magic. Just people and animals with gifts.

Master Lillain faced off with a rebel. The rebel had a sword and wielded shadow powers. He was very aggressive and impatient. He immediately flashed his way around Lillain. Black and mysterious shadows followed wherever he went. And his speed was super fast. Lillain tried to maintain her focus on him. But he evaded and zigzagged around her. Then he started moving in with the attack. The shadows confused Lillain a lot. He was moving one way but it seems like he moved the other way. But Lillain managed to dodge his strike. He moved around again, now trying to deceive Lillain, his shadows all around, appearing and disappearing. And he occasionally appeared to strike with his sword. Lillain dodged and dodged. But she got hit one time, the sword slashed her skin on her right arm. But it wasn't deep. He attacked again. Lillain just lost it. She exploded in anger. In a ripple effect, soil and rocks left her body trembling the ground in a small radius around her and let out a little bit of electric currents, killing the rebel instantly. The shadows disappeared.

'Such a waste of power' Lillain said.

Master Mousy was handling a rebel riding a beast, a really bad looking bull with snake-like scales as its skin. The rebel has no powers, but the crossbow he's holding was getting really annoying. He kept shooting at her every ten seconds as the beast tried to kill her with its horns and tusks. Indeed, this bull has tusks on both sides of its head. Mousy hopped around onto the bull, back down, away, and back on top, and away. And at every opportunity to do something else, she summoned the soil to pull the beast into the earth.

The royals and some reinforcements arrived. A soldier gave Queen Flyangel a bow and a quiver of arrows, she aimed at the rider and fired. The rider fell backwards and got squashed by the beast trampling everywhere. The king's guards charged and stabbed the beast.

King Edward and Prince Jake took on a group of rebels. Two rebels charged at Jake who blocked and struck them with ease. Two more rebels at the same time charged at Edward. Edward sent two quick shots of water from both his hands, one line froze one rebel, the other sent the rebel flying. Two more rebels wielding powers. One was a Sprite, the other had a forcefield and a protective shield. The Sprite grew tree vines out of her hands and sent them growing towards Edward. While the other sent forcefield at Jake. Jake rolled out of the way and found another coming at him. He didn't make it in time, the forcefield sent him back a few metres. Edward formed a sword out of ice, he cut the continuously growing vines repeatedly. The forcefield rebel turned his focus on Edward. An arrow from Flyangel came at him. But his shield deflected the arrow. He looked across the field. Flyangel was quite far away. Jake rejoined the fight. He sent more forcefields but his focus had to be divided because Flyangel's arrows kept coming. The Sprite extended her vines towards Jake now. She let them out from everywhere, her entire body was now covered in vines. Edward cut his way to her and attempted to strike. But the forcefield rebel shielded her. That distraction helped Jake to finish him off. He struck with his sword, the forcefield rebel died. And Edward struck the vines with his ice sword. The sword miraculously went through smoothly like it was all vines and no body. There wasn't even blood. The vines stop growing, which means the Sprite is dead. But the battle wasn't over.

Lydia's force has made it into Town Park. They faced a greater resistance there, holding them stationary for the time being. Bobby and Sir Everos led their men here. And it wasn't long later that Master Nvago appeared to assist. Lydia has always fought alongside Pertum and it is still the same now. Both of them killed the soldiers coming at them with ease. They were enjoying their time until Nvago challenged them.

'I wonder who you are' Lydia said mockingly.

'Never seen this old man before' Pertum added.

'Less talk during battle children' Nvago replied and disappeared as mist started forming around them. Lydia grinned, loving a challenge at last compared to all the boring soldiers. Nvago appeared behind Pertum.

'Duck!' Lydia exclaimed. Lydia sent a fireball as Pertum ducked. Nvago disappeared.

'Playing games old man' Lydia continued to taunt. But Nvago maintained his calmness. There's no reason to get angry over words with no meaning. Nvago appeared again in between them. They both sent their fire. Nvago disappeared and the fire collided. Lydia exclaimed in anger.

'We need to be more careful' Pertum said, not wanting to get hurt by Lydia's fire if that happens again.

Nvago appeared in between them. Lydia sent her fire. Nvago disappeared and the fire hit Pertum right in the face. He screamed as the fire burned his eyes and tongue and everything else. The pain was so much that he immediately gave up fighting and died. Lydia yelled in anger. The mist was very thick now. Lydia could only hear the fighting everywhere else but it was fading.

'Come out and face me you coward!' Lydia yelled furiously.

'Calm down my dear' Nvago appeared a few steps in front of her. She sent her fireballs at him. He moved so fast it would seem like he has superspeed but it was the mist's manipulation. The fireballs went past and into the mist.

'What powers' Lydia cried in disbelief. But she got angry back again as fast as she was shocked. Nvago went in for the attack. No one had seen Nvago's fighting skills before. Lydia is now the first, and it is truly impressive. It was just arms and legs combat. But Lydia was having a hard time catching up. This old man was faster than her. Punch, blocks, kick, blocks, and other combinations. They continued on until Lydia was too tired to continue. Nvago ended with a kick on her side. She fell down exhausted. The mist cleared up and the sound of the fight came back.

'Stop this attack now' Nvago told her.

Lydia groaned as she tried to move away from him. As a final effort, she surprised him with a fireball which he caught in his hand easily and wiped it out.

'How did you... Who are you?' Lydia asked weakly.

'I am Master Nvago, protector of Trading Village and portals, keeper of travellers, portals, and businesses. I am one of The Fifteen' he said. Lydia stared in shock before fainting from tiredness.

LIZYATI'S RETURN

The whole attack was just a distraction. They have more planned in the future but the rebels only wanted a team to secretly retrieve magical artifacts and a certain prisoner from the castle. But their secret didn't stay a secret. As Master Kitty, Captain, Bale, Oliver, and some other forest animals of Forest District 1 were heading towards the fight scene, they noticed the guards at the castle gates were dead. They went up the castle steps and found more dead guards. The doors were wide open. In the doorway were some more dead guards and servants.

Five rebels came into the dungeons. Two went to the artifact chamber while the rest inspected the cells. Quite a number of men in red coats, one blue coat, and other people. At the end was a cell with a table and a book on top.

'This the one?' one said.

One of them stepped closer to the iron bars. It seems empty.

'Anyone inside?' the same one said.

Lizyati stepped into the light.

'Are you the one whose magic is like no other?' the rebel near the bars said.

'Is there something you want?' Lizyati said mysteriously.

'Help us, kill the king of Combination. Take the city and Ciaran will reward you with a high position' the rebel said.

'Interesting' Lizyati said. 'If you can get me out of this cell'

The rebel wanted to blast the cell doors open.

'No! It's anti-magic' another one said.

'The keys!' the rebel exclaimed. The first rebel handed her the keys. She struggled with the locks.

'I believe it's that one' Lizyati pointed to the key. The rebel unlocked the cell door and Lizyati stepped out breathing in deeply.

'We're not in fresh air yet, lady' the third rebel said. Lizyati gave him a cold stare.

'There's something I need first' she said. 'Where's the objects room?'

'You mean artifacts?' the second rebel said.

'Whatever'

'This way' the first rebel led them to the artifact room. They regrouped with the other two who had found what they're looking for. Majuza's amulet and the cursed bracelet.

'Let's get out of here' the rebel holding the amulet said.

'No, she needs something first' the first rebel said.

Lizyati was scanning the entire room for two objects. She found them within seconds. Two vases side-by-side. She grabbed one first, open the lid, nothing came out, but there was a mix of cold and warm temperatures all of a sudden. She then smashed the vase on the floor. The same thing happened with the other.

'What was that about? Anger?' the rebel with the cursed bracelet said.

Lizyati simply smiled.

(Hiss…)

They turned to see a very fierce cat, Master Kitty, and the others blocking their exit. Before the rebels could react, Lizyati had done something. Kitty was lifted off the ground and was flung into some crates. One by one the animals were flung in random places even though they tried to fight this invisible force.

'That's pretty normal magic to me' the first rebel said. Immediately after that, the two jinn revealed themselves. The rebels jumped in shock at how hideous they look. Hati and Uri then turned their faces into one of them.

'They're impersonators?'

'Shapeshifters?'

'They're much more than that' Lizyati said.

'Why are we trusting her? One of those things pretended to be Marcala' the third rebel said.

'Do you want my help?'

'Yes!' the second rebel said. 'Enough talking guys' But the third rebel was very unsure.

'Let me make it easy' Lizyati said. One of the jinn, Hati, rushed into the third rebel's nostrils, possessing him. But this was no ordinary possession, he began floating and gasping in pain as his insides were torn apart by Hati.

'Stop it!' the amulet holder said. Hati left the third's body. He fell down dead and most of his skin were gone making his bright red flesh visible. Hati rushed into the amulet holder. She dropped the amulet and the same thing happened to her. The bracelet holder immediately placed the bracelet around Lizyati's wrist, hoping that it would stop the magic. But Hati was still active.

'What's this?' Lizyati said, looking at the bracelet like it was nothing. 'Looks nice'

Hati went into the rebel that placed the bracelet. As the rebel died, the bracelet detached from her wrist. Lizyati picked it up and examined it before throwing it aside. There were two rebels left. They stared at Lizyati fearfully.

'Do you want to join your friends?' Lizyati asked sweetly.

One of them sent a fireball at her. The other jinn, Uri, smoke-travelled in front of her, absorbing the fire and stepped aside. Immediately after that, Hati entered the rebel attacker's body and the same thing happened. One rebel left.

'Please, I'll do anything' he begged.

'That's so nice!' Lizyati said cheerfully. 'You'll be my sacrifice'

The rebel stared in horror as Lizyati widened her smile. Hati and Uri both entered him. But they didn't do the same thing to him like Hati did the rest. They just restrained him from movement. Lizyati went to find a sharp object in the chamber and found a shiny black dagger. She approached the rebel, uttered some strange words and stabbed him in the chest. As the blood flowed down his body, he gasped, unable to even scream. After a few seconds, the two jinn exited. Lizyati breathed in deeply and threw the dagger aside.

'*Bebas semula*' she whispered. (Free again).

The jinn disappeared as Lizyati made her way out of the dungeons. However, Master Kitty attempted to stop her again in the main hallway.

(Meow...) Kitty meowed with a deep cat voice. Lizyati turned around. There Kitty stood on all four paws staring at her.

'What happened to your voice?' Lizyati laughed.

Kitty dashed past her. The strong wind almost made Lizyati lose her balance. She turned and Kitty sent strong wind in her direction. Lizyati was flung backwards. But then Kitty started feeling some presence around him. Kitty knew what was coming. He dashed out of the way just as something grabbed the empty space he used to be in. The jinn were coming to get him. He ran past Lizyati and stood behind her now. Lizyati regained herself only to be flung again by Kitty's strong wind. The presence came again. Kitty dashed out of the way as the same thing happened. This time, he didn't run past Lizyati, he used the air to grip Lizyati's neck and began removing all the oxygen around her. She began suffocating. He would have succeeded if it weren't for the jinn. The jinn grabbed him where he stood. One of them entered his body and tore every organ inside him. Kitty cried out in his cat voice as the jinn left and he fell hard onto the floor dead. The air powers stopped and Lizyati regained herself again.

'*Tempat ini sudah dibuka. Uri, pergi bawa keluarga kamu datang. Penuhkan tanah ini dengan keturunanmu*' Lizyati said, stepping into the fresh air. (This placed has been opened. Uri, go and bring your family here. Fill this land with your legion).

'*Apa perlu saya lakukan?*' Hati appeared and asked. (What do you need me do?).

'*Sekarang kita tunggu. Nanti bila dah ramai, baru kita teruskan*' Lizyati replied. (Now we wait. Later when there's many of you, then we'll proceed).

THE ARRIVAL OF
THE DUTCH NATION

*Before you start reading the next
chapter, finish what you're supposed
to do first. Done? Carry on!*

S ir James, a knight of White Woods, has been
assigned to lead the troops at White Shore
outpost. He had enough experience fighting, having
fought in the Battle of Alhora alongside Sir Everos.
But the Dutch was nothing compared to anyone
he's encountered before. Firstly because he doesn't
understand them. And second, he made the mistake
of striking first. At the sight of their ships, they
started firing the artillery they got from the British
ships. Whether the Dutch mistook them for being
radical British or not, it didn't do them any good as
the dutch have guns as well, and they began shooting
and disarming them one by one as they got closer.
There were many casualties and a few deaths. James
made the right choice to surrender. Where are the
SHAWs when we need them, James thought. It was

very unfortunate that none of the soldiers are magic-abled. That made it easy for the Dutch. They were mostly wearing dark blue uniforms and they behaved quite differently than the British.

'*Gegroet, ik ben kapitein Noah van de Koninklijke Marine*' the captain said. (Greetings, I am captain Noah of the Royal Netherlands Navy).

Sir James stared at him without any clue what he's saying.

'*Brits?*' Captain Noah asked further. (British?). James shook his head, unable to handle the confusion. Noah sighed.

'Mai Engliz... not good, not good' Noah continued. '*Spreekt iemand hier Javaans?*'. (Anyone here speaks Javanese?).

'Java? Anyone?' Noah continued asking.

'I absolutely have no idea what you're talking about' James said, getting more annoyed every second.

'*Is dit het achtste continent? Een nieuw land, prachtig!*' Noah said. (Is this the eighth continent? A new land, magnificent!).

'*We gaan niemand pijn doen. We willen gewoon een vreedzame regeling tot stand brengen*' Noah continued. (We are not going to hurt anyone. We just want to set up a peaceful settlement).

'Whatever your name is, I don't understand you not a single bit' James said. But the Dutch were already leaving them alone, they moved west along the coast. Their ships sailed in the same direction.

'What was that about?' James looked at his men with confusion.

'Send a letter to Combination. Mention that they don't speak English' James instructed.

THE RETREAT

*Before you start reading the next
chapter, finish what you're supposed
to do first. Done? Carry on!*

The five rebels tasked to retrieve the artifacts and Lizyati were taking so long. Ciaran believes they failed. He called his forces to retreat. They did accomplish one thing, they had caused lots of damage in the northwest side of the city. But they did something even worse, they unleased a certain evil. The rebels retreated back to Alhora and Barenge.

It was time for the cleanup. Queen Flyangel and Prince Jake supervised Forest District 2 and mainly the academy. King Edward went on to join Master Nvago, Bobby, and Sir Everos in the central districts. In the evening, citizens were already re-entering their homes. Although Village District 5 and Forest District 3 suffered lots of permanent damage, a lot of the people and animals are willing to share their homes temporarily with those who have lost them. The royals returned to the castle to find the servants and some king's guards busy handling the dead bodies and the minor damage done to the castle.

'What happened?' Flyangel asked.

'There has been an attack' Annie was there to report the whole event. Captain, Bale, and Oliver were there to provide her with more information as well. Annie seems to be understanding Captain as he speaks in his chipmunk voice.

'The whole attack in the northwest districts were all distraction' Annie explained.

'Wait, Annie, you understand him?' Edward asked.

'Don't we all? They're speaking as per normal' Annie said.

'No Annie, it has been a few days since any animal can talk'

Annie stared in confusion.

'She has the gift of communicating with animals' Master Nvago said.

'You have magic!' Flyangel cried excitedly and sounding very supportive.

'I have?' Annie cried in amazement.

'That's good!' Flyangel said. 'You can tell me more'

'But the five rebels died. And we lost one prisoner' Annie continued.

'Let me guess, Lizyati' Edward said. Annie nodded.

'And we lost a very important person' Annie continued sounding very sad.

And at that moment Master Mousy's squeak was

very high pitched. They looked up to see a king's guard carrying a motionless Master Kitty in his arms.

'Kitty' Edward murmured in sadness. At that moment, he remembered all the fun memories he had with both masters, Kitty and Mousy. His first favourite master, Master Jackenzie died when he was 8. Now Master Kitty. Master Mousy is all he has left among the people and animals he look up to. Tears rolled down his cheeks. He don't remember when was the last time he had felt this sad.

That very night, a huge farewell was conducted in honour of Master Kitty and the fallen soldiers. People filled The Royal Court, outside, and all the way in both directions of King's Road. They brought lanterns and lit them up as a sign of peace and they sang Sofya's song together. It was magical.

PART 9

THE
BATTLE OF
SOUTHERNERE

MEETING WITH
THE DUTCH

Before you start reading the next
chapter, finish what you're supposed
to do first. Done? Carry on!

Sir James' letter from White Shore Outpost arrived at the castle a few hours before the farewell for Master Kitty and the fallen soldiers commenced. King Edward replied with a letter requesting James to send a scout and a representative to find out where the Dutch are settling and inform them about a meeting Edward is planning. The Dutch settlement is way past the snowy mountains of the Valley of Sorrows and is between White Shore Bay and Cappidop Bay. A few miles away from Flyra's Stand. They named their small camp Diederik. James' scout stayed behind as the representative engaged. If anything happens to the representative, the scout could escape and report what happened. Knowing they don't understand English, the representative immediately held his hands up in the air the moment they noticed him. A rolled up parchment in his right hand.

'Peace! Peace!' the representative shouted.

The soldiers brought him into their camp to meet the captain.

'*Wat is uw bedrijf hier?*' Captain Noah asked. (What is your business here?).

'What is what?'

'Biznez?' Noah said.

'Oh, I want to deliver this letter, a peace meeting with the king' the representative said. Noah took the letter. It was fortunate that Master Nvago is with them now as he is fluent in all languages. Being the keeper of travellers, from young he's been trained to study all languages be it new or old. And because of the meeting he had with the council of The Fifteen, he knows that the only nation left after the British and the pirates are the Dutch. Nvago helped write the letter in King Edward's words.

The letter read "Greetings captain of the Dutch, I am King Edward of Combination and I welcome you to Southernere. I come in peace and hope that we could have a peace meeting in the heart of Combination. Guessing where you might settle your people, there should be ravens in the trees. Write a letter in response to mine, and ask them to deliver it to Combination. I await your reply captain".

Captain Noah looked up at the representative with amusement.

'*Spreekt uw koning Nederlands?*' he said. (Your king

can speak Dutch?). The representative just smiled, having no clue what he's saying.

'*Ik zal de brief schrijven. Laat hem gaan*' Noah said. (I shall write the letter. Let him go). Immediately after that, the soldiers let the representative make his way.

Noah proceeded to write a reply letter and went to look for the ravens. True enough, there are many of them. He was about to ask but the raven already flew down towards him, grabbed the paper and flew back up.

Captain Noah's letter arrived at the castle after the farewell.

'Here is the letter your majesty' one servant passed the paper to Edward. Edward noticed his hand was bleeding a little.

'How did that happen?' he asked. The servant was suddenly very shy.

'You're too kind to notice your majesty. The raven. It's wild'

'There's no such thing as too kind Ferdinand. And perhaps, next time you can wear gloves' Edward suggested, smiling. The servant nodded his head and walked away happily. Edward unrolled the letter which read Dutch. He smiled amusingly and went to find Nvago. Later Nvago translated for him "Greetings King Edward of Combination. I am honoured to be invited to your home for this peace discussion. However, I do not know your location. I shall reach your military base in the morning, and your men will take me to your place. I look forward to meeting you. Captain Noah".

The next day came very fast. By around eleven in the morning, Captain Noah and some of his men, led by James' men arrived at the castle gates. Noah and his men had brought weapons but they were asked to surrender them at the gates for the peace conference. They were led up the castle steps. Noah looked around in awe. The meeting was held in the ballroom. The royal servants had set up a long table in the centre with buffet tables by the sides. But it wasn't for those seated to walk around freely. The servants will be the ones serving the dishes to the table. All according to the agenda Queen Flyangel had planned. It was a very large table. Two chairs can be placed on each of the shorter sides. King Edward and Queen Flyangel sat on one side. Captain Noah and his men sat on one of the longer sides. Master Nvago and the rest of the royal council sat on the other.

'Je bent niet wat ik had verwacht' Noah said, looking at Flyangel, Dewi, and then the rest. They were clueless of what he said and waited for Nvago to translate.

'He's saying that you are not what he expected' Nvago said.

'En ik dacht dat de koning Nederlands kon spreken' (And I thought the king could speak Dutch).

'Nee, praat via mij' Nvago replied. (No, talk through me). Edward looked on curiously at Noah

and Nvago. He was expecting Nvago to translate everything for him but it seems not.

'*Dus, hoeveel talen kun je spreken?*' Noah asked. (So, how many languages can you speak?).

'*Alle*'

(All).

'*Javaans?*'

(Javanese?).

'*Ja*'. ("Yes" in Dutch). '*Kepiye kabarmu dina iki?*'. ("How are you doing today?" in Javanese).

'*Geweldig*' Noah cried in awe. (Marvelous).

'*Hoe dan ook, vertel je koning dat hij een heel mooie stad heeft*' Noah said.

'He's saying to tell you that you have a very beautiful city, your majesty' Nvago translated.

'Tell him thank you' Edward said, smiling at the captain.

'*Zijne majesteit zei dank u*'

(His majesty said thank you).

'*Oké, ik ben klaar om deze vrede discussie te voeren*' Noah said.

'His ready to have this peace discussion, your majesty' Nvago said.

'Great! Firstly, welcome to Southernere' Edward began. At the same time, Nvago translated for the captain.

'*Super goed! Allereerst welkom in Southernere*'

'And welcome to Combination. This city is the capital of Inland'

'*En welkom bij Combinatie. Deze stad is de hoofdstad van het binnenland*'

'Where you are settling is the Outlands but we can set up trade routes and joined festivals to get to know one another'

'*Waar je je vestigt is* the Outlands, *maar we kunnen handelsroutes opzetten en festivals sluiten om elkaar beter te leren kennen*'

'*Dat klinkt haalbaar*' Noah said. (That sounds doable).

Nvago was about to translate when a king's guard pushed the doors wide open, rushing towards Edward and Flyangel.

'Your majesties, forgive me. The rebels are attacking again' the guard said.

'I'm sorry Noah' Edward said and left to assess the situation. The Dutch were left with Nvago and Flyangel trying to entertain them.

THE SECOND ATTACK

*Before you start reading the next
chapter, finish what you're supposed
to do first. Done? Carry on!*

The rebels came in from the same direction. Forest District 3 has been taken over by the rebels. The animals had fled to the centre of the city. Soldiers and king's guards were deployed to defend Forest District 2 and Village District 5. The citizens of the village district and the students of SHAW Academy were evacuated immediately to the southern districts.

'We cannot keep on evacuating the people to White Woods, it's not helping them. We need to make sure the Outlanders can't move forward' Edward told Bobby to spread the word.

Bobby led most of the king's guards and soldiers in Village District 5. King Edward and Sir Everos led some king's guards, knights, and soldiers at the forest district. The SHAW masters joined to defend the school.

This time, Ciaran was leading the attack in the village district. Two king's guards faced him. One struck his sword at him. Ciaran blocked with his sword and counterattacked which the guard blocked. The other guard moved in for the attack. Ciaran blocked and sent a gust of wind. The guard dodged out of the way as the other guard attacked Ciaran. He blocked again, sent another gust of wind. This guard failed to avoid and was flung backwards. The other guard moved in while Ciaran was distracted. But Ciaran blocked his attack. They continued sparring for a few seconds while the other guard regained himself and charged. Ciaran grabbed hold of both of their necks using the air and choked them.

Bobby was fighting with a Helaze rebel. The rebel sent waves of fire at him which he managed to duck or jump every single time. Bobby got close and struck but the rebel pushed the sword back with a high pressure of fire. Bobby's sword was so hot that it started turning reddish-yellow. Bobby pressed on his attacks. The rebel continued on blocking the fire, but Bobby was gaining speed. The rebel ran out of energy and Bobby struck him.

Over at the forest district, the rebels were led by a hot-headed Sprite, Anani. He is very annoying. He kept on moving the ground where he stood. The earth broke apart, moved up, or down. As a result a lot of the trees toppled. Then one Sprite SHAW master faced him. Whenever Anani tries to move the ground up to avoid her, she pulls it back down. When he moves the ground down, she jumps down to join him. And when he breaks the ground apart, she jumps across or joins it back. Then they fought in hand combat. Occasionally, Anani pulls the roots from trees to wrap around the master's legs. But the master got free within seconds and blocked his attacks.

Edward faced three rebels. Two with magic, one without. The two are a Winterain and electric powers. The electric rebel zapped at Edward who dodged out of the way. But the sword rebel managed to strike him in the leg. A little cut. Edward froze the sword rebel in his place with water turned into ice. The winterain attempted to free her friend but Edward created an ice wall separating the sword rebel from them. The electric rebel continued zapping. This time, Edward covered him in water and the massive amount of currents got him electrocuted even though it was his own. The winterain faced off with Edward in a water combat. Edward and the rebel sent and blocked using water. They went back and forth until suddenly a horn was blown from Forest District 3. The rebels retreated. The ground trembled and a giant earth wall came up separating Forest District 3 from the rest of the city.

'What was that about?' Master Lillain asked. She had been fighting in Forest District 2 as well.

'I have no idea' Edward replied.

'Perhaps they are taking a break. Highly unlikely they're retreating' one SHAW master said.

'Agreed, we need men here at all times' Edward said.

MASTER NVAGO'S QUEST

*Before you start reading the next
chapter, finish what you're supposed
to do first. Done? Carry on!*

The Dutch weren't happy at all. Queen Flyangel and Master Nvago's attempt to entertain them failed. They even showed their powers, but that somehow angered Captain Noah even more.

'Het is heel duidelijk dat je in oorlog bent. Hoe kunnen we je vertrouwen voor vrede?' Noah said in frustration. (It is very clear that you are at war. How can we trust you for peace?).

'Now now, *kalmeer* Noah, *we hebben er niet voor gekozen om deze oorlog te voeren. Er zal vrede zijn'* Nvago replied. (Calm down Noah, we didn't choose to have this war. There will be peace).

Noah went silent for a while.

'Ik ga weg' he said. (I am leaving). He and his men left.

The horn was blown and the battle stopped for

the time being. Edward came back to the castle and found out about the failed meeting.

'Matters are getting worse everyday' Edward muttered.

'We'll get through this' Flyangel said and gave him a hug to calm him down.

They were all gathered in the castle library with Master Nvago, Masters Lillain, Mousy, Bobby, Sir Everos, Dewi, Annie, and some other servants.

'Are your men positioned Bobby?' Edward asked.

'Yes sire, both in Village District 5 and Forest District 2'

'Your men, Everos?'

'Same as the king's guards, your majesty'

'The SHAW masters are positioned as well' Lillain said.

'I may have a solution' Nvago said. All eyes turned to the old master.

'I have not been able to return to Gratultyn. And I strongly believe now, something bad has happened. Southernere has been sealed from the presence of Gratultyn magic. And because of that, common magic has also been sealed. But there's a way for me to open a new portal. It requires a very strong magic and a very strong conductor. If we succeed, I can find out what's happening and get help'

'Is it in the Valley of Sorrows?' Flyangel asked.

'No, it's in the Marina Islands' Nvago replied.

'I thought there's nothing there' Everos said.

(Squeak...) Mousy squeaked. Whatever she meant

to say, nobody knows except Annie who repeated her words.

'Master Mousy said she read about it before'

'I've read every book in this library, I've never come across the Marina Islands' Edward said.

(Squeak…)

'The book is in Trisnarim Palace' Annie repeated what Mousy said.

'It's a wand. The first wand ever created. Ancient Sages created the wand with one purpose. If Gratultyn is in danger, people in the realm of reality can find the wand and save Gratultyn from destruction. As time went by, the artifact became a legend. And the books containing the information became fiction. If the information I received from the Sage's Library is still relevant, it should be in the Marina Islands'

'How many men do you need?' Edward asked.

'Not men, but specific people'

'Oh, I was expecting you to say you don't need men, as you always travel alone' Flyangel joked.

'I'm afraid this time, I can't be going alone' Nvago said in a very serious and low tone. It almost sounded devastating.

'Among the information I read, the sage master that placed the wand here set some conditions in order to retrieve the wand. Each of the four elements are needed and a drop of royal blood'

Royal blood, they looked at Edward and Flyangel. But Flyangel knows it doesn't mean her at all. She was not royal, her mother was only the half sister of

King Henry, Edward's father. If anyone should have pure royal blood, that would be Edward.

'We can't go now. Given the current situation' Edward protested.

'Eddie, you need to go' Flyangel pulled him aside for a private discussion.

'I can't leave you! And you're pregnant, you can't fight' Edward argued, but he toned his voice down to a whisper.

'Edward, I'm more than capable of taking care of myself. This is more important. Without this, we'll stay the same way with the Outlanders, and the newcomers, and every other problem. And we still don't know where is Lizyati, that is another very big problem'

'I'm afraid if anything happens to you' Edward pulled her for a hug.

'Complete this mission, and you'll see me again' Flyangel pulled her head back and gave him a tender kiss.

They both rejoined the conversation.

'I'll go and also represent Winterain for water' Edward said.

'Count me in for Sprite' Lillain raised her hand.

'No, I need you here. I have someone in mind who is a Sprite' Edward said, thinking of Oliver.

'We still need air and fire' Nvago said.

'And we need the stronger ones, the more experienced ones to stay and guard the city' Edward said. 'Any good students you have who would like to volunteer?' he asked Lillain.

'As a matter of fact I do, Baron, a Helaze, but his mother will give consent if the best friend comes along. But the Ardni twins, there's no chance' Lillain said.

'How about one SHAW master, I believe it would be alright to take just one SHAW master from the school, your majesty' Nvago said.

'Who?' Edward asked.

'Master Alya is an Ardni, but she rarely talks' Lillain said.

'Everos and Annie will come with us. Send a letter to White Shore, tell James to replace your position while you're gone. Queen Flyangel will be your sole in charge while I'm away. Fight well everyone, for the good of Southernere' Edward said and dismissed the informal meeting.

Edward went around informing some of them to prepare quickly for the mission.

'Lillain, help prepare your students, light travel only'

'Annie, pack some food, light travel'

'Everos, two swords and a crossbow would do'

It wasn't long later that the group assembled. A horse carriage with two horses at the front and two other separate horses belonging to Edward and Bobby were waiting at the castle roundabout. Edward will be riding his horse. Nvago will be riding Bobby's.

Everos will be the coachman. And the rest will be sitting in the carriage. They all had their adventure gear on. Edward wore a simple button up shirt with a vest and black pants. Nvago wore the same with a different colour. Everos had his armour off and was wearing the same as Edward. All the boys wore the same thing but with different colours and sizes. Oliver has his cat fur on as per normal. And Annie and Master Alya wore their outdoor dress with a simple headscarf. They bade goodbye and galloped away.

THE FIGHT GOES ON

*Before you start reading the next
chapter, finish what you're supposed
to do first. Done? Carry on!*

The earth wall came down. The rebels started attacking again, pushing towards Forest District 2 and Village District 5, now stronger and more aggressive than before. The students at the academy and the civilians in the village had to be evacuated as the defenses could no longer prevent the rebels from entering the districts. Powers were thrown and swords were swung everywhere.

Queen Flyangel was rushing towards Forest District 2 but Bobby and everyone else were telling her otherwise.

'Your majesty, King Edward wouldn't want you to be fighting right now' Bobby said.

'Edward isn't here Bobby' Flyangel snapped. That ended the whole conversation. Flyangel had her bow and arrow ready. As they reached the battle scene, Bobby charged in with his men and Flyangel drew her arrow and fired at every rebel in sight. Those that came up close, she hit them with her bow or used her powers to freeze them in place. But she soon encountered a challenge with Ciaran and another rebel. Everyone else was very occupied to notice that Flyangel needed help.

'The queen' Ciaran said. 'The one who destroyed the successor. What an honour to kill her'

The other rebel charged at her recklessly and Flyangel swiftly caused an arrow to pierce through him. Now the numbers were fair. Ciaran immediately blew a powerful gust of wind in her direction. Flyangel almost tried to control the air but fortunately remembered that Gratultyn magic doesn't work anymore. She dodged out of the way but found another wind coming at her. She got thrown backwards and her bow fell out of her hand. Fortunately it wasn't bad. As she was getting back up, Ciaran stood in her line of sight. She touched the grass, turning it into ice. The ice spread in Ciaran's direction. Ciaran stepped back slowly at first. But the ice gain speed according to his movements. Ciaran turned around to run. A big mistake. Flyangel took the opportunity and went for her bow lying a few steps away. She drew her arrow and released. The arrow went straight through Ciaran's left shoulder. He exclaimed in pain. The ice caught up to his shoes and went up his body, freezing the outer layer of his skin. The arrow got stuck in the ice as well as it moved up and stopped at his neck, leaving the head vulnerable. Flyangel headed towards him, intending to talk. Along the way, some rebels tried to stop her. Flyangel froze them completely, threw them back with a violent flow of water, and knocked out the rebel that tried to melt the ice with a swing of her bow.

'It's cold!' Ciaran exclaimed painfully. He couldn't bear it anymore. The ice was working on freezing his skin tissues.

'Maybe if you cooperate with me, I'll let you go' Flyangel offered a solution. But Ciaran's hateful eyes explain his opinion.

'Seeing how they treat you, I say you're the leader. Where's Alphaga?'

'Gone' Ciaran replied simply.

'What are you doing here?'

'What we have always been doing. We're avengers, we avenge Majuza'

'That stopped a few weeks ago. You are all nothing but rebels'

Ciaran blew cold icy wind from his mouth into Flyangel's face. The cold didn't bother her. It was nothing compared to what she is capable of.

'Leave and never return' Flyangel said.

'You know my answer to that'

Ciaran was shivering very badly.

'You're not helping yourself' Flyangel said.

'I don't need to'

Another rebel had creeped up to Flyangel from behind and swung her sword. Flyangel sensed it at the last moment, she nearly got hit. She ducked and the sword hit the ice instead. Flyangel turned and pushed the rebel. The rebel fell backwards and quickly got back up. Flyangel had already drawn her arrow and aimed directly at the rebel's head.

'Go on' the rebel dared her. But behind Flyangel, Ciaran was already taking advantage of the crack the sword made to the ice. He called on the surrounding air to blow across the surface of the ice. Taking advantage of the sun as well, the melting process took a much shorter time.

'Step back' Flyangel told the rebel. She stepped back, keeping Flyangel's attention on her while Ciaran melted the ice. Just then, Bobby came running and saw what was happening.

'Flyra!' he managed to say. The ice broke into a thousand pieces spreading in a short radius around. Bobby jumped in between Ciaran and the queen. The small ice pieces cut him in many different parts. At the same time, the shock made Flyangel release her arrow into the rebel's eye. She turned around to find Ciaran still shivering but free and Bobby lying on the ground, gasping in pain. Sharp ice pieces did not manage to hit the parts of his body that were covered in armour. But it did a lot of damage to some vital areas like the face.

'Bobby!' Flyangel cried, falling to her knees. She had blocked her focus from the surroundings and didn't realise Ciaran had escaped. She held Bobby in her arms. His face was bleeding from the ice pieces cutting his cheeks, forehead, and one was very close to the eye.

'I can fix this' Flyangel said.

'No' Bobby said weakly. There's no magic Flyangel can do that will fix his face.

'Let me just…' Flyangel said and proceeded to melt the ice pieces. Seconds later, all that's left were cuts on his face.

'It'll only be a while. You're strong' Flyangel cried, tears rolled down her cheeks.

'My queen, I'm old. It's time for me to go. Please say to Edward for me that I love him like he is my own son' Bobby said weakly. To move his mouth means to move his cheeks as well and the pain was a lot.

'You can tell him yourself, there's still time' Flyangel stubbornly said and pulled Bobby up with her. Reinforcements had just arrived and she asked two of the soldiers to bring Bobby back to the castle. Her attention went back to the fight and noticed that Ciaran was nowhere to be seen.

THE GLOSEDAURS

Before you start reading the next
chapter, finish what you're supposed
to do first. Done? Carry on!

A 2 hour journey can be made into half an hour or less when Master Nvago uses his powers. Misty teleportation and manipulation. They stopped somewhere in the woods, in the far south of Southernere. They abandoned their carriage and brought the horses along as they continued their journey on foot through the narrow pathway.

'A few hundred metres more, can be less, to the coastal town' Nvago said.

'How do you know there's a town here? There's nothing recorded on the map' Annie said.

'The map was last updated before Edward's grandfather was born. And besides, I frequently travel the world. I know places'

'Are we still in the Inlands or the Outlands?' Cardinal asked.

'There's no Inland or Outlands in the south my

child' Nvago replied. 'People rarely come here because of the unpredictable weather'

They looked around. True enough, there were dark clouds forming further south, but it was very bright where they're standing. The air was very cold. Fortunately Annie had brought extra cloaks, scarves, and gloves.

'Stay close' Nvago said. He was about to use his powers again. Mist circled around their group. It was important that they could see each other, which means they can teleport as a group. If they can't see each other, they might separate ways. A few seconds later, the mist disappeared and they were at the entrance of a small coastal town. Very few people were walking, covering themselves in at least 3 layers of clothing. They entered the town. No one seems to care about their presence.

'Leave the horses in the stable there' Nvago said, pointing to a small stable with a skinny young man standing in front, most likely the stable boy.

'Don't we need to pay?' King Edward asked.

'This town doesn't care about money' Nvago said. 'Now we need boats'

The docks were very small compared to the ones in White Shore. There were only 3 rowing boats that could fit 2 people each.

'That's not very safe-looking' Baron said.

'Agreed. That won't help us against what's out there' Nvago said.

'What's out there?' Sir Everos asked.

'You'll see'

'You don't think we need to prepare or anything for what's out there?' Edward said, repeating "what's out there" in the same tone as Nvago and Everos.

'We have wielders from each element. That should be enough to prepare' Nvago sounded very positive. He was looking around the docks for anyone.

'Wait here' he said suddenly and left.

He came back a few minutes later with a short old man.

'I found someone with a boat' Nvago said cheerfully. The old man led them away from the docks to a small building built into the water.

'What's the name of this town?' Edward asked.

'It doesn't have a name. I think. Well I never bothered to ask' Nvago said.

Inside the building was a single dock and a boat with a single sail. It was big enough to fit all 8 of them. Much better than rowing boats.

'Much better' Nvago said and thanked the man. He left the building without asking for anything in return.

'I like the people here' Baron said.

'They are far from civilization I'm afraid' Everos said.

'Let the boy have his opinions, Everos' Edward said softly.

'I agree with Baron' Nvago said. 'Alright everyone, get on board. Let's find this wand'

They boarded the boat and Nvago sailed it out through the opening and away from the land.

'Master Nvago, why do you not just use your powers to teleport us straight to the wand?' Cardinal asked.

'My powers don't work that way. No teleportation powers do. Teleportation takes effort from all your cells to appear on a different plane of existence and travel quickly and reappear in the main plane'

'That sounds painful' Baron said, making a frightful face.

'I'm used to it. But travelling straight to the wand would probably kill me, given my age'

'I understand' Cardinal said.

'Hey Cardinal, magic duel?' Baron suggested. The two boys grinned at each other.

Baron conjured fire on both of his hands. Cardinal conjured water in between his fingers.

'Same thing all the time' Baron said.

'You as well!' Cardinal laughed. Whenever they duel, they always start the same way. Baron sent fireballs at Cardinal. He wiped them out with the water and sent a wave of water towards him. Baron rolled out of the way, almost crashing into Oliver at the side of the boat. He got up quickly and sent a wave of fire. Cardinal jumped out of the way, the fire went past and disappeared.

'Your skills are impressive for rank five' Edward said, absolutely impressed.

'Thank you, your majesty' Cardinal and Baron said together.

'I wish Gratultyn magic was still here. I was getting good at it' Cardinal said proudly.

'You are?'

'Me too!' Baron cried excitedly.

'Alright everyone, I'm going to move us further, but stay alert, we're entering dangerous water' Nvago said.

Mist appeared again surrounding their boat. During that time, the water was calm. A few seconds later the mist disappeared again but the view seemed to be the same, except for a very dark sky. They were in the middle of nowhere in the Marina Straits with no land in sight. The waves were very aggressive. Water splashed onto the boat.

'Stay alert!' Nvago exclaimed.

It wasn't long until a threat came onto their boat. A dolphin-like creature with a seahorse's head and tail and lobster legs at the bottom jumped out of the ocean and landed on the deck. It's whole body was glowing bright blue.

'What is that!' Baron cried, staring in horror.

Mist surrounded the creature and threw it back into the water.

'That's a glosedaur. A creature that loves meat' Nvago said. 'If they get to you, they will start sucking your flesh through their small mouth holes'

Another jumped out of the water. Nvago did the same thing to it. The mist surrounded them and sent them back further away. More jumped. Some climbed the sides of the boat.

'Annie, get the children inside!' Edward exclaimed. Annie brought Cardinal and Baron into the small cabin behind the wheel.

'We can fight!' Cardinal said. But Annie wasn't about to agree to that idea given the current situation.

Everos drew his sword and cut one glosedaur in half.

'They're amazingly easy to kill' Everos said.

'Don't get too confident' Edward replied.

Edward shoved massive amounts of water into the glosedaurs, throwing them back into the ocean. Oliver couldn't find time to conjure soil or dirt, so he jumped on the glosedaurs and started scratching their bodies with his sharp claws. They made noises mixed between a dolphin, a whistle, and a clicking sound as they screamed. Master Alya sent the wind in multiple directions, throwing the glosedaurs overboard. A glosedaur broke into the cabin from the back of the boat. As Annie screamed in shock, Cardinal and Baron teamed up against it. Baron sent a continuous line of fire at it, burning it alive. The glosedaur screamed in pain as it charged to attack its attacker. Cardinal summoned the water from the ocean, grabbed the glosedaur's tail and pulled it back out of the cabin. Some glosedaurs surrounded Nvago. Nvago spun the wheel. The boat took a sudden turn, everyone slipped and fell to the side. The glosedaurs fell as well and slid towards them. Edward and Everos sliced some of them. Oliver jumped on top of one and made it bleed. Alya blew them away with the wind. Nvago disappeared and appeared, also sending his mist to suffocate the glosedaurs or carry them away.

'Hold on!' he cried. Mist surrounded their boat. Edward and Everos killed the remaining glosedaurs and threw them out of the boat as the water became calm. The mist disappeared. The sky was brighter now and in the distance, they could see 2 islands about a few kilometres apart. The light from the sun made the mess of the attack clearer. Everyone was in a mess. Those outside the cabin especially were covered in glosedaur blood. The whole boat was covered in it. Glowing blue liquid. Annie, Cardinal, and Baron stepped out of the cabin.

'I'm guessing the blood is the reason they're glowing' Baron commented.

(Meow...) Oliver meowed.

'He's saying why can't we just take another route to the island' Annie translated.

'Because that would take days. The glosedaur territory is massive. To go around it is to waste time' Nvago replied.

'This thing is sticky' Everos said, reacting in disgust to the blue stains on his clothes.

'The sooner we get to shore, the sooner we can clean ourselves' Nvago said.

'Which island?' Edward asked.

'Tiny Island' Nvago replied. They sailed towards the smaller island on the right.

LAND OF THE JINN

*Before you start reading the next
chapter, finish what you're supposed
to do first. Done? Carry on!*

The rebels had stopped their attacks again, separating themselves from the rest of the city with a tall earth wall. They did not manage to conquer Forest District 2 but Village District 5 had fallen into their hands, part of it.

'We need to stop them before more innocent lives are taken' Queen Flyangel spoke to the members of the council. Aside from King Edward and Sir Everos, Bobby wasn't there as he was recovering from his injury. Only Flyangel, Prince Jake, Masters Lillain and Mousy, Dewi, and Flyangel's handmaiden, Laura, were present.

'Fighting is the only thing they want. We can't give them that' Lillain said.

'Perhaps there is another thing we can give them' Flyangel said.

(Squeak…) Mousy squeaked. But sadly no one understands her.

'They attacked the castle the other day, perhaps they want the artifacts' Laura said.

'That's definitely right' Flyangel agreed.

(Squeak…) Mousy squeaked in a very high pitch, like she's saying "that's what I said!".

'I won't be long' Flyangel said.

She approached Sir James who had just arrived from White Shore Outpost a few minutes ago.

'James, take me back to the castle' she told him.

James and three king's guards who were Flyangel's personal guards for that shift, escorted her back to the castle. She proceeded to the artifact chamber in the dungeons. Majuza's amulet and the cursed bracelet were now kept even more securely, locked in a large chest. Flyangel has the key in her dress pocket. She took them out and proceeded back to Forest District 2. As if on cue, the moment Flyangel reached the rest of the council, the earth wall came down and the avengers were all standing in attack position, lining the edge of the district. However, there's no sign of Ciaran anywhere. But before anyone could start hurting anyone, a warm and cool breeze blew throughout the area. Everyone felt a scary cold presence. Some people even started shivering. It was very quiet here that they could hear in the village district, a battle had started. Suddenly, someone came from the trees, attracting everyone's attention. It was Lizyati looking at everyone with her death stare.

'Somebody catch her now' Flyangel said without taking her worried eyes away from Lizyati.

'I'll get my father' Dewi replied, running off.

Lizyati somehow got almost everyone captivated. The few left were worrying if anyone was gonna start attacking. This is probably the work of her jinn.

'Everyone, today we enter a new era. This land was incomplete, and now I complete it' Lizyati said out loud. And immediately afterwards, most of the people there, from both sides, were suddenly possessed. They started attacking one another, regardless of which side they're on. Lizyati laughed, enjoying the chaos outbreaking. She walked on the field towards anyone who didn't seem to be affected.

'Hmm, you have a strong mind, the jinn can't enter you' she said to a rebel.

'It's painful!' he cried. Lizyati carefully took his sword away from him, uttered some words, and pushed the sword deep into his chest.

Across the field, Flyangel was going around trying to help those who couldn't move and stop those fighting one another.

'That's not what you're supposed to be doing my queen' Lizyati said. Flyangel turned around in shock. Lizyati was suddenly standing there smiling.

'Stop this' Flyangel said.

Bunuh dia' Lizyati said with determination. (Kill her) Lizyati told her jinn. Flyangel didn't understand that, but she knew something not good was going to happen. She didn't know what else to do. She knew either Hati or Uri was going to come and kill her. The jinn entered her body, attempting to rip everything apart. Flyangel started screaming, dropping the cursed bracelet onto the grass. Immediately, the amulet in her other hand glowed and she started feeling relieved as the jinn rushed out of her body. Smoke exited her nostrils along with a cold shriek. Flyangel felt her insides healing from the pain and she looked at the amulet. Majuza's amulet, it's deep magic awoken by the successor, Princess Erieka, during the battle of Alhora. Now, it's magic is available for anyone. It wasn't working earlier due to the cursed bracelet being held in her other hand. The cursed bracelet's purpose was to block all magic from the user. She inserted her hands under her headscarf to put the amulet around her neck. Lizyati stared in disbelief, understanding what this meant. All of a sudden, everyone who was possessed turned their attention towards Flyangel.

'If the jinn can't hurt you, everyone else will' Lizyati said. 'And by midnight tonight, the whole entire land will be home for my people'

Cold wind blew everywhere and all the possessed started making their way towards Flyangel, killing anyone who tried to stop them. Flyangel released her water and ice powers. But it wasn't enough. She felt a greater power within. She knew that magic isn't gonna work but there's no harm trying. She sent a massive forcefield in the direction of her men. It works! The forcefield sent them far behind. This amulet has Gratultyn magic, Flyangel thought. The rebels were also very close. She sent another forcefield which sent them back the same way. Lizyati didn't take any more steps towards her, she knew she'd be defeated easily. Instead she focused on other people who were not affected by the jinn and let the possessed get to Flyangel. Uri had successfully returned with jinn from anywhere, a huge number of them, that is how Lizyati could possess many people at once. And according to her, there should be more since she mentioned by midnight, the whole land will be filled with her people, the jinn.

Flyangel looked around the field for anyone who was normal. Master Mousy was in one area fighting a few soldiers. Four king's guards and a SHAW master had gotten close enough to Flyangel for a melee attack. The king's guards impressively moved forward with their swords as the master conjured water. Flyangel ducked and dodged and pushed two of the king's guards with a forcefield. The master sent the water towards her. But a shield appeared in a spherical motion, preventing the water from getting close at all. So it's just like the seed of Gratultyn, automatically immune to magic attacks, or in this case additionally, jinn attacks. Damn, Majuza must have been very powerful to be able to create this magical object, Flyangel thought. She made her way towards Mousy, grabbed her, and ran away from the district. Flyangel's disappearance doesn't mean the possessed get back to hurting each other. They started chasing Flyangel as she ran. When looking towards them, it would seem like zombies were chasing her. A few of the possessed got close and Mousy softened the soil or road where they stood and they sank underground very quickly.

'Hold on Mousy!' Flyangel cried. Almost every part of her body was already in pain.

'Build a wall Mousy!' Flyangel cried as they neared the castle.

Mousy did exactly that. An earth wall came up, cutting the top length of King's Road, separating the possessed from the castle and Business District. Just as they thought they were safe, more horror was discovered. It wasn't just the field around the academy. It was everywhere. The Business District was filled with possessed citizens, soldiers, and king's guards killing one another. Those who were not possessed were sadly involved in the violence as well.

'We need to get out of here' Flyangel said and ran past the castle gates, ignoring the guards who were fighting with one another. She ran around the castle through the East Garden, past the main pond, cutting through the castle field. Combination Woods was just ahead. She glanced to the left at the Main Garden, a few servants were hitting each other with brooms and trays. She didn't stop. Up ahead, she noticed some animals were calling for her to come quickly. Suddenly, one of the royal gardeners stepped out from behind some shrubs and stood in her way. She stopped, feeling very bad to do this. She knows him, a dear friend, Joe is his name. But he raised his shovel like he was going to come and attack her. She had to. So she sent a forcefield to his side, throwing him into the north pond. She started running again and entered Forest District 1.

TINY ISLAND

Before you start reading the next
chapter, finish what you're supposed
to do first. Done? Carry on!

The Marina Islands, there are 2 islands in the south. Separated from the mainland by the Marina Straits. If you are facing the south, the bigger island, Marina Island, is on the left, and Tiny Island is on the right. Both islands have their own unique nature. Marina Island is filled with snow-capped mountains and beautiful green trees with leaves that repel anything but green and they are not seen in any other places. There is a small town somewhere within the trees. Tiny Island has one huge volcano in its centre surrounded by rainforest. Generally, this island isn't known to have any visitors over the years, so whatever lives here or the things you might find is a mystery. Only one thing is known, the first wand should be somewhere on this island. And their best guide to its location is Master Nvago.

'So, how do we get to the wand?' Sir Everos asked. They had just finished washing away some of the blue stains on their cloaks and placed them on the beach to dry. They were in the first layer of clothing they had worn since they left Combination. If they were still in the mainland or the ocean, they would start shivering. But the island gives off natural heat that helps keep them warm.

'It's underneath the volcano' Nvago said, pointing to the volcano.

'That sounds dangerous' Cardinal said.

'Very' Baron added.

'Don't worry, the volcano has been dormant for a very long time' Nvago said.

'That's a relief' Annie said.

(Meow...)

'However I'm not sure from which direction we should be going' Nvago said.

'That's alright, we can go in from here. See where it leads us' King Edward said, pointing to the trees in front of them.

'The trees look different' Cardinal said.

'This is a rainforest. And it's not a natural climate to have in this part of the world. The whole island exists by magic. Stay close, I don't know what's in there. And make sure we have lots of water, dehydration is your worst nightmare in there'

'I can conjure water if we need' Edward assured.

'Me too' Cardinal said.

'Let's go then'

Nvago led the group into the trees, going over a thick root in the ground and stepping on some huge leaves in the process. After about a few minutes in, something happened.

'Ah! What is that!' Baron shouted. They all turned to look at him trying to get something off his back. He turned around hoping to show them so they could help. It was a huge spider with a red body and eight hairy yellow legs. Nvago swiped his hand in its direction. Mist kicked the spider away into the giant leaves on the ground.

'What was that?!' Baron asked. He looked at his best friend's disgusted face and he wished he hadn't asked.

'It was a spider. A rare one actually. Very beautiful. Completely harmless, if you're not moving' Nvago said, sounding way too calm.

'That's horrifying!' Annie exclaimed.

'Now we best be quiet, I believe the spider is only a little of what's around here' Nvago said.

They immediately kept quiet and continued walking.

'These branches are too thick' Nvago said a few minutes later. Their leafy path was blocked by thick branches and leaves dangling from surrounding trees.

'Give me your sword'

Everos passed him his. Nvago swung the sword on the branches, breaking them, and cutting the leaves. Suddenly, there was a very loud clicking noise in the distance which made them all stay completely silent.

'I don't like this at all' Baron whispered.

The clicking noise came again, but softer than

before. After a few more minutes of silence, Nvago got to work again.

'Whatever that is, I don't want to come face to face with it' Baron said and Cardinal nodded his head in agreement.

'But I wish our friends would have been here, I would like to see the look on their faces' Cardinal said. And they both laughed. Everos immediately shushed them.

(Hiss…) Oliver hissed at something. They all looked down, a cluster of small black spiders were crawling towards Oliver.

'Not again!' Baron exclaimed.

'Burn them' Nvago said.

'What?'

'Burn them!'

Baron let out his fire towards the spiders. Their tiny bodies popped with black liquid or blood. The ones still in the leaves fled deep inside. The fire spread to the other leaves.

'Water' Nvago said.

Edward swiped his hand, a wave of water splashed on all the fire, wiping them out all at once.

'Why can't we just burn the entire forest?' Baron asked.

'No. Like I said before, this island exists by magic. Killing it, far away the chance it will be for us to obtain the wand' Nvago replied.

They continued their journey which brought them

up a hill. The base of the volcano was now quite visible among the trees in the distance.

'Once we reach the base of the volcano, there should be a cave entrance, watch out for that'

'It's getting hotter' Cardinal said. 'Is there still water?'

Annie took out a bottle from her backpack. The bottle was still half full.

They were about to make their way down when the trees from their side started moving vigorously. Some of the trees toppled and there were sounds of branches breaking. Suddenly, a huge lizard, the size of three boats, came out from the trees. It stuck out its tongue repeatedly and made the clicking noise, making its way up the hill towards them.

'Oh my so that is what we heard just now. That thing is hideous!' Baron exclaimed, stepping back.

'We need to use our weapons for this creature' Nvago said. 'Give me the crossbow'

Everos handed Nvago the crossbow and Nvago gave him back the sword. He and Edward went closer to the lizard with their swords in hand.

'Oliver and Alya, distract it with your element powers' Nvago ordered. 'The three of you, I need you to look out for anything that might come in this direction. Anything. Preferably a hissing sound'

'Wait, there's more?!' Baron said.

'Just do it child'

Oliver moved the leaves in one area, successfully attracting the lizard's attention. Alya sent some of the leaves flying into the air. As the lizard looked up curiously, Nvago aimed the crossbow and fired. It turned its attention to where the arrow came from. But Nvago was not there. Mist started feeling the area. Oliver searched through the dense foliage for the ground where the lizard stood. He obtained control of it and started making the roots underneath jump out and tie themselves around the lizard's feet, and dragged them back down. Alya controlled the wind to blow the lizard down as well. Edward and Everos worked on striking its feet and body. The lizard clicked. Up close, the sound was super loud, if anyone placed their ear to it, they could hurt their eardrums and also suffer a bad headache. Nvago appeared elsewhere and shot another arrow. Although it didn't do any damage, it did annoy the lizard.

Over on the other side, something else was making its way through the trees.

'Um, Master Nvago! Something is coming here!' Baron said as loud as possible for Nvago to hear.

'Step away from the hill' Nvago said, suddenly appearing in front of them. The three of them moved down the other side of the hill. The trees moved apart as another giant creature, much larger than the lizard, came out of it. Annie, Cardinal, and Baron stared in horror. It was a very large snake with fern green scales and black spots in random parts. It raised its head, surveying the ground. Its 2 huge curved pointy white teeth came into view as it hissed at the fight that was happening.

'Let the lizard go!' Nvago exclaimed. Everyone stopped what they're doing and ran as far away from the scene as possible. The lizard was no longer interested in them, it was more interested in saving its life. It turned around and crawled quickly back into the trees where it came from. The snake was very delighted to see its meal. It slithered into the trees, chasing after the lizard.

'What other creatures are out there?!' Baron exclaimed.

'I have no idea' Nvago replied. He wasn't lying. Not everything he has the answer to.

'Let's go'

They proceeded towards the base of the volcano, hoping to find an opening to a cave or something on this side. And there was an opening, a hole in the rocks, partially blocked by plants and vines from the trees. They entered with caution.

FALL OF SOUTHERNERE

*Before you start reading the next
chapter, finish what you're supposed
to do first. Done? Carry on!*

There was chaos everywhere. Combination, White Shore Outpost, White Woods (outside the hidden city), Silverside, Arstar, Trisnarim, the new Dutch town (Diederik), Flyra's Stand, and every other city and town in the mainland of Southernere were all affected by the black magic of the witch, Lizyati. She had gotten help from her two friends, the jinn, Hati and Uri, who had brought more jinn from their old home. And with Lizyati's knowledge in black magic, she had made herself the master of the two jinn and gotten herself quite an army.

The whole of Combination has fallen, most of the jinn were here and possessing everyone who has a weak mind to turn them against one another.

White Shore Outpost has fallen, the soldiers who were clueless of what's going on fled into the woods.

White Woods was still strong, being hidden by the magical barrier, the knights and everyone else had no idea what was happening outside. The camping area, the tents they have outside for the people who evacuated from Combination were in chaos. Even families were turning on one another.

The new rebel base in the fallen Barenge and Flyra's Stand were no different. Those who were not affected fled into the woods or to the Valley of Sorrows.

Silverside suffered the same fate. King Harold was still very sick, the moment the jinn entered his body, it killed him. Princes John and James, and their soldiers and archers were left trying to defend their home against the possessed, including their sister, Princess Jane, who was sadly affected. The princess screamed as she tried to fight the jinn inside from time to time. But when she lost control, she charged at her brothers with a sword in hand. John and James could only block her attacks as they didn't want to hurt her. Within an hour, the whole of Silverside has fallen. Jane had killed one of her brothers. No one could confirm who was the one who died and who was the one who fled out of the city walls and into the forest. There were also other survivors who fled into the forest in many directions.

Arstar managed to control the possessed for quite some time. There weren't that many jinn that came to the northwest part of Southernere. But what's happening involves trust issues and betrayals. From the moment everything went wrong, Arstar fell in a much shorter time than Silverside. King David was killed in the process and Arstar was completely ruined having no royal blood at all for a chance to reclaim the city.

Trisnarim did well, to be the only city left that the leader, Queen Lady Lith, still has full control on. Being the city that Lady Feramein always secretly visits, they have lots of magical shield, and because of the trisnal stone which amplifies the magic. Trisnal stone like any other jewels and rich stones, they are good conductors of magic. Only a few of the jinn figured out some loopholes and made it through and possessed a few people, but they were contained in the icy cells of Trisnarim Palace.

Currently, Queen Flyangel and Master Mousy were on the run from their own city. The animals from Forest District 1 stayed with them the whole time as they too wanted to leave the city. One fact was discovered, the jinn don't possess the animals. Maybe they couldn't because the animals are full of magic or maybe it's just nature, Flyangel can't tell. But whatever the reason is, no animals are possessed. Captain and Bale were there too with many other animals, making their way quietly through the forest of the Encampment District. Flyangel was intending to go to White Woods. She is determined that the small city is still standing. Some animals went in other directions along the way. Wherever they want to go, Flyangel isn't going to force them to follow her. They were now at the edge of the training camp, about to enter Forest District 6. They bumped into another group escaping the city. The group had more animals and a few people that were bleeding in some areas. Flyangel recognised one of them, a young girl, from among the representatives of rank five at SHAW Academy, Izalora. But their short rest was interrupted by soldiers charging into the area, killing one or two people and a few animals.

'Run!' Flyangel cried as she led the group through the forest. Village District 2 came into view. The path to White Woods is just beyond the district, a little to the left. But Flyangel wasn't going to risk going into the village and encountering more problems. She led the group to the left and curved her way around the perimeter of the village district. Some magic wielders attacked them from behind. Flyangel put up a shield so large, it protected the whole group. The village was now far behind. They were officially out of the city and heading for White Woods.

In the heart of the Merchant's District, Dewi and Aditya were hiding in a dark corner between two buildings. At some point, the possessed came into the alley and Aditya struck them with his dagger. Dewi had been crying. Before the outbreak, she had left the battle between Combination and the rebels to seek her father. She came across her husband and her father in the Merchant's District defending themselves against some folks and soldiers. Her father was killed in the process. Dewi immediately pulled her husband away from the scene and they hid for as long as it took.

'*Dewi, kita tidak bisa hanya bersembunyi di sini*' Aditya said. (Dewi, we cannot just hide here).

'*Ayah telah meninggal, tidak ada yang bisa menghentikan Lizyati sekarang*' Dewi replied. (Father has died, there's no one who can stop Lizyati now).

'*Mereka punya sihir bukan? Mereka akan menemukan jalan keluarnya*' Aditya said. (They have magic don't they? They'll figure the way out). It didn't take Dewi long to agree with what her husband said. He took his hand and they both ran out of the alley and headed south towards the end of the city. There were dead bodies everywhere and people still fighting with each other.

West Coast is a very small town, but it was no different than the big cities. The jinn came possessing the peaceful people. One minute they were relaxing, the next minute they were killing each other. Even the ones who would never hurt small creatures were violent. Alphaga could not control them, so he fled again into the woods.

Lizyati went up the stairs at the entrance of Combination Castle, enjoying the view. She breathed in, this time with pleasure.

'*Sekarang tanah ini jauh lebih bersih*' she said. (Now this land is much cleaner). She grinned as Hati and Uri appeared behind her with their appearance, very frightening as always.

THE STONE OGRES

Thanks to Baron's fire, they all could see their way through the cave. They were deep inside and the heat was overwhelming. But they could still feel the wind coming in from the cave openings. Until one time, the wind sent a message. King Edward, Master Nvago, and Master Alya felt it. Though Master Alya never told them that she did.

'Something's happened' Edward said.

'I felt it too' Nvago agreed.

'Why? What is it?' Cardinal asked.

'Chaos has occured on Southernere' Nvago replied.

'I didn't know the air could give a message, that's so cool!' Baron said.

'Southernere is a magical place. And we are in the most magical place in all of Southernere' Nvago said. 'The wind do deliver messages'

'I hope Flyangel is okay. I hope everyone is okay' Edward said, full of worry.

'We have to complete our quest' Nvago said. 'Find the first wand, open the portal, find out what's going on, and get help'

They went deeper down into the cave. There was natural light coming from an opening in front. As they got closer, the area became clearer that it is very beautiful. There were trees here underground. Large natural pillars of stones stood in equal distance from each other in a circle, holding the ground above from breaking. The light was coming from holes with lava resting inside. Mossy stones were in random places, decorating the area. In the centre of the circle is a huge pedestal with four corners and a one-line hole in each one. A small stone bowl sits at the top of the pedestal. Nvago was very delighted to see it. He wasn't expecting the next thing that was going to happen. The moment he stepped into the circle, some of the mossy stones started moving. They either broke apart or formed together into big fat stone ogres.

'Ogres' Nvago muttered.

The ogres have glowing green eyes, moss all around them, and a big stone weapon which they hold with both hands.

'Destroy them' Nvago said. Mist appeared and he started disappearing and appearing. The ogres, four of them, charged, raising their weapons to strike. King Edward and Sir Everos drew their swords. Edward slid underneath the ogre's strike and struck its legs. Baron and Cardinal fought together with Annie against one. The ogre slammed its weapon on the stone tile. The stone broke apart like a small explosion. Baron sent his fire but it wasn't working, nor did Cardinal's water. Annie was using the crossbow. And the arrows are not doing any damage. Master Alya and Oliver took on one ogre. Alya sent an ogre-sized tornado which effectively carried the ogre around but because the area was too small for a tornado, she got Oliver stuck in the vortex as well. And the ogre was still here and suffered no damage. Oliver tried to control the stones but couldn't. These things have minds of their own, he needs to be able to control minds before he can control them. So he tried to attack it with huge rocks. It resulted in a scratch on the ogre but nothing more. Nvago took on one ogre himself. He teleported the ogre away from him a few times but the intention of making the ogre dizzy and confused did not happen. Edward struck the ogre repeatedly as it was busy smashing its weapon on Everos' sword. The ogre got annoyed and turned its attention to Edward. Everos struck it but his sword shattered into pieces due to the damage it had taken. The ogre turned back to him, Everos rolled out of the way just as the ogre smashed the stone tiles with its weapon. Oliver conjured a stone wall to trap all the ogres inside their own circle. They were about to say that was a smart decision, but the ogres started smashing their trap. Within seconds, the stones fell apart. Thinking that this difficult situation must be part of the test, Nvago asked Edward to give some of his blood into the bowl at the top of the pedestal.

'Edward, blood in bowl, top of pedestal' he said.

Edward glanced at the pedestal and back at the ogres. He understood, they need to try something. These ogres seemed magically indestructible. He hopped on one side of the pedestal so that he could reach the bowl. He cut a short line on his palm and clenched his fist over the bowl. Blood dripped from his hand, flowed down the bowl into the small hole in the centre. He turned around to see one ogre smashing its weapon into Everos' head. Everos was thrown to the wall of the cave, there wasn't much of his head left. Edward cried in anger. He moved away his bleeding hand, stepped down from the pedestal's side, and charged at the ogre. But the stone ogres moved back to where they originally stood and shaped themselves back into the mossy stones they saw before. Edward struck but all he did was scratch the stone. It was no longer alive, it was over. He had given his royal blood and that passed the test. But they lost someone. Annie couldn't bear to watch Everos, she looked away and covered Cardinal and Baron's eyes. Though they held her hand up to take a peek. Everyone else crowded around Everos. Edward kneeled by his side, touching his arm. Blood and other liquid were splattered around the head area, whatever that remains.

THE REBELS
FIGHT BACK

Before you start reading the next chapter, finish what you're supposed to do first. Done? Carry on!

Lizyati walked down the stairs to the dungeons. She approached the cells to where the British prisoners are.

'Are you going to kill us now?' one of the British soldiers said.

'We heard lots of shouting going on outside. Quite a disaster it seems' said Lieutenant Greenwood.

'I have a deal for you' Lizyati said.

'No deals! We don't take deals. Especially from the enemy' Captain Charles snapped.

'So I'm your enemy?' Lizyati asked in a very mysterious way.

'We're behind bars. You're outside. That explains enough'

Lizyati raised her eyebrows questioningly.

'If you say so' she said. What happen to Charles

next happened very fast. Charles began hovering above ground, gasping for air. His eyes turned reddish-black and his veins on his face became visible. His face turned blue and he fell to the ground dead.

'Witchcraft' Greenwood murmured.

'Anyone else wants to join your captain?' Lizyati asked sweetly. Everyone shook their heads.

'Good. Now here's the deal, I'll let you out and give you my protection if you fight for me' Lizyati said.

'We don't fight for anyone else but Great Britain' Greenwood said.

'I suggest the rest of you rethink again after this...'

Lieutenant Greenwood gasped in pain as the same thing that happened to Charles happened to him.

'Father!' his fifteen year old son cried. 'Please! Let him go!'

'Join me then'

'I will!' the son shouted in desperation. Greenwood fell to the ground unconscious.

'He'll live' Lizyati said. She took the keys hanging on the wall at the entrance and unlocked the cells.

'Now listen, everyone else not in here is your enemy. Kill them when they're going against you. Your weapons are in the treasure room. Now go out and do rounds around the city' she said.

'You mean patrol?' one soldier asked.

Lizyati gave him a death stare. The soldier flinched. They all proceeded to do their task.

'You, bring your father to a room and stay with

him until he is awake. Then bring him with you to do what you promised me' she said to Greenwood's son.

'As for the rest of you…'

Lizyati turned to the remaining people who were just servants, maids, or ship crew members.

'You'll be my sacrifice'

There were screams from the people, that was the last the son heard of them as he dragged his father out of the dungeons.

'Is that everyone?'

Three men and a woman came into the forest clearing. The rebels who survived the chaos have regrouped in Alhora Woods.

'That's everyone who's not affected Ciaran' one of the rebels replied.

There were many casualties. But everyone was still eager to fight.

'Alphaga was right! We have a common enemy' one rebel suddenly spoke. He continued.

'The Inlanders are not our threat. We need to take down that old lady. She killed Marcala. She doesn't belong here! I say we join the Inlanders and kill her!'

There were shouts of agreement and disagreement from the rebels.

'Silence!' Ciaran bellowed.

'We are Majuza's avengers. We don't act this way just because of a failed attack. The Inlanders are still our enemy. But first, we will kill this lady. Then we'll continue our fight' he said.

Everyone shouted in agreement.

Evening came on Southernere and the rebels were standing in the Combination Border Woods, ready to charged back into Combination.

'Remember, everyone else is not to be confronted. They are all influenced by her. We find her, kill her, and finish what we started' Ciaran said.

They charged into Forest District 2 and SHAW Academy. No one was there. Only dead bodies were found scattered around the area. They moved forward onto King's Road and found some people still fighting with each other. They proceeded down, the castle and the royal grounds could be seen from the distance. They arrived at the castle gates. All but one of the guards were found dead. The one remaining guard, bleeding from head to toe, charged at them upon sight. Ciaran blocked his strike and struck him on the side. He gave one more strike and the guard fell down dead.

Suddenly, some of the rebels were having a bad headache.

'I think the creatures are trying to get into me' one of them cried.

'Two of you, stay here with them, the rest follow me' Ciaran ordered. Five rebels were pulled away from the group. And two left to look out for them. There were fourteen remaining. Ciaran led them into the castle.

The rebels left outside were fighting mentally with the jinn as the jinn were trying to possess them. The two watching were getting worried that they might have to fight them. But things got worse when three British soldiers came to their location.

'What is happening?' one soldier asked.

'You don't have the right to walk around here like that outsiders' one rebel said and drew her sword. The soldiers stepped back and pointed their rifles. The other rebel drew his sword as a response to that.

'We have a new command and don't make this difficult for us. She ordered us to kill whoever that go against us. So lower your weapons' one soldier said.

Suddenly, one of the rebels fighting mentally lost and got possessed. He screamed in a scratchy voice.

'Die!'

He immediately turned to attack his fellow rebels. The two rebels had no choice but to end him. They both struck with their swords, decapitating his upper and lower parts of the body. The soldiers stepped back in shock.

'You're not our fight outsiders. Your leader is. So go away' the male rebel said.

'We can't do that' one soldier said, still pointing his rifle at them with trembling hands. All the other rebels got possessed and they attacked the two. Although they were outnumbered but they defended really well. It is unimaginable how strong the force of the jinn is and the person that is being possessed by it.

But the soldiers shot their rifles. The two rebels died and the possessed rebels started hurting each other.

Inside the castle, the rebels have split into 2 groups of 7. Ciaran led his group to the east wing. While a rebel named Kesh led his group to the west wing. Kesh's group was the unfortunate one to come face to face with Lizyati. Kesh sent a fireball towards her but one of her jinn wiped it out. Hati and Uri appeared frightening everyone with their horrifying appearance. More jinn revealed themselves and an intense battle began. The rebels swung their swords and sent their magic powers. The jinn defended Lizyati, possessed a few rebels, and killed some of them.

In one of the chambers on the second floor, Lieutenant Greenwood had just gain consciousness.

'Father' his son cried and hugged him.

'Why George?' Greenwood said. 'Why did you agree to her. We are man with honour. We don't deal with the enemy this way'

'You were dying!' George argued.

'Then let me. At least I'll die with honour'

George looked away, disagreeing with his father's opinion.

'That lady is our enemy. She proved it after she killed the captain. She's threatening us. We must not fall for such threat'

David Greenwood got up and looked into the

mirror by the side of the bed. He straightened his uniform and everything.

'Come on, let's fix this' he called on his son. They both left the room to find Ciaran and his group. Ciaran drew his sword.

'Peace' Greenwood raised his hands. 'We want to fight the lady as well'

Greenwood guessed that Ciaran was also after Lizyati. Good guess.

There were sudden screams and magic explosions coming from the west wing. They ran in the same direction. It was coming from the level below. They proceeded down the stairs, turned the corner, and found Lizyati had just stabbed Kesh in the chest.

THE SAGE'S MEMORY

*Before you start reading the next
chapter, finish what you're supposed
to do first. Done? Carry on!*

King Edward had washed the blood away from Everos' body. They stood around him as he lay motionless.

'He was a brave man. A good knight. We'll have a proper farewell for him when we return to Combination' Edward said.

They were still mourning but there was no time to lose. Southernere was in danger. Nvago explained to them what had to be done. Each element must be placed into the four one-line holes on the pedestal's corners.

'One corner for one element' Nvago said.

King Edward, Master Alya, Oliver, and Baron, each stood in front of one corner.

'Now, you will release your element, send it into the hole, and you will be teleported into another dimension for the final test. Remember, work together' Nvago said.

Edward, Alya, Oliver, and Baron all released their element from between their fingers. Edward sent the water into the hole. Alya sent the wind into the hole. Oliver sent the dirt into the hole. And Baron sent the fire into the hole.

The next moment everything went blank for all four of them. To everyone else, they vanished into thin air.

The four of them opened their eyes to find themselves in the centre space of a library. A huge magical library with its second level overlooking the first. Books and papers are flying everywhere. The candles and lamps are hovering over tables, walls, and ceiling. The windows are tall light red stained glass. The whole library has red as the major colour.

'Where are we?' Oliver said. Everyone was in awe at the library's beauty that it took them, even Oliver, a few seconds to realise that Oliver had just spoken in human voice.

'I can talk!' Oliver cried in amazement.

'Must be this place' Edward said.

'You are correct, Edward son of Henry' a voice said. The voice was coming from the library entrance. Three huge double doors stood behind towering over him, an old man in a sorcerer's cloak.

'Welcome to Sage's Library' he said. 'And welcome to Gratultyn'

All the doors opened magically to reveal a clear sky. They briskly walked out with curiosity. There weren't any clouds. The sky was very clear and bright too. Though there wasn't any sun. But the land is just too small. Huge magnificent trees are found around the library. And some small flying creatures and small glowing plants. But that's it. The land stops a few metres away from the library like they were on a floating island. They went to the edge and carefully looked below. Many other floating islands could be seen in the distance below. The library island is hovering just above a magnificent castle island. And in other areas are some nature islands. The depth of this world is unimaginable. There were still formation of rocks way at the bottom, depending on how far their eyes could see. But what was more curious is that the islands far at the bottom are just rocks or dirt. They could see some islands just below here with that same rock and dirt underneath it. So it could possibly mean the islands far below are inverted. And they have their own sky at the bottom.

'This is Gratultyn?' Baron said in awe.

'I wonder what happens when you reach the bottom' Oliver said.

'You'll turn the other way around. The sky is like a sphere. We're standing this way, the people at the end are standing inverted. For them, they look at us that way too' the old man said. 'The gravity line in Gratultyn is in the centre where the Mother Isle is'

'So we really are in Gratultyn?' Edward asked.

'No. You're just in my memory. I'm already a dead man I suppose' the man replied. He extended his right hand for Edward to shake. 'I am Quillon. The sage that created the first wand and hid them. You are here for that, am I correct?'

'Yes' Edward said.

'Do you still want to look around or do you want to start immediately?' Quillon asked.

'Start what?' Baron asked back. Quillon smiled and swiped his hand in the air. Purple fog surrounded them completely and moments later they found themselves on a different floating island. There were a few islands above them. One unknown, a few smaller ones, the big castle island, and the library where they were before is way at the top. This island was nearer to the side of the world, if the world has a side. Because all around is just sky, light from unknown sources, and lots of mist. The mist is like some kind of a protective layer and who knows what is beyond the mist.

'Welcome to the Isle of Nature' Quillon said. 'Your test will be here. If you passed, I shall give you the wand'

'What is the test?' Edward asked.

'That's your start' Quillon smiled and he disappeared behind the purple fog.

'So we have no instructions' Oliver said. 'What are we going to do?'

The Isle of Nature is very beautiful. One giant tree, with the perfect brown bark and branches and millions of different shades of green leaves, stands in the centre surrounded by a shimmering lake. Two small mountains behind the tree with mossy rocks formed so perfectly to give way to a glorious waterfall. Everywhere else is filled with magical plants. There were a few small human-like beings with wings, fairies. And some brown rock creatures that wield elemental magic, three times bigger than the stone ogres. They could be seen influencing the nature around them, sending wind into the big tree, and creating small waves in the lake. Beautiful maidens with tails, mermaids, were hanging out near the waterfall.

'It's so peaceful here' Alya said softly. But everyone could hear her. That was the very first time she spoke ever since she was with them.

'Yeah, but what are we supposed to do though?' Oliver said. They all looked around for signs. But there was obviously no indication.

'We have to make it back up there' Edward said, looking intently at the library island. 'He's the only person that can explain to us what this is about. And I have a feeling this is part of the test' Edward said again upon noticing their questioning looks.

'Well, how do we get up there?' Oliver asked.

'Master Alya can float us up' Baron said.

'No' Edward said. 'Remember, we are being tested for our element. We need to make use of our own element. Maybe that's the whole test. Alya, you make your way up there, the rest of us will figure out a way'

'We go together' Alya said.

'How can fire help me get up there?' Baron asked.

'Or dirt' Oliver added.

'Wait, just wait' Alya said. 'Master Nvago told us to work together. So I think it's okay for me to bring all of you up'

Edward kept quiet, thinking.

'We can try that' he said after a while. 'Though I don't think it's that simple. Watch out for anything. Stay cautious at all times'

They all nodded obediently. Alya summoned the wind to carry all four of them away from the Isle of Nature. Being in the air, they now have a more fascinating view of the whole world or what's within the mist at least. The Isle of Nature is much closer to the Mother Isle somewhere below. The Mother Isle is the largest floating island with a city that looks like each district was built in different eras of history, not sure the history of the real world or Gratultyn. Everything else below the Mother Isle are inverted, facing the other end. Alya brought them up past another floating island which was filled with all kinds of flowers. They thought this was going to be easy but then their first challenge started. Diagonally above the flower island is the castle island. A fire-breathing dragon flew out of probably one of the castle's courtyards and began chasing them. Alya brought them down below the castle island, narrowly escaping the dragon's fire. She brought them over the huge city below, heading straight for another island up ahead. A large tree, smaller than the one on the Isle of Nature, but has more sparkling lights around it. As they got closer, they realised that the island was filled with fairies and their little homes and other magical plants and tiny creatures. The dragon is now making a big turn to get back to them. It roared as it flew above the city. Before Alya could land them on the island to take a quick break, the dragon's fire got in the way and she circled them back towards the city. The fairies fled in panic as the dragon got close. The dragon turned to follow Alya and the rest.

'We have to land in the city!' Alya exclaimed.

'The dragon will destroy it' Edward said.

'We'll have more cover to fight it'

Alya brought them down into one of the city's districts' central squares. The citizens reacted to their arrival with curious faces. There were so many types of people and other unknown creatures, with different skin colours, and shapes and sizes. The dragon roared above. The citizens fled into buildings and other streets. Edward was about to conjure a shield around the square but the dragon stopped. It turned around and flew back up to the island above. The citizens came back out of the buildings and acted as if nothing had happened. The four of them were treated like they belonged there and that there was nothing weird going on.

'What just happened?' Baron said in confusion. Suddenly a male voice echoed throughout the city.

'Citizens of Champion City, good morning to all of you. Sage Master Quillon wishes you a good day'

They looked around but couldn't find where the voice was coming from. As they started paying attention to the details, they realised this city, or the district they were in could be from a different time period. Most of the citizens were walking and looking at an object in their hand. The object is a small circle that projects a small translucent image in front of their eyes. The buildings are not made of stone for sure.

'I think the dragon is tasked to only attack us. So we're safe as long as we're in the city or anywhere else other than in the air' Edward said.

'So how do we get up there? The moment we leave this city, the dragon's sure to come back out' Oliver said.

'That's our only option. We fight in the air' Edward replied. Alya carried them out of the city and they heard the dragon's roar.

'Go to that island. We stop there for a while' Edward pointed to the fairy island. Suddenly, the dragon flew down in front of them, catching them off guard. Alya lost her grip on all of them, they started falling down towards the Mother Isle. Alya tried to catch them back but managed to only catch Baron and Oliver. Edward continued falling towards the clear field outside Champion City. Alya went after him, bringing the rest with her. The dragon circled back and headed towards Alya. It breathed fire and Oliver let out a huge amount of dirt from his paws and formed a rock wall, blocking the fire. The gravity then pulled the rock down. Edward already created a floating pool of water for him to safely fall into. The rock wall came down faster than him, breaking the pool formation and broke apart as it touched the ground. Edward formed another pool just in time and landed inside. He brought the water down with him onto the field as Alya caught up with him. The dragon roared and was already charging at them. Edward sent a massive forcefield in its direction. The forcefield managed to disrupt the dragon's wings and it fell, hitting the edge of the Mother Isle and continued on below. They thought it was over and Alya was about to float them up again. But the dragon came back up like it had been falling from the other side. It came back down again, and a few moments later, it stopped in midair at the gravity line. The line that separates the top half of Gratultyn and the bottom half. Now that it has come to a stop, it was able to free itself off the gravity and flew back up into the air.

'We have to kill it' Edward said.

THE RED SPRITE

*Before you start reading the next
chapter, finish what you're supposed
to do first. Done? Carry on!*

Bodies scattered and blood spattered. Those are what they found the moment they arrived at the small camp in White Woods. The camp was set up for Combination citizens when the British took over White Shore the other day. During the rebels' attack, some of the citizens from Village District 5 had been evacuated to the camp. And after recent events, it seems none of them survive from killing one another. They looked upon the dead bodies in horror.

'If White Woods suffered the same fate, we have nowhere else to run' one woman said.

'Let's hope otherwise' Queen Flyangel replied. She led them through the camp and further into the woods. The trees here are much thicker and whiter. As they reached a small clearing, Flyangel stepped into it and disappeared as she went through an invisible barrier. They all followed.

White Woods, a very small town, but very magnificent. The whole town is like a huge castle courtyard with small buildings inside for the different houses and other needs. Walls surround the buildings and connect to a large structure, White Woods Keep, a little bit smaller than Combination Castle. Outside the walls, big white trees stretched as far as the eye can see. A huge amount of the stone used for building is white marble. And the foliage that covers the entire town looks like the city was magically formed in a garden. They appeared through the town main gate entrance and were relieved to find that the town was not affected by the black magic. The townspeople stopped whatever they were doing the moment they saw the queen and bowed or curtsied in respect. Flyangel nodded to them and they continued on with their jobs. A few kids laughed and ran around the town centre and waved at Flyangel when she looked at them.

'Holly' Flyangel called one of the ladies carrying a laundry basket and heading towards a building.

'Yes my queen' Holly replied, attending to her immediately.

'Would you be so kind and help provide our guests with wonderful hospitality?'

'Of course, your majesty' Holly said and gestured for the group to follow her.

'Mousy, come with me' Flyangel said. They both proceeded up the stairway leading up to the keep.

'Queen Flyangel wait!' Izalora's voice called from behind.

'Yes Izalora?'

'We have to fight back! We need to stop the witch' Izalora said with determination.

Flyangel gazed into her eyes for a moment.

'Sweetheart, we will fight when the time comes. Right now, everyone's tired and we don't have the numbers to win'

'I'm sure the rebels are fighting with us given what's happened' Izalora replied bluntly.

That angered Flyangel. She suddenly remembered of the many times the rebels or formerly avengers were given many chances and they still are the same.

'No!' Flyangel snapped and walked away immediately. Izalora was shocked by her short outburst. She wondered if she said something wrong. Master Mousy took her hand and gave her a calm look. Although she couldn't speak, Izalora understood what she was trying to convey. Give it time, Flyangel needs some rest, soon she will be ready to fight again, furthermore she is pregnant.

There were only 6 knights guarding the keep as most of the knights were assigned to Combination and White Shore Outpost. At every landing of the stairway, a pair was standing straight on opposite sides facing each other. They greeted Flyangel by holding their sword straight up in front of their face. Flyangel led Mousy inside to a small meeting room.

A rectangular long table fitted with 8 chairs in the centre. There was nothing else except for candles on side tables and torches on the walls and a small window at the end of the room. They both took a seat near the entrance.

'So based on what I saw. I think the jinn cannot control animals. And people with perhaps strong minds too' Flyangel said.

Mousy stared into her eyes for a while and nodded.

'I'm so glad you can still understand. Things will be so much worse if you couldn't'

Flyangel sighed with relief as she was finally able to rest.

'But what happened to Kitty means that they can still kill us' Flyangel continued.

There was silence for a moment.

'Izalora wants to fight. I want to as well. But only us three? We'll die before we even get to the castle'

Suddenly, there were screams from outside the keep. Flyangel and Mousy rushed out the door to find Izalora standing there, having been eavesdropping the whole time. They ran outside. There was a battle at the town entrance. Five soldiers from Combination have entered and it seems like the jinn controlling them want to kill everyone here before killing each other. The knights had gone down to defend the townspeople. They were already in a tense sword fight with the soldiers. Flyangel rushed down the stairs to assist. She sent a strong flow of water to one soldier, throwing him back out the magical barrier. Mousy also went down and sent a strong flow of mud in one soldier's direction. The soldier was thrown back out the barrier. Izalora also came down to help. One soldier managed to kill one knight by driving a sword deep into its chest. As it pulled the sword back out, the knight fell and Izalora sent a big boulder in his direction. The boulder pushed the soldier back out the barrier. There were 2 possessed soldiers left. One caused some heavy injuries to 2 knights while the other started swinging his sword at the townspeople. A knight knocked his sword off of his hand. Angered, the soldier turned his attention to the knight and lunged himself at him. Another knight struck the soldier's back just as smoke exited his mouth and into the first knight. The soldier died from the painful strike but now the jinn was in the knight. Unbeknownst to the other knight, the first knight got up, struck the knight's side and grabbed a woman from the townspeople and drove the sword into her back.

'Mother!' Izalora screamed in shock and frustration.

Flyangel sent the other soldier out the barrier as everyone heard Izalora's scream. The possessed knight pulled the sword back out and was ready to attack some more. But before anyone could do anything something extraordinary happened.

Izalora let out a short scream as she pushed her hands forward. Her eyes glowed red. Her veins started to show. Unknown red magical substance like gas appeared in the air around her hands and charged with high speed at the possessed knight. The red gas seems to be the one carrying the knight into the air but it's all just Izalora. The knight stared into nothing with an open mouth as the red gas surrounded him and started glowing very brightly like a light bulb with high intensity. Everyone covered their eyes but Izalora kept looking. The possessed knight was already screaming in pain like he was being tortured. Some people were already running away into their homes to hide. Flyangel came up to her.

'Izalora, stop this please' Flyangel said softly. But Izalora was acting like nothing else around her existed. Then green gas appeared over the red gas and made its way up to the knight. The high intensity glow was no more. Now they could see what the glow and the red gas had done. The little bit of armour on the knight had melted onto the floor below. Now the green gas is attacking the body in a spherical motion, in and out. With one final deafening scream that doesn't sound like the knight's voice, smoke came out of the knight's mouth. The knight fell to the ground below, half naked with burn marks. The smoke was now trapped in Izalora's powers. The green gas kept on attacking. The smoke transformed into a figure. A jinn with a very hideously frightening face. Bloody eyes and face with cold black skin and long black hair. Its scream echoed. Izalora sent a final attack. Crimson gas appeared over the other two colours and charged up to the jinn. The jinn shrieked as smoke appeared randomly around it. The crimson gas seems to be the one killing it. The other colours disappeared and the crimson gas took over. Smoke tried to leave the sphere of gas but couldn't. There was steam coming out at the top and the jinn slowly disintegrated. All the powers disappeared as Izalora's eyes stopped glowing. She fell down unconscious.

'Izalora!' Flyangel cried, catching hold of her before she hit the ground. Everyone else was equally shocked as to what had just happened. Had they discovered a powerful force that can free Southernere from evil hands or had they discovered a force that will bring about Southernere's destruction?

'Izalora, you're okay' Queen Flyangel's calming voice soothed Izalora's nerves. She woke up finding herself lying on a comfy bed in the keep. Flyangel, Master Mousy, and one townsperson were there. The woman had been attending to her, making sure she was okay.

'What happened?' Izalora asked, putting her hand on her forehead, trying to ease the sharp pain inside.

'You were in your trance, I've not seen that in a long time since the war' Flyangel said. 'And your powers, I certainly have not seen such a thing before. Given that Gratultyn and common magic are no longer around, you have a very powerful gift'

Suddenly the events that occured before came rushing back into her mind. She moaned softly as the headache got worse.

'Stop thinking about that Izalora. You need rest' the woman said. Izalora started to cry. Tears rolled down the side of her eyes.

'My mother' Izalora sobbed.

'There there'

Flyangel lay her head beside Izalora's.

After a few minutes, Izalora sat up.

'You need to rest' the woman said.

'No, I'm okay' Izalora replied. She turned to Flyangel.

'Is the knight okay?' she asked.

'He's okay' Flyangel said reassuringly.

They kept quiet for a while more.

'We need to fight' Izalora said.

'Look at what happened to you. And there's so many of those creatures out there' Flyangel argued.

'I'm fine, like you said I was in a trance. It doesn't always happen. I know. I studied at the academy. It happens with extreme emotions. I am fine now. I can control my powers. I didn't know that I had that in me. Now that I do, we can fight back'

Flyangel gave her a good long look.

'You don't know when to quit do you?' she smiled.

'We can free Southernere. We have the Outlanders with us I'm sure of it'

Flyangel disagreed with the part about the Outlanders but Izalora has a point.

'Okay, we shall fight'

UNITY IN SOUTHERNERE

*Before you start reading the next
chapter, finish what you're supposed
to do first. Done? Carry on!*

Ciaran and the remaining rebels, and Lieutenant Greenwood and his son were standing in the hallway facing Lizyati who had just killed Kesh and his group. She grinned at them. Hati and Uri, and a few other jinn appeared in front of her grinning as well (in their own way).

'Who else?' Lizyati said.

The rebels with no powers charged while the others sent their powers towards the jinn. Greenwood aimed his rifle while his son charged with the rest. Unfortunately for some, the jinn entered their bodies and killed them. No matter how many attacks they were doing, no one could even get close to Lizyati. Greenwood's bullets weren't doing anything. Everytime he fires at Lizyati, a jinn would do something and the bullet just disappears. When someone almost gets close, Lizyati would step back and more jinn would guard her. Later on however, when the opportunity arose, she made a run for it while everyone was preoccupied. She ran out one of the exits from the west wing into the Fountain Garden and stumbled upon two castle servants fighting one another using metal trays. One took a swing at her which she ducked and pushed him back in retaliation. He fell to the ground and the other servant jumped onto him. Lizyati continued on down into the West Garden. The wall surrounding the royal grounds was up ahead. She turned left towards the castle gates. Once outside, a small group of men stopped her. They are neither the people of Southernere nor the British men that Lizyati forced to work for her. These men were wearing dark blue uniforms. And most of them were pointing their guns and rifles at her. Captain Noah was standing bravely in front of them.

'Je hebt de rust in Diederik uitgelokt. Zwarte magie mag niet heersen. Weg met heks, of ik kom in actie' he said. (You have provoked the peace in Diederik. Black magic is not allowed to rule. Begone witch, or I will take action).

Lizyati stared at him with clear confusion as she did not understand a single thing he said.

'Sampeyan bahasa Indonesia kan? Miwiti saiki utawa aku bakal ngirim pesen bali menyang Indonesia kanggo ukuman sampeyan' Noah spoke in Javanese. (You are Indonesian right? Begone now or I will send a message back to Indonesia for your sentence).

However, Lizyati still couldn't understand the majority of what he said. She doesn't speak Javanese but she somehow understood what he meant.

'Coba dan hentikan aku' she replied. (Try and stop me). She started murmuring some words which called some of the jinn to her aid and they remained invisible so the Dutch can't see them. Noah watched while trying to remain calm. He had expected the witch to react in this way. Which is why he was ready. He looked back to his men. One of them nodded his head and proceeded in front. The man brought with him a wooden bowl and a kind of doll in the other hand. He placed the bowl on the ground in between them and Lizyati. The jinn, unbeknownst to the Dutch, started charging at them but the man uttered some airy-words and the jinn were deflected by another force. The deflect made them visible for a while. Suddenly, a fight started on a different plane. Everyone except for Lizyati and the man with the doll could not see what was going on. But everyone can feel the presence. A scary cold presence around them. On a different plane of existence, the jinn were fighting with another group of jinn, the ones on the side of the man with the doll.

'You brought with yourself a shaman' Lizyati pointed out. Noah understood what she said a little.

'Hiz name Liam' Noah said, feeling very proud of Liam for saving their souls.

'Maak je wapens klaar!' he exclaimed. (Ready your weapons!).

Noah's men aimed their weapons at the witch.

Lizyati was in a panic, she took out her dagger and cut herself. The bullets went flying but smoke blocked their view. When the air cleared up, Lizyati was gone.

'*Waar is ze heengegaan?*' Noah asked. (Where did she go?).

'*Ze heeft haar bloed opgeofferd om meer tijd voor zichzelf te winnen. De demonen aan haar zijde hielpen haar ontsnappen*' Liam replied. (She sacrificed her blood to buy herself more time. The demons on her side helped her escape).

'*We gaan nu het kasteel binnen. Iedereen moet bij elkaar blijven. Niemand mag scheiden. De demonen zijn nog steeds overal*' Noah said. (We enter the castle now. Everyone should stick together. No one should separate. The demons are still everywhere).

They entered the castle and followed the sound of the ongoing battle. They found Ciaran's group and Lieutenant Greenwood in the west wing. The rebels are down to only five. The seven of them were too busy fighting the jinn to even notice the Dutch coming in. Liam placed his bowl on the ground and murmured some words. Suddenly the air became calm but cold, as the presence of the jinn in the other plane fighting could be felt amongst them.

'Dutch' Greenwood said.

'*Engelse mannen*' Noah said. (English men).

'What happened?' Ciaran asked while trying to

calm himself down. The seven of them were almost out of breath. Some of them were covered in blood.

'The Dutch apparently have someone who knows black magic and he helped us' Greenwood replied.

'Why?' Ciaran asked, turning his attention to Noah who's behaviour was obvious that he is the leader. Ciaran felt surprised and weirdly honoured as to why a stranger who wasn't born here, doesn't belong here, and shouldn't have come here in the first place would stand up for this land and protect it.

'Black magik cannot rule. Iz no no' Noah replied.

Just then, Liam picked up his bowl and proceeded back out the castle in a rush. They all followed him. To their dismay, everyone else in the city who were survivors of the brutal fight between one another were standing at the castle gates, ready to kill all of them. One lady charged past the roundabout fountain towards the castle steps. Liam placed his bowl down, held up his doll. He has a needle in his other hand, he said some words and poke the doll with the needle. The lady stopped abruptly and fell to her knees clutching her stomach. That was just one lady. Upon seeing this, everyone else started charging towards Liam.

'We need to protect this guy so he can do his thing' Ciaran said, calling the remaining rebels to fight with him. The five of them went ahead to battle some people.

'There's not enough of us to stop them without killing. I'll have to shoot them' Greenwood said.

'I'm with you dad' George Greenwood said.

'Me too' Noah agreed.

'Bescherm Liam' Noah said to his men. (Protect Liam).

Lieutenant Greenwood pointed his rifle up while his son joined Ciaran's group to do some melee attacks with his sword. Greenwood shot a few men armed with a knife or a sword. Ciaran sent some man-sized tornadoes. While everyone engaged in combat, Liam did his thing. The lady was now lying unconscious. The jinn possessing her had come out and was already fighting other jinn on the other plane of existence.

As the battle raged in Combination, elsewhere, the message of unity has spread. The winds carried the presence of comradeship to all of Southernere. From White Shore Outpost and Arstar in the north to Silverside in the centre and Trisnarim in the south. Those who are not affected by the jinn had stayed hidden all this time. But now they all joined arms together and headed out to fight the possessed survivors and drive away the evil jinn from their lands however possible.

Alphaga had come across another town (more like a village) not far away from the previous one. Unlike West Coast, Waterfront doesn't seem to be affected by the jinn. As he got closer to the village walls, he noticed the people guarding the walls were dressed nothing like the rest of Southernere. One of the reasons are, they were more revealing. The men have long pants but their tops are uncovered. The women also have long pants, but their hair revealed, and their top only covered the top parts, revealing their belly button. They have spears for weapons and most of them have their faces painted in many different colours and patterns. The leader, called himself Master Griffin, brought with him everywhere he went, a walking stick with raven feathers at the top. Fortunately, Alphaga found a common interest with them that made him a friend instead of a foe. Firstly, they speak English. Secondly, they stand with the Inland. Why has no one heard of them before? Guess Southernere has more to be discovered than we thought, Alphaga wondered.

'The creatures from the other side can't get in while I'm still standing, so you're safe' Master Griffin assured Alphaga in his supreme deep voice.

'Creatures from the other side?'

'Call it what you want, the other side, the other dimension, the demon realm, they're all the same' Griffin replied.

'So these creatures are from the realm where demons and monsters are from?'

'They are everywhere. Anywhere can be their home. Any forest, any ocean. And if they bother humans, it is either because we bother them or someone is doing some naughty magic. But if not, they are just like us, capable of disturbing others and ourselves, perhaps just for fun. Black magic could be useful, but in evil hands, it could bring about destruction. And I've read that in some beliefs, it is forbidden'

'How do you know all this?' Alphaga asked, still wondering how no one has talked about this village before.

'We have a library filled with books by Southernere explorers who went to the world where the foreigners came from. Unlike the rest of Southernere we chose to learn and never forget our history. Which is why we understand why the avengers are attacking'

'And why's that?' Alphaga asked innocently, trying not to reveal yet that he was one of the avengers.

'Majuza wanted revenge, so her people are not stopping until Combination falls under them' Griffin said. Alphaga tried not to frown. Griffin mentioned a very wrong answer. Yes Majuza wanted revenge but the reason isn't complete. Whoever the historian that wrote that down is the main reason no one knows the truth. Or at least that's what the avengers believe.

'I see' Alphaga said simply.

Just then, strong wind blew into the village spreading the message of comradeship.

'They are fighting together as one' Alphaga said, getting excited. 'We should go to West Coast and help them'

'No' Griffin replied immediately, turning to walk away. Alphaga hopped up in front of him and blocked his way.

'Why?' he asked in disbelief.

'West Coast is lost. I sent my scouts hours ago

and they came back telling me everyone has started killing one another'

'We can help them!'

'I'm not risking my people's lives!'

'Why did Southernere send this message? It's because she wants us to fight! She wants us to stand up and fight for our home!' Alphaga argued. Their argument had drawn the attention of the villagers. Griffin stared past Alphaga into nothing. He has no more points to argue back. He was in a dilemma, the thought of sacrificing his people for others and also the thought of abandoning the others who live on the same land as himself.

'My answer is no' Griffin said, walking past Alphaga. Alphaga looked back at him in disbelief. To his surprise, all the villagers walked up to their leader.

'I want to fight' one man said with determination.

'Me too' one woman said.

'We want to fight' they said together.

It was probably the most beautiful thing Alphaga had ever seen. He smiled as the leader turned back to him with a grin.

'We fight then'

THE FIRST WAND

*Before you start reading the next
chapter, finish what you're supposed
to do first. Done? Carry on!*

King Edward and Oliver ran closer to the edge of the Mother Isle as the dragon glided down towards them. Master Alya controlled the wind to circulate around the dragon, causing it to be stationary for a while. Oliver raised the ground where Edward was standing until a few metres away from Alya's wind. The dragon flapped its wings in anger, trying to break the wind chain. Edward sent a flow of water into the wind as Alya lowered down the temperature. Edward separated the water into small droplets and the wind brought it around, cooling the temperature around the dragon. Snowflakes started to form in the cool air and the dragon's wings started to freeze. Unable to flap its wings anymore, the dragon started to fall at very high speed towards the ground.

'Let me help' Baron said.

'No Baron, fire will only help it' Alya replied sternly.

Oliver dug a large hole in the ground and Edward filled it in with water. The dragon fell inside, causing a huge splash. As the dragon was about to get up again and attack, Edward froze the water, trapping the lower half of the dragon's body. The dragon's stomach glowed red. It was heating itself up, trying to escape. Oliver formed a long metal spear and handed it over to Edward. Alya carried Edward in the wind towards the dragon's chest. Edward jabbed the spear into its heart. First time, the dragon roared in anger. Edward jabbed again and the dragon roared in pain before dying.

'Now that was impressive!' Baron cried in admiration. That was probably the best teamwork he had ever seen.

Alya brought them all up. They saw the fairy isle and the hundreds of colourful tiny fairies as they passed. The castle isle has very few people wandering the courtyard, they dress the same way as Quillon. Probably other sages. Finally they reached the Sage's Library and Quillon was waiting for them at the bottom of the library steps.

'Well done' Quillon said. 'I agree with the child, that was impressive'

He had a genuine impressed look on his face.

'Was that the test?' Edward asked.

'There are no tests, there never has been. What you have to do is prove yourself worthy to me' Quillon replied. 'And you have done so. So here's the reward'

He held up his hand and a very short straight

black stick appeared floating above his hand. Edward reached out to grab it but the stick made its way to Edward's hand by itself.

'Is this the first wand?' Edward asked, feeling sceptical.

'Why wouldn't it be?'

'No, I just thought it would be longer, more... more grand' Edward said.

'Of course it would be more grand, the first wand, probably still the only best wand in all the realms! But what you have in your hand is only one piece of it'

They looked at Quillon with confused looks.

'When I hid the wand, I divided them into four pieces. What you have is the piece in Southernere' Quillon explained.

'Where are the others? This won't do any good in reopening a portal to Gratultyn is it?'

'Oh, something bad happened. That's why you need the wand' Quillon said, staring into each of their faces. 'Well this piece can restore magic if restoration is needed, but you need all the pieces to reopen a portal to Gratultyn'

Quillon paused for a second.

'If you seek the other pieces, you need to find Cyler Raider'

'Cyler Raider?'

But Quillon had swiped his hand, surrounding them in purple fog and everything went black.

The four of them opened their eyes and found

themselves back in the cave, standing around the pedestal. Master Nvago, Cardinal, and Annie had been sitting on the cave floors waiting for them as they stood there with their eyes closed. Their minds were in Quillon's memory but their bodies were here the whole time. The three immediately stood up when the four of them woke up. And in Edward's hand, he held the piece of the first wand.

'How did it go?' Nvago asked.

'It was amazing!' Baron exclaimed.

'Beautiful' Oliver said.

'Confusing' Alya said.

'Still got lots to do' Edward said, handing him the wand.

'This is not the full wand' Nvago said examining the wand.

'Yes, Quillon divided them into four pieces and hid them in different locations' Edward said. 'To find the rest, we need to find Cyler Raider'

Nvago looked at him, in deep thought.

'What can this do?' Cardinal asked, pointing to the wand.

'Restore magic. I think that will allow Southernere to have all the magic again, including Gratultyn magic' Edward replied.

Nvago held out his palm and Edward handed the wand over.

'We can talk about it more later, right now, our people need us' Nvago said. He moved the wand in a circle motion and flicked it upwards. A spark came out of it and exploded in a tiny golden firework.

'What did that do?' Baron asked, not feeling any different.

'Restore magic' Nvago replied.

Edward tested it out by casting a simple magic. He sent a forcefield so powerful, one of the motionless stone ogres exploded into thousands of pieces. Now that all magic has been restored, they could do more than what they were gifted with. With that, they set off for Combination while force-carrying Everos along.

RISE OF
SOUTHERNERE

*Before you start reading the next
chapter, finish what you're supposed
to do first. Done? Carry on!*

Alphaga and some Waterfront villagers led by Master Griffin scouted the town of West Coast from a distance, waiting for the right moment to move in. A few townspeople were fighting one another near the forest and Alphaga recognised some of them. After a signal from Griffin, they both went to engage. Griffin banged his stick which startled the villagers. If it wasn't clear before, it is clear now for Alphaga, Griffin knows some black magic himself. The townspeople couldn't move and their eyes raised such that the black part wasn't visible. Muttering some words as he passed by, Griffin gently touched each of the townspeople's forehead which made them unconscious and drop down. The rest of Griffin's men then followed after him and Alphaga as they made their way stealthily through the town. There were a few dead bodies lying. Soon they came across another group involved in a more violent fight. Some have knives. One held a sharp wooden object that was probably broken from a chair or table. Griffin banged his stick again, it worked on only a few of them. Wooden object guy literally growled before charging at a Waterfront villager. The villager blocked his strike successfully with a spear. Trying not to kill him, the villager engaged him in a spar while waiting for Griffin to do his thing. Suddenly, all around them, torches were lit as the other townspeople surrounded them in a circle. They had no expression on their faces. Their eyes were lifeless. They definitely outnumbered Alphaga and the Waterfront villagers. Griffin banged his stick but it didn't work on all of them. A few of the townspeople charged into the circle without warning. Subconsciously in response, Alphaga sent a forcefield in their direction which worked to his surprise.

'Magic is back?!' he exclaimed with excitement. More townspeople charged. Alphaga and magic-abled Waterfront villagers sent more forcefields or shielded the area. But the townspeople were very strong and the main reason is obviously because of the jinn possessing them. It would seem like they would go down fighting soon when suddenly, a strong force came to their rescue. Men and women dressed in ice blue uniform marched in with powers and weapons made out of trisnal stone. Queen Lady Lith herself was leading the Trisnarim army, marching in dressed mostly in white from her headscarf to her pants. Within seconds, the townspeople were made unconscious or immobilised.

'Your majesty! We will be forever grateful for your arrival' Griffin said. The queen smiled.

'Just doing my part as a citizen of this sacred land. Southernere herself wants us to fight' Lady Lith replied. She then noticed Alphaga among the villagers. Although she knew Alphaga had made peace with Inlanders for quite some time, she only remembered him for the time when they fought on opposite sides in the war. And furthermore she received a letter from the late Queen Darleen a few days ago about the rebels' attack on Barenge.

'Your majesty, I am...'

'Yes I know who you are' Lady Lith cut short Alphaga's words which surprised Griffin as well as he does not know who Alphaga was.

'Were' Alphaga corrected her which she ignored and proceeded to look around. When she was satisfied that her work here was done, she asked her men to head back to their ships, the Guardians.

'Your majesty! Don't mind me asking, you have your whole army with you?' Griffin asked.

'This isn't an army master, this is just one unit. Many others are heading east to Silverside and Combination with my daughter' Lady Lith said.

'Where are you heading to?' Griffin asked again.

'Arstar, to make sure they're alright' Lady Lith answered. Griffin offered his assistance which the queen agreed, even Alphaga, but she wasn't too happy about the latter.

As her mother was leaving for Arstar, Princess Nathaliya was just making her way through the forest, leading her men up towards Silverside. The surroundings drastically change as they near the city walls. The trees had fallen over. Some of them got burned by fire conjured with magic. A part of the Silverside wall was ruined. And that is saying something because Silverside has the largest wall surrounding its city compared to other cities with walls. There were very few people left still fighting with one another. They immobilised them within seconds and checked out the entire city.

After ten minutes, they gathered near the ruined wall and everyone reported their findings. They found a few survivors among the soldiers, citizens, and servants who were not affected by the jinn. But none of the royals were found, except King Harold and Prince John's dead bodies.

'King Harold has no marks on his body, he possibly died from natural causes' one of the honour guards told Nathaliya.

'Or those creatures killed him' Nathaliya replied.

'Prince John has a stab wound in his chest. He was killed by a person, your majesty'

The honour guard just stood there as Nathaliya stared at him, thinking for a moment.

'Princess Jane and Prince James are still alive

somewhere, we need to find them' Nathaliya said. She sounded very relieved that those two were still alive. Her men started going separate ways into the forest to look for the royals.

Nathaliya, two honour guards, and two Ocean Masters went north of Silverside for the search. Their plan was to regroup back at Silverside after half an hour.

The Guardians of the sea with Queen Lady Lith, Master Griffin, and Alphaga arrived in Arstar after twenty-five minutes. They were surprised to see the people had taken control of the city after King David's death. A lot of them have amazingly strong minds. The few who got possessed were no match for the majority. They locked the possessed behind bars and buried their king. A citizen named Lewis had taken charge of the situation. He respectfully passed the responsibilities to Lady Lith which she kindly accepted.

'You did very well in protecting the people of Arstar' Lady Lith complimented Lewis.

'Arstar was very devastated when those things took over. We hope whatever that is happening will come to an end soon' Lewis said.

'Let's hope our friends in Combination stay strong for the upcoming battle. Things will turn out fine' Lady Lith said with full of hope.

Princess Nathaliya and her four men walked

further north. But they were already losing hope as they will soon have to regroup with the rest.

'Your majesty, permission to speak my mind' one of the Ocean Masters said.

'Permitted'

'It's like the avengers are not enough, we are faced with more problems and it seems like it'll never end' she said.

'Be careful of your words Alicia. Life will always have challenges, because without them, we will never have the chance to improve ourselves' Nathaliya replied.

'I'm going to kill the person responsible if he's not dead…' one honour guard said. But he was shushed by Nathaliya before he could continue speaking. He looked at her in surprise. She seemed like she had heard something. The other honour guard also heard it. They all listened and true enough, they heard voices. Nathaliya immediately took off after the voice.

'Your majesty, wait!' her men called. The voices became louder and clearer. Someone was pleading. Nathaliya passed a few more trees and came upon a clearing. There was Prince James with his sword in hand, ready to charge at the person he was facing. His sister stood opposite him also with a sword in hand. More specifically, the sword was a few inches away from a man who was on the ground. Beside him was a lady who was the one pleading. It was Dewi and her husband Aditya.

'Please don't, please don't hurt him' Dewi pleaded.

'Hey!' Nathaliya let out a short aggressive exclamation. That caught Princess Jane's attention. She turned and Nathaliya swung her trisnal sword in front of her eyes. The magical force rippled out causing Jane to let go of her sword and drop to the ground.

'Jane' James cried and went to his sister. He looked at Nathaliya gratefully. Nathaliya felt sorry for him. His father and brother died on the same day. And his sister was possessed.

'Dewi, what happened? Is Combination okay?' Nathaliya asked. Dewi shook her head in a way more like she was refusing something. She was still affected by what happened to her father.

'Hey, it's okay' Nathaliya cupped her hands on Dewi's tearful cheeks. 'It's okay. Come with us'

She gestured to one of her men to help them up. And they returned to Silverside.

After fifteen minutes of waiting and regrouping, Nathaliya and her men were already formed up to make their way to Combination.

'I can come with you. I want to see the person responsible for all of this to be punished' James said to Nathaliya.

'You need to stay here. I need one royal who is still sane to look after the survivors here'

Tears formed in James' eyes.

'Why? Did I say something wrong?' Nathaliya asked with a very gentle tone, and full of worry.

'I know Jane couldn't control herself, but I can't

find myself looking at her after what she did to John'
James cried.

That surprised Nathaliya. Well, she didn't know
it was Jane who killed John.

'Hey, hey, I'm here, I'm here' Nathaliya said,
giving him a warm hug. She let him let out his tears
for a few minutes. He pulled back, smiling.

'Who knew the knight in shining armour would
be the one to cry on the shoulder of the princess'

She smiled back, caressed his cheek and kissed
him tenderly. Their foreheads touched for a few
moments.

'I'll await your return my princess' James said.
'Stay safe'

NOW AND
FOREVERMORE

*Before you start reading the next
chapter, finish what you're supposed
to do first. Done? Carry on!*

While Queen Lady Lith was on her way to West Coast and Princess Nathaliya to Silverside, the battle was raging in Combination royal grounds. Ciaran and his group, and the foreigners were too focused on the front that they forgot to secure the back. Lizyati came from inside the castle, grabbed Liam and slit his throat. A few of the Dutch soldiers exclaimed in anger and attacked the witch. But she was too skillful for them. She threw red powder at one, swiped her hand at another, and stabbed the last with her dagger. The red powder erupted in flames, burning the soldier alive. The swipe sent a jinn flinging the soldier away. And the dagger killed the soldier as another one of Lizyati's sacrifices. Immediately after that, Captain Noah led some of his men to face the witch while Ciaran and the Greenwoods stayed focused on the front. They were getting tired but more and more possessed were coming through the gates. They had no choice but to kill.

Suddenly, a glowing red spark illuminated the evening sky from the south. The ground trembled. For a few seconds, everyone was trying to keep their balance, expecting an earthquake while some of the possessed fell down clumsily. Then, the trees started to move. Tree roots from the forest districts nearby dug their way through and out of the ground to grab the possessed and pull them under. The ground beneath them behaved like liquid, hardening back only after they were underneath, leaving them stuck with only their heads above ground. Followed by that, the presence of a powerful magical force rippled around the area. Outside the castle gates, they could see Queen Flyangel making her way through the crowd of possessed, blasting them away or the jinn inside them away, while completely protected by the shield from the amulet under her headscarf. Following after her were five knights of White Woods, fighting the possessed that gets near. The townspeople of White Woods were also there to fight alongside the queen. Flyangel's presence gave the survivors hope. With a commanding shout, Ciaran led his people to bring down the possessed. They no longer need to kill them as the amulet's magic overpowered the jinn controlling them and made them unconscious. Flyangel and the knights stepped onto the royal grounds as Noah and his men faced an intense battle with the witch.

Lizyati turned 360 degrees while striking with the dagger, slitting one Dutch soldier's throat when he attempted to close in on her. She lunged at another with the dagger. The soldier successfully avoided and another left a deep cut on her back. She groaned in pain and turned aggressively while swinging the dagger. But the soldier had backed away. The soldier who avoided earlier saw this opportunity to strike her again. But Lizyati was not stupid. She back-kicked him in the groin area which caused extreme pain. And after that she threw red powder on the floor. Fire grew in its place, blocking the soldiers in front from getting to her. She turned to face the soldier covering his groin, whimpering. She charged at him and drove the dagger deep into his neck. Noah charged at her angrily, thrusting the sword forward. Lizyati dodged and swung her dagger at his face. Noah hopped backwards, merely avoiding the hit. He attempted to strike her again on the side. She blocked it with her dagger and threw more red powder on him. Noah pulled himself away as fast as he could. Most of the powder fell onto the floor. The little amount that fell onto his gear fortunately did not catch fire. He moved around the fire to face the witch again. Lizyati gave him a daring look. She is one strong woman Noah had to give her that. But Noah knows the deep cut on her back is going to eventually kill her. He just needs to find a way to strike her in the same place. So another spar began. Noah and Lizyati exchanged strikes and blocks to each other's weapons which ended with Noah knocking the dagger out of her hand and his sword inches away from her neck. Something was preventing the sword from touching her. Noah knew he'd lost when Lizyati formed a creepy smile. Suddenly, Noah felt something enter him. His insides were torn apart. He gasped as the jinn killed him and the last thing he heard was Lizyati's voice.

'The witch defeats the captain' she said. She turned around to see Flyangel was already wiping the fire out to get to her. And so she made her escape.

The townspeople of White Woods were making their way into the Business District. They chanted "for Southernere" as they charged. Those in hiding from Business to Merchants' Districts heard their cries and were motivated to come out and join them. They were surprised by the number of people that were still normal. They could easily fill the ballroom of Combination Castle.

The red sparks glowed brighter than before in the darkening sky. Over at the South Districts Market, Izalora was making her way up to Village District 1 with Master Mousy, Captain, and Bale leading a large group of animals. Izalora was actually floating her way. She had let herself loose. Red gas spun around her as she floated. Every few seconds she sent red sparks into the air, influencing the natural forces around her to react. So far she has successfully convinced the trees to move. The possessed were randomly scattered on the streets and they moved to attack upon seeing them. Izalora sent red and green gas to those who got close, making them unconscious or burning the jinn inside. All the while, her eyes glowed as red as blood. Mousy sent minor earthquakes and trapped the possessed in between. Captain and Bale attacked with sticks and pebbles. They managed to stop every possessed person in the district within a few minutes. Izalora floated back down and the whole magical aura disappeared and her eyes turned back to normal. Just then a small boy's voice called her. She looked to where it was coming from, recognising the voice. At the doorstep to one of the houses, she saw her ten year old brother, Isaac, standing there. His face showed that he had been crying.

'Isaac?' Izalora called longingly. They both ran to each other and hugged.

'Oh I'm glad you're okay' she cried.

'I killed someone Iza, he tried to kill me' Isaac said, his voice sounded like he was very guilty for it.

'It's okay. It's okay'

Isaac pulled away from the hug.

'I couldn't find father and mother. I thought you were all dead, so I just went to hide' Isaac said.

'I thought you were dead too' Izalora cried, her tears rolled down her cheeks. She doesn't know if she can tell him the news that their mother died. Or that she couldn't find father too and probably he's gone as well. Mousy came to be by their side.

'I wish I can talk to you like before so I can comfort

you' Mousy said without realising that they can now understand her.

'Master, you can talk!' Izalora cried. The second good news she had heard all day after knowing her brother's alive.

'Gratultyn magic is back? Edward's done it!' Mousy said, staring into the distance. Her thoughts shifted back to what she wished for earlier.

'Come here child' she said, asking to hug Isaac and then comfort him with the nicest words Mousy can think of. After a while they let go.

'Do you know what this means?' Mousy questioned Izalora.

'We can defeat that witch and her army very easily' Izalora replied.

'Exactly'

Their group pushed on towards the Merchants' District. Izalora let her powers out again. This time with the presence of Gratultyn magic, it amplified her powers. Her Sprite energy called on the forces of nature to assist her. This time, not only the trees move. The wind started blowing the possessed far away from anyone normal. It started raining. Every water droplet that fell on the possessed, froze them in their place. Reaching out to feel every one of them, Izalora controlled the water droplets once they touched the ground, turning them into bubbles and enlarging their sizes. She sent them towards the possessed, trapping them inside.

Over at the castle, Flyangel, her knights, and Ciaran had searched the castle for Lizyati but she was nowhere to be found. They exited the castle back again. The rest were waiting for good news.

'She's gone again' Flyangel said. She kept looking at the foreigners, avoiding the rebels' eyes. She couldn't push the thought away that it was all their fault. If it weren't for them, none of this would have happened.

'That is not good' Lieutenant Greenwood said. Flyangel responded by shaking her head in agreement.

'Nevertheless, I will go around the city, to make sure everything is alright' Flyangel said. She proceeded down the steps with the knights following closely behind.

'Stay behind, they shouldn't roam around without supervision' she told the knights. And so the knights stayed behind to keep watch on the rebels and the foreigners. The rebels and the Dutch weren't very happy about that, but they cooperated. Flyangel then went off to the Business District. The moon was shining brightly in the dark sky when she arrived. The townspeople of White Woods and Combination survivors had stopped every possessed from causing further harm on anyone. They trapped them behind barriers in different rooms and different buildings. No one can deny that during the process there were some killings involved. That explains the dead bodies lying around.

Flyangel continued on to Forest District 2. The field where the chaos began earlier in the afternoon was completely empty except for the many bodies lying around. While there, she looked for familiar faces but was grateful to find none. That means Bobby, Prince Jake, Master Lillain, and Laura must be elsewhere. She searched the school and found a big group of students hiding in the great hall. She had to break through a few barricades that they set up to get in. The students were on their feet and ready to attack, thinking that she was another threat but were relieved to find the queen completely sane. She asked them to remain there safely as the threat is still out there and then proceeded to Village District 5. The district was as silent as the Alhora cemetery. No one was there. Bodies that were lying around are casualties from before when the rebels attacked. Still no sign of Lizyati.

She met up with a few survivors among the citizens when she reached Town Park.

When she headed down to Village District 4, a possessed lady caught her by surprise, coming at her from around a corner. Her natural instinct made her send a forcefield towards the lady. Gazing up at Traveller's Hill, she saw figures moving in the darkness. As preparation, she played with ice and water around her fingers, ready to strike anytime. She was about to hurt someone when the first person she got a clear view of was Princess Nathaliya.

'Nathaliya?'

Nathaliya was looking around very worried. She saw how deadly quiet the place was.

'Who did this?' Nathaliya asked.

'Someone from the outside world' Flyangel replied.

'Where is everybody?'

'Not many of us left. But I believe a lot of the people ran into the forest. While the others got controlled by the jinn'

'Jinn?'

'Yes'

'And Edward?'

Flyangel thought of that question for a while. Now that she thought about it, it worried her even more. What if Edward couldn't fight the jinn? What if they failed their mission? But everything slowly cleared up as she remembered that Gratultyn magic is back. So that means they succeeded.

'He's on a quest to bring back Gratultyn magic, and I believe he succeeded' Flyangel said.

'So the person from the outside world caused magic to disappear?'

'I don't know' Flyangel said sadly.

'The whole land of Southernere was affected by that creature you mentioned'

Flyangel looked at her, full of worry.

'At first I thought the Outlanders did this because Queen Darleen sent us a letter before she was killed. She mentioned that in the letter…'

'She was killed? By who?'

'You don't know?'

Flyangel shook her head furiously.

'The Outlanders took over Barenge. And I

thought they went to take over Combination after that. But I guess their plan was interrupted by this outside worlder'

Flyangel was lost for words. She couldn't believe what she had just learned. The rebels killed Darleen. Her husband's aunt. The news triggered her anger. Before she could control herself, the anger, the frustration, and the vengefulness took over. The amulet under her headscarf glowed blindingly. It exerted a single wave of magic in a circle radius all the way throughout Southernere.

The surroundings, everything started to change. The rain that was just falling in the Merchants' and Business Districts started falling everywhere else. The night sky turned into the darkest shade of red. Flyangel's blue eyes started glowing and her veins also turned blue.

'Flyangel'

Nathaliya called out many times but nothing could stop her. She has entered her rage outburst. Frost covered every part of her skin. Her feet left the ground and she started gliding up towards the castle, turning rain into snow wherever she went. She passed over the Town Park and the Business District and all the survivors watched in fear and curiosity.

The rebels and the foreigners were still at the castle steps watched over by the knights. The moment they saw her, they became uneasy. The rebels followed Ciaran's lead and stood defensively.

'What is she doing?' Lieutenant Greenwood asked.

'She's in a rage' Ciaran replied. Flyangel flew down closer towards them and force-grabbed Ciaran. Ciaran was choked as he was lifted off the floor by the neck.

'Do something!' Greenwood exclaimed.

'We can't, there's nothing we can do to a rage outburst!' one rebel replied.

Greenwood raised his firearm to shoot but was stopped by one of the knights.

'If we don't do something, we're all next!' Greenwood retaliated, pushing the knight away. The other four knights went to stop him. But then the others joined in to help Greenwood. The Dutch took on three knights while the rebels took on the other one. Greenwood aimed his rifle at Flyangel and took a shot. But the bullet was stopped midair by a red gas. Down near the gates, Izalora was just walking in and saw what happened. She stopped the bullet before it could kill the queen. Master Mousy and some other animals and human survivors came after her.

'She's going to kill him!' Greenwood protested the moment Izalora reached the fountain at the roundabout.

'He deserves it' Izalora replied.

Princess Nathaliya had just reached the gates with some of her men.

'Flyangel!' she called out. 'This is not the way!'

But it was too late. Flyangel had finished. She dropped Ciaran onto the steps below, already dead. Flyangel herself fell down as she had passed out from exerting a lot of energy while being pregnant. Mousy caught her magically just in time to slowly bring her down. The rebels and the foreigners looked at Ciaran horrifyingly. What used to be a handsome face was now bloody and distorted.

Izalora, Mousy, and Nathaliya went to check on Flyangel. But their problems aren't over yet. Without warning, Flyangel got up all of a sudden, her eyes seemed liveless. It wasn't bad until she started speaking in a cold demonic voice. The jinn had entered her body while she was vulnerable. She began laughing crazily.

'You will never be able to defeat me now. All of your lives will be mine!' Flyangel cackled. Everyone stepped back and Izalora immediately sent her red and green gas surrounding Flyangel. She resisted, taking advantage of the amulet's powers to break through the magical barricade Izalora was forming. But Izalora got help. Nathaliya and Mousy both made use of Izalora's magical gas to increase their power over Flyangel and the amulet and the jinn inside her. The glow the magic brought to the area was getting brighter and brighter. Everyone else went to find cover while the soldiers and knights remained in place, covering their eyes with their shields. When it got blinding, Nathaliya and Mousy let go to cover their eyes and Izalora continued on her own. Izalora's eyes glowed red, the blinding lights did not affect her in any way. She soon released the crimson gas with a little bit of sunshine yellow. A few waves of magic rippled in a circle throughout the royal grounds. The jinn around the area that got hit by the magical waves were disintegrated. The jinn inside Flyangel left her body and Flyangel fell to the ground unconscious. There had been two of them inside her. They showed themselves and it was Hati and Uri. Izalora did not stop her magic. The jinn were still trying to fight Izalora but Izalora was not backing down. She pressed on her powers, ripping Hati and Uri inside out. Shadows revolved around them and broke apart, revealing Lizyati had been hiding behind their jinn magic the whole time. With a final push, she sent the jinn's own magic towards them, engulfing them with shadows and disintegrating them with her crimson gas. Lizyati fell out of their protection as the two jinn she devoted her life to were destroyed. She was now powerless and vulnerable. She could call on the other jinn that were still lurking around Southernere but Izalora scares her. The knights immediately went to grab Lizyati. Just then Flyangel gained consciousness. She saw Ciaran's dead body first and then Lizyati being apprehended by the knights and realised what was going on.

'Wait' she called on the knights before they could bring her away to the dungeons. The knights brought Lizyati to face her and she stared into her eyes.

'You won't be put behind bars again. For your evil deeds, you deserve to be punished. I hereby sentence you to death. Tomorrow you will be beheaded at the city square. Now and forevermore, anyone who dares disrupt the peace that Southernere has, there won't be any sentence for her except the death sentence'

THE PEACE TREATY

King Edward, Master Nvago, Annie, Master Alya, Baron, Cardinal, and Oliver arrived at Combination Castle in the morning, bringing Sir Everos on a giant leaf which Nvago carried with magic. Seeing the aftermath of the jinn attacks was very shocking.

After Lizyati was defeated, everyone who was possessed regained their own selves. It was like the jinn had switched allegiance or no longer worked for Lizyati. The survivors from among the soldiers, king's guards, citizens, everyone helped in cleaning the mess up. By the time Edward and the rest arrived in Combination, they had cleared up every single dead body lying around the city.

As the sun rose, everyone stopped whatever they were doing to attend one of the most important events in history. The death sentence. There had only been one death sentence before. And the person was

Majuza. People gathered in the city square to witness the second death sentence in Southernere history.

A small stage was set up beside the fountain. The executioner, who is one of the king's guards, waited on top with a very sharp sword in hand.

Everyone watched silently as two soldiers escorted a smug looking Lizyati from the carriage towards the stage. King Edward and Queen Flyangel walked into the square from another carriage behind. Both of them gestured for the other to proceed up the stage.

'You should go, you were here the entire time' Edward said to her. Flyangel went up the stage, heart beating heavily. The look Lizyati gave her made her sure of this decision. The soldiers pushed her down onto her knees and her neck on the wooden board placed on the stage.

'Ready, your majesty' the executioner said.

Flyangel nodded and addressed the crowd.

'We are gathered here today after a series of terrible events. When Majuza faced the death sentence many many years ago, it was for the many unimaginable things she did. And today, this foreign lady had done many unimaginable things in the few days she's been here. Lizyati, I hereby sentence you to death by beheading. May this be a lesson for anyone who dares to cross with Southernere ever again'

The executioner raised his sword. The sword went smoothly through Lizyati's neck. And the last thing people saw her did was smile.

The rest of the day was less tense. More of

sadness and reconciliation. A massive farewell was conducted for all the casualties of the jinn attacks for all of Southernere. A raven carrying a letter from Queen Lady Lith reached Combination that morning, updating what had happened and what is going on in the west. She also informed the death of King David. Among the names mentioned in the farewell were Sir Everos, King David, King George, Prince John, Izalora's mother, and many others.

Afterwards, the royals returned to the castle with the four remaining rebels, the Greenwoods, the Dutch, and a few others among the royal council to have a peace meeting. Among the matters discussed were, Barenge, the foreigners, and moving on.

Firstly, Barenge had been under the rebels' control for a few days. It wasn't easy for Edward to hear what happened to his aunt. But he wasn't feeling vengeful for it. And besides, the person leading the rebels is dead. The four rebels promised to return to Barenge, gather the other rebels left, and leave the Inlands. But Edward told them otherwise. If they can rebuild Barenge in memory of the previous royals who ruled Barenge within one year, he'll let them stay there.

Secondly, the British, only two of them left, father and son. Initially, Lieutenant Greenwood wanted to return to Australia but Edward offered him an advisory position in Combination. Since he can speak English, and was just recently from the outside world compared to Dewi. Greenwood could give advice and teach them a few things that Southernere doesn't have.

Master Nvago helped them understand the Dutch. The Dutch made a decision to leave. They mentioned that it was Captain Noah's idea to come here in the first place. And they said it was clearly a mistake. So they will return to Indonesia.

Lastly, Flyangel proposed how they can move on from there. One rule was updated to better fit the current situation. It is that all nations, cities, towns, villages, Southernere born or foreign, whose Southernere is their home, is responsible to maintain the peace that Southernere has together.

From this day onwards, there are no more Inlands and Outlands. Southernere won't be divided by who they represent. The old ways, the feud has to stop. Instead, Southernere will be divided into regions. The regions are a good way to indicate the different atmosphere Southernere has from the north to the south. There are six regions. White Capital, Iron Centre, Wild North, Wetlands, Frozen Point, and Marina. White Capital is where Combination, White Woods, and White Shore Outpost are. The Iron Centre includes Barenge and Silverside. Wild North has Flyra's Stand and the new Dutch settlement Diederik, which will be removed as the Dutch had decided to leave. In the Wetlands are Arstar, Waterfront, and West Coast. Frozen Point is where Trisnarim is. And Marina is the two small islands in the south, Marina Island and Tiny Island.

The meeting ended afterwards and the individual

parties left to do what they promised or what they had decided to do.

'Do you think this will work?' Flyangel asked Edward. Edward smiled playfully at her. This was the first time they had alone time together since they reunited.

'Don't you want to talk about something else instead?' Edward teased. Flyangel got up to his chair and kissed him on the cheek.

'I have a good feeling about this' Edward said, smiling confidently. 'This will work'

TO BE CONTINUED
(Next book in the series is Volume Three: Parts 1, 2, 3)

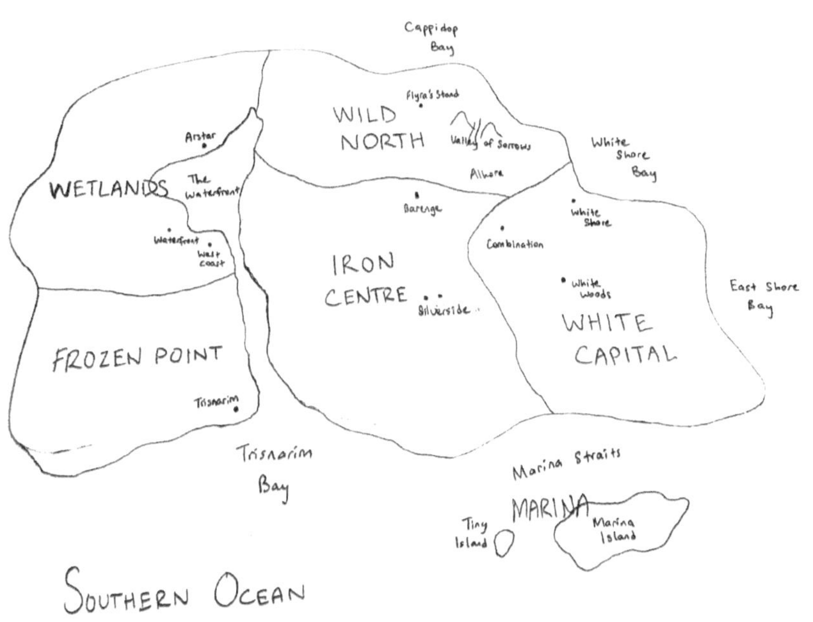

Map of Southernere 1931